A SEA OF SPECTRES

NANCY TABER

PRAISE FOR

A Sea of Spectres

"In A Sea of Spectres, a mystical talent that's passed down through the women of the Doiron family is also one that might kill. Nancy Taber deftly weaves together multiple timelines, the history of the Acadian Expulsion, and Maritime life for a gripping story that's ultimately a tale of family, trust, and identity."

—Janie Chang, bestselling author of *The Library of Legends*, *The Phoenix Crown*

"Prepare to be captivated by Taber's tale, which expertly weaves folklore with feminism and heroics with heart. A Sea of Spectres will keep readers on the edge of their seats with a sweeping epic of masterful storytelling that expertly combines research, Acadian history, and stunning use of craft. Above all, it's the characters that will stay lodged within the reader, echoing power through all the generations captured in this beautiful debut, in which women triumph beyond all boundaries."

—Kelly S. Thompson, national bestselling author of *Girls Need Not Apply* **and** *Still I Cannot Save You***.**

A Sea of Spectres

ISBN: 9781773661575

Printed in Canada

Cover: Tracy Belsher
Designed by Rudi Tusek
Edited by Penelope Jackson

Library and Archives Canada Cataloguing in Publication

Title: A sea of spectres / Nancy Taber.
Names: Taber, Nancy, 1971- author.
Identifiers: Canadiana (print) 20240355563 | Canadiana (ebook) 20240355571 | ISBN 9781773661575 (softcover) | ISBN 9781773661582 (EPUB)
Subjects: LCGFT: Detective and mystery fiction. | LCGFT: Novels.
Classification: LCC PS8639.A22 S43 2024 | DDC C813/.6—dc23

Canada

The publisher acknowledges the support of the Government of Canada, the Canada Council for the Arts and the Province of Prince Edward Island for our publishing program.

ACORNPRESS

P.O. Box 22024
Charlottetown, Prince Edward Island
C1A 9J2
acornpresscanada.com

To all Doiron women,
past, present, and future,
especially my mother.

“Fiction is the autobiography of the imagination.”

—Pat Schneider

CHAPTER 1

Raina, present day

Raina squinted into the rays of the early afternoon sun that glinted off the Northumberland Strait. Flashes of light danced like fireflies over the water towards the red sandstone cliffs. The seas were clear. No ghostly vessels, no spectres. That would change once day turned to night. She'd need to shore herself up. She pinched the bridge of her nose to stave off the headache she knew was coming. Over these last few days, she'd spent more time than she liked too close to the ocean.

She turned her attention to the only thing keeping her sane: her work as a police detective. She scanned the people seated in the outdoor patio at Crossings Pub, searching for anyone who seemed too aware of their surroundings or overly concerned with anything other than their companions, fries, or beer. Normal people noticed almost nothing outside themselves, which was why pickpockets were so successful, why the otherworldly was so hidden. Most would be shocked at how vulnerable they were. Ignorance wasn't bliss. It was hazardous.

She sipped her tea, which had long gone cold, as she leaned her slim body against a low wooden fence at the edge of the parking lot. No one paid her any attention. More importantly for her purposes, no one switched out a set of car keys for another.

It'd been a good trick for a while, she had to give them that. One person smuggled something over the Confederation Bridge in one car, met another at the pub, sat for a moment, talked, then traded cars. The guns or the drugs or worse—trafficked women—travelled towards Charlottetown and across Prince Edward Island while the courier departed with an empty vehicle, ready for another run.

The police force had only caught on to the tactic when a toll taker noticed a man who'd just arrived leaving in a different car. A search of camera footage noted a similar pattern over the past several weeks. They'd set up surveillance in the area, discovered the key switch, and established traffic stops under the cover of routine checks. Several arrests had boosted the success rate of the departments collaborating on the case.

She'd been involved in a few of the recent apprehensions, welcoming the exhilaration and adrenaline that rewarded a job well done, protecting the public, maybe saving a life downstream. She couldn't stop the smuggling—no one could, it wasn't like an organization that fell apart once you got the ringleader, but a hodgepodge of people with an assortment of reasons and ways to break the law—so she didn't expect an ultimate win. Victory was the stuff of folklore and fairy tales. As long as humans existed, there'd be people trying to take advantage of others. So if she couldn't eradicate them—though that would be a power worth having—she could trip them up, slow them down, send them to jail for at least a few years. That was something.

The smugglers must've decided to change strategies, because the arrests had dwindled, so this was Raina's last shift at the bridge. The police planned to redouble their efforts at the airport and the ferry terminal, the Island's only other easily accessible entry points. She'd volunteer to investigate at the airport. That'd get her away from the water. She could handle being somewhat near it; she did after all live on a two-thousand-square-mile, narrow, canoe-shaped island. But being this close always split her attention and resulted in nightmares that not only rocketed her awake long before dawn but stayed with her all the next day. Real ghosts were bad enough. She didn't need to add her own creations to the mix.

Her phone pinged. Liam. Another detective from her detachment in Wellington, where she'd moved years before when she'd been accepted to the nearby police academy. Her hometown was only an hour's drive from there, but Wellington seemed like a world apart. Inland and away from family.

Liam was at Tim Horton's, just around the corner from the pub. Said he had an update. She texted him to order her another tea, tossed her paper cup in the garbage, and strode towards his unmarked black sedan. He was just pulling out of the drive-through and into a parking space as she arrived. She sat in the front seat and nodded hello.

"Your eyes are bloodshot again," he said.

"Nice to see you, too."

"Nightmares chasing you?"

Raina had mentioned them to him after one particularly bad night when she couldn't explain away her sluggishness. Not what they were or why she had them, of course.

"I have some aspirin." He handed her a cup of tea, reached a long arm over to click open the glove compartment, and dug through papers, napkins, straws, and ketchup packets.

She took a gulp of the hot liquid, not much caring if it scalded her tongue. It'd keep her focused. "No, thanks. I slept fine last night." Fine for her, anyway. Tonight, however, was likely to be different.

"Family, then? Let me get you something stronger. Extra-strength Tylenol?"

She shook her head and grinned. "Haven't heard from my mother in a while. All's quiet on the northern front."

"How are their tours going?" He closed the compartment and sat back.

"Busy as ever, supposedly."

"Any more sightings?"

"Depends on who you ask." A key part of her family's ocean sightseeing business was attracting tourists with promises they'd glimpse the phantom ship. So, it was in her mom's interest to say she'd seen it, even if she hadn't. Not that she lied on purpose. She just had an active imagination. To most people, the phantom ship was a fun Island myth about a flaming vessel with a crew of ghosts. If they knew how real it was, like Raina did, they'd do anything but seek it out.

It hadn't always been this way. She used to work on the tour boat—it wouldn't be a family business without the kids roped in—passing out oatmeal cookies and lemonade. Comforting picnic food paired with stories of drowning, burning, and melancholy. Her dad worked the helm, steering the boat one way, then another, at each shout from her mom. "There, can't you see it?" she'd always say. "Just there, under the setting sun." Raina's brother, Brian, sat at the stern, life preserver close at hand, equally terrified and thrilled at the prospect of having to rescue someone. Her favourite part was watching the eyes of the tourists grow wider with each shivery tale as darkness fell.

Until that last summer of high school, when the ocean's call almost overwhelmed her. Then no power on earth—not even her mom—could convince her to get back on that boat. She shook away the memory.

Liam picked at a spot of something on his cuff. "Crap. Must've gotten stained when I was cleaning the highchair. Damn homemade jam."

"How are the boys?" She cared about the answer—they were rather adorable—but she was more interested in the mix of emotions that crossed a parent's face when they talked about their kids. Love and pride warred with frustration and exhaustion. It was good practice to predict which feeling would emerge. Entirely based on knowledge of facial tics and body language. Nothing supernatural about it. And nothing to do with her family.

Liam grimaced. Frustration for the win. "I'd rather go through basic training than potty train another toddler."

"I loved basic training." Run, shoot, study, repeat. Simple.

"Of course you did." Liam chugged his double-double coffee. "There should be basic training for parents."

"Knowing you, it would be called *Cuddle 101*."

"I like that. Maybe my wife can write that into her blog."

"She has my permission," Raina said. "I'll never use it." She glanced at her watch. By her estimation, time for small talk was over. "So, what's up?" she asked.

"Finally got my informant to meet with me. Smugglers aren't switching to the airport or the ferry. They're on boats. Again."

Entering a cove, offloading cargo, and sailing away was an Island tradition from the rum-running days. Though it wasn't as favoured a method anymore. With modern tracing and communication gear, tracking a ship that crossed the Northumberland Strait was easier than monitoring the thousands of cars or hundreds of plane passengers that arrived daily. At one time, before cell phones, and with cars outlawed on the Island, it didn't much matter if a smuggling ship was spotted. The vessel would be long gone before law enforcement managed to get anywhere near its anchor point, the contraband hidden or relocated.

"What'd the chief say?" she asked.

"He just got off the phone with his Coast Guard buddy. They're going to assist with enforcement support. It's a one-week tasking."

"Good idea. I can scour the airport. A few smugglers are bound to mingle with tourists, sneak whatever they can in. There's a baggage handler who's been helpful before. I'll—"

"Chief wants you with the Coast Guard. You know he doesn't trust anyone other than police officers with chain of evidence."

Shit. She was the only one in her detachment with experience on boats. You didn't need it to work with the Coast Guard, but it helped. She tapped her fingers on her knee. Tap-tap-tappity-tap. Such a simple thing, but the tapping never failed to help her breathe through her emotions. If only it worked against the phantom ship.

She couldn't say no. Turning down an investigative opportunity would not only piss off the chief, it'd hurt her career prospects. She was so close to her next promotion she could almost taste it, like the whisky that helped her ease into a few hours of oblivion after her head hit the pillow. Besides, even if refusing wouldn't blow back on her, it wasn't as if she could explain the reason.

"When?" she asked.

"In three days. Evening sail."

She nodded. An image of a young woman with purple hair and a nose ring flashed in her mind's eye. She blinked it away. Paying attention to her premonitions only increased her link to the phantom ship. The premonitions weren't connected to the spectres themselves, just that, as far as she could figure, her abilities lived in the same part of her brain. Enabling one opened her to the other. While the premonitions might be helpful, the phantom ship was decidedly not.

But who was the woman? Smuggler, victim, just a random thought? That was the problem with her visions—forerunners, premonitions, whatever they were called: they weren't that specific.

"I'll go over the files again," Raina said. "Check with informants. Maybe we missed something." If she could plan a big bust, then she'd need to turn her attention to that. Chief would have to assign someone else to work with the Coast Guard. Three days wasn't much. But if she dedicated her attention to it, cut down the little sleep she managed to get, she'd find a lead. Get her promotion without stepping foot on a ship.

Her phone pinged. She looked at the screen and her hopes plummeted. A text from her chief. He had a missing person case he wanted her on. Worse, the last GPS lock they had on the woman's cell phone was near Rustico. Raina's hometown.

A FEW HOURS LATER, RAINA ARRIVED IN RUSTICO. IT WOULD'VE BEEN A WASTE of energy to avoid her family. Even if she weren't immediately recognized, which was highly improbable, the gas station attendant would wonder who the familiar-looking stranger in the Jeep was, then cross the street to ask the baker if he knew, which the restaurant owner would overhear, and she'd tell the cashiers at the market. Within ten minutes information would zip along the town's gossip lines faster than high-speed internet. *Raina's back in town* would be on everyone's lips, and a call-and-response would begin, until news of her presence reached her mother's ears.

Annoying, but not dangerous. No, the peril lay elsewhere, in the call of the ocean as it lured her towards its mysteries, legends, and shimmering, treacherous beauty. The temptation was strongest in Rustico, the home of her ancestors.

She parked beside the local police cruiser. The town's nod to law and order was one full-time and one part-time constable, both under the purview of her own department, reporting to the same chief she did. She texted her mom that she was here. Raina didn't have to worry about getting a quick response. Her mom would be on the tour boat for at least a few more hours.

Raina reached over to the passenger seat and picked up the thin missing person file. Simone Robichaud. A tourist, female, Caucasian, and nineteen years old. No record, though her fingerprints were on file for a vulnerable sector check, probably for a volunteering job. The company she'd rented her car from had tried to contact her when she didn't return it as scheduled but got no answer on her cell. The car's GPS indicated it hadn't moved from the lot of a Cavendish motel in days, even though she'd checked out. A quick social media search showed her steady stream of selfies at various tourist traps had stopped.

Disappeared like sea spray merging with fog, her mom might say. Raina bit her lip. The closer she'd gotten to Rustico, driving along narrow curved roads with intermittent views of the glinting waters of the Gulf of St. Lawrence as the sun set, the more thoughts of her mom surfaced. Raina didn't need her superstitious mumbo jumbo. What she needed were facts. She'd started in Cavendish, searching the rental car, then levering out information from ice cream vendors, souvenir shop cashiers, and lobster supper waitresses. Nothing. The Island teemed with tourists this time of year. Tracking down one woman would be arduous, even one with purple-streaked hair and a nose ring. When she had first seen Simone's photo and recognized the woman from her premonition, Raina had flinched. Simone was important, that much was clear. Raina needed to find out why.

After a quick courtesy call with the town's full-time constable, who had actually been a neighbour when they were kids, Raina went to check into the Oceanwaves B&B. When she entered the two-storey Queen Anne-style house, rooms stretching in all directions with multiple add-ons over the years, the owner apologized for the top-floor garden view, explaining the only unoccupied room was in back. Raina tried not to look relieved. She wouldn't have to keep the blinds closed to block out the sight of the ocean. The windows were sealed well enough to occlude the sound of the waves and their briny scent. She could've returned to Wellington and commuted back, limiting her time in Rustico, but it would've taken too long. If Simone had come to any harm, time was the one thing that couldn't be wasted. And if she was somehow involved with smugglers, she could have vital information that might lead to exactly the sort of breakthrough Raina needed.

Staying at the B&B was sure to cause a fight with her mom, but she planned to win it. Working out of her childhood home would do nothing more than remind people she was once little Raina, with braided auburn pigtails and a gap-toothed smile. That girl had vanished, replaced by Detective Cormier, with a professionally-cut angular bob and perfectly straight teeth. That was the official explanation for her mom. The unofficial and more important one was that she would quite literally go out of her mind if she had to live with her mom and next door to Brian. She had the therapist bills to prove it. Though she'd told her therapist only half the story. The other half might've gotten her committed.

At 11 p.m. she was still sitting at the wooden desk set in the back corner of the room, searching Simone's credit card history and social media profile for clues. Raina had her earphones in, the music in her phone's playlist turned up loud to cover the whispering phantom ship that was even now calling to her. The opening chords of Great Big Sea's "Captain Kidd" pounded in her ears. Pirates, battles, and death. A safe way to satisfy her obsession with the ocean.

When her cell rang, she didn't need call display to know it was her mom. She would've just arrived home after saying goodbye to the tourists, pocketing their tips, and battening down the boat. Brian would've had a beer with her dad and walked to his own house, complete with picket fence, wife, and the requisite 2.2 children. They had two girls and were trying for another.

"Raina, are you really here?" her mom said. "Where are you? I have leftover clam chowder I can heat up. I think there's a few doughnut holes left, if your father hasn't already scarfed them down."

Tempting, but she'd have to pass. "Mom, I'm staying at Oceanwaves."

"What? Why?"

Raina gave her the official explanation.

"You can't do that. People'll think I'm a horrible mother. Bad enough you moved away."

"Tell them I'm on police business and need private space to work," Raina said. Her mom wasn't horrible, of course, but that didn't mean Raina wanted to sleep in her house.

"We could set up a cot in the basement. There'd be space if we moved aside your dad's boxing equipment. He barely uses it anymore. Or we can leave it for you. You still box, right?"

"Yes." Raina had picked up the sport in high school, as a way to connect with her father, who used to be an amateur boxer.

"Wonderful. I'll make up the cot. I'd put you in the spare room, but—"

"No, Mom. I mean yes, I still box, but no, I'm not staying there. I'm already settled in at the B&B and you know they don't refund deposits after check-in."

"What do you expect? Dang tourists searching for the best bargains, asking for Airbnbs. Who around here is going to rent their house to strangers? And then where would you yourself sleep?"

"It's better if I just stay here."

"Fine, but you have to visit tomorrow."

"I'll try, but it depends on my investigation," Raina said.

"We've missed you. Or rather, you missed Christmas," her mom said.

"I told you I had to work." Such an old habit between them, weirdly comfortable, with Raina's evasion ramping up her mom's passive-aggressiveness and vice versa.

"If you worked in the family business, you wouldn't have to choose between one and the other," her mom said.

Choosing between them was actually a key benefit of working somewhere else.

"We could use the help, you know," her mom said, then turned back to her Airbnb rant. "It's as bad as this whole self-serve business. Did you know that someone asked if they could just rent a boat themselves and listen to our tour on an app? An app? You can't replace us with an app. Where's the ambience, the personal touch? Of all the nerve. It's as bad as whistling on a ship. And another thing ..."

Raina let her rail while she continued her back-trace on Simone. Once her mom got going, nobody could stop her. Raina had hung up on her once. Not quite hung up. Said she had to go, sandwiched a goodbye in between her mom's words, and ended the call. Her mom called right back, said they must've been cut off, and restarted her story from the beginning, in case Raina had missed anything. Easier to let her wind down.

Simone had withdrawn a fair amount of cash at her hotel's ATM. That was the last time she'd used her card. Had someone forced her to do it? Or had she done so on purpose, so she couldn't be found?

"So, what do you think?" her mom's voice cut through Raina's thoughts.

"Hmm?" Raina said.

"Excellent. We'll see you then."

Crap. What had Raina just agreed to?

"Do you have your own galoshes or do you need to borrow a pair? The transom is leaking again."

"I'm not going on the boat." Even if she wanted to, which she decidedly didn't, she didn't have time for social calls.

"Shouldn't you confront your fear, instead of running from it? A terrible thing, what happened to you." Her mom swallowed. "But you survived, and you need to get over it. For your family." She'd dropped the passive in favour of the aggressive. Great.

Besides, Raina did confront her fear. Every night. The memory of icy water closing over her head. Filling her lungs. But that wasn't the worst of it, though her mom didn't know that.

"Our family has always been in symbiosis with the ocean," her mom continued. "For centuries. Even after getting shipped to France and stealing their way back, our ancestors didn't abandon the ocean. And they had good reason to hate it."

"I have work to do."

"Well, at least tell me how all that promotion stuff's going. It's so complicated. Lists and rules and points. Union reps. Why can't they just see you're the best and promote you already?"

Raina couldn't help but laugh. "Because they're not my mom."

"I could write them a letter. Would a reference help? Maybe from your time working with us?"

"No, Mom, that would not help." It'd tank her chances for sure. "Do not send them anything. Promise me."

"Fine, fine." There was a pause as her mom was doubtless shifting her home phone receiver from one shoulder to another. "You said your written examination went well, and your interview. You have the seniority. What's the holdup?"

"They still have to assess my performance, I told you that. Which they can't do until the chief writes my evaluation for this year." So she couldn't afford any missteps. She had to find Simone and then dig up a smuggling lead. "If this evaluation is as strong as the last four years, I should have enough points to top the list." A promotion would mean more responsibility, a raise, and more overtime, though she didn't need the money. She needed her mind occupied and her body busy. "I have to go. Maybe I'll see you at the pier tomorrow."

"Great. There's always room for you on board."

"No, Mom, I'll be working. I'll start in town and make my way towards the harbour." With her feet firmly on the docks.

Not long after, she choked down a few shots of whisky and lay on the double bed, tossing the heavy quilted comforter over the rounded metal footboard. As usual, her sleep only lasted a few hours. She opened her eyes to a room that was not as dark as it should have been. Flashing light crept through the blinds.

Chanting voices slipped into the corners. *Raina. Raina.* Her name danced on the lips of the dead.

She slowly sat up. Placed her feet on the floor and stood. She swayed to the call as it thrummed through her body. She opened her door and snuck down the creaky hallway, towards the large window that overlooked the harbour. There, in the distance, was the phantom ship.

Her treacherous friend.

Flames soared from its masts and sails, illuminating the night sky. She smiled at the promise of the icy firestorm welcoming her to their crew. Readied herself to burst down the stairs and race to the shore, throw herself into the ocean.

A spectre separated itself from the ship. *Not yet*, it whispered, breaking the pull between Raina and the water. Raina jerked backwards. Ran to her room, slammed the door, and slumped to the floor. She rummaged in her bag, removed a pair of handcuffs, and locked herself to the bedframe. She peered at the key, finally deciding to stuff it into her sock. Yes, it was within reach, but it would take conscious thought to remember the key, extricate it, and unlock herself.

Conscious thought would remind her that although joining the ship's crew would open her to its mysteries, it would mean her death. Hardly a fair trade.

CHAPTER 2

Raina

Dawn finally arrived. Raina's arm screamed with pins and needles. She unlocked herself and worked feeling back into her limb, berating herself for letting her guard down the night before. But the call was stronger than ever. Something had changed. She just didn't know what.

She needed to shake off the night so she laced her sneakers for a five-kilometre run inland. Then she showered and forced herself to eat a protein bar, the routine steadying her. She tugged on jeans, a grey T-shirt, black blazer, and Blundstone boots, and placed her files into a backpack. Find Simone. That was her task. So she could get out of Rustico.

The fishers were already up and out—it was best to talk with them after they'd gotten their catch for the day, when they weren't anxious to get on the water—so she started with Your Morning Sludge. The café was an old one-room house tucked into a bluff above the red, orange, and blue fishing shacks that lined the harbour. Contrary to its name, it stayed open all day and was run by a coffee aficionado, Raina's best friend from high school, Hattie.

Raina opened the door to the clang of the bell and stepped inside, over the broom that was set into the bottom of the door frame. Hattie had installed it first thing when she'd bought and renovated the place. The broom supposedly attracted good luck. But just like hope, luck was not a strategy.

"Raina Cormier, as I live and breathe," Hattie said. "I'd heard you were in town but didn't believe it." She rushed over and pressed Raina into her plump body.

"Great to see you." Raina hugged her back and took a seat at the long counter. A group of teenagers in the corner laughed as they shared jokes with each other. It was the same table where Raina, Hattie, and Brian used to sit, when the café was a fish-and-chips place. They would pool their allowance money to share a seafood platter every Saturday afternoon, chat about their week, and gaze out the wall of windows at the harbour beyond. It'd been years since Raina shared anything with Brian, other than the occasional family dinner.

"So, what's the case?" Hattie asked.

"You have to ask?" Raina said.

"Missing woman," Hattie said. "Least, that's the news from the B&B."

Raina pulled out Simone's photograph. "Seen her? Woulda been sometime in the last few days."

"Nope, sorry. Just the regulars, a few young families, and middle-aged bus tourists. Tea? You look like you need it."

"God, yes."

Hattie poured the tea, glanced at the Anne of Green Gables calendar on the wall, and then plunked the mug in front of Raina. Hard. The liquid sloshed up its sides.

"What's that for?" Raina asked.

"Just realized it's been almost a year since I saw you last."

"Has it been that long?" Raina knew exactly how much time had passed. Counted out the days and months. She preferred at least one year between each visit. She usually timed it for Christmas, but her eldest niece's sixth birthday had messed up her system. Maeve said the only thing she wanted was for Raina to be at her party. Hopefully Nora, almost four, wouldn't have the same idea. She didn't mind seeing them, just not in Rustico, if she could avoid it.

"I brought you a present." Raina pulled a canister of Cow's hot chocolate out of her backpack. The store was famous for its bovine-themed T-shirts and ice cream, but Hattie had enough clothes, and frozen treats didn't travel so well.

Hattie's eyes lit up. "You're forgiven. Want a mochaccino?"

"Just the tea, thanks." Raina took a grateful sip.

"What about meeting at Griff's later, for french fries?"

Raina had worked the occasional shift there as a teen. Fries were great. The waitressing, not so much. "Sorry, no time for side trips. Any interesting gossip about a tourist that could be my missing person?"

"Nah, you know I pay that no never mind. Maybe she's just partying somewhere."

"With no social media posts? I doubt it." Plus, Raina's premonition of Simone, followed by being assigned the case to find her, meant whatever was going on was attached to Raina. It had to be connected to the smuggling case. Somehow.

"Why don't you just do your walking-through-a-wardrobe thingy?" Hattie asked.

"What?" Raina said, though of course she knew what Hattie meant.

"Like you used to when we were kids. I got a copy of *The Lion, the Witch, and the Wardrobe* kicking around, I'm sure. You want to borrow it? I'm guessing kids' books aren't standard police issue—you don't have 'em in your kit along with the fingerprint powder and all."

"Come on," Raina said. "We were just playing a game." Her premonitions had initially come in the form of novel covers. As a way for her to process them, maybe, though she'd never really figured out how the premonitions worked. The Narnia series was the first, after she turned thirteen. In the books, the wardrobe was a literal passage between a rational world and a magical one. Her own visions were metaphorical, with Raina remaining in one world and opening herself up to a mystical one within it.

"A game? That's a bit of an understatement," Hattie said. "Come on, this is me you're talking to, not Brian." She perched herself on the next stool, settled her own mug beside Raina's, and wiped the spilled tea off the counter with her rag. "So?" she said.

"It got scary," Raina confessed. That was an understatement.

"You never did tell me what happened, that night."

"Nothing to tell," Raina said. "Just falling back on the old Sherlock Holmes thing these days—observation, deduction."

"So long as you leave off the smoking opium that old Sherlock was into," Hattie said.

"Whisky's better anyways," Raina said.

Soon after, fortified with caffeine and her time with Hattie, Raina waved goodbye and walked down Main Street. Next stop was the bakery. She hadn't met a tourist yet who could resist Anna's date squares. Her stomach rumbled, but she pushed away the urge to order a tray. She'd end up leaving town pounds heavier than she arrived if she wasn't careful.

"Raina!" Anna lowered her copy of *The Guardian* onto the counter in front of her. She always had the Island newspaper close at hand, as well as the local one, *The Northern Star*. A few specks of flour stuck to her forehead. "So great to see you. Look how thin you are. Mercy. What can I get you?"

"Nothing, thanks." When Raina was anywhere else, being slender was positive. Here, it was like a familial insult, a refutation of home cooking. "I'm here on police business."

"So I heard. Nice you're back. Why don't you visit more often? Your mother misses you, you know."

"I do."

"Always talking about how successful you are, top of your class at the academy. Made detective in record time. But isn't it odd, working with men all the time?"

Ed bellowed a "hello" and a "well bless your heart" from the back. Yeast and cinnamon wafted towards her. He must've been making sticky buns.

"You work with your husband," Raina said.

"Ha! He doesn't count as men. One man, yes, and my favourite, obviously." She leaned towards Raina. "Speaking of which, have you met anyone special?"

Raina ground her teeth and handed over Simone's photograph. "Have you seen this woman?"

"My, look at that nose ring. Looks uncomfortable. A few days ago, a teenager came in with those—whaddya call them—spacers in his ears."

The bakery door opened and a woman with a toddler walked in, each wearing a *PEI Dirt Shirts*. Tourists.

"Welcome," Anna said to them. "Hope you're hungry. Got lots of goodies to choose from."

The toddler mashed her nose into the glass case. "Cookies!"

Her mother pulled her back. "Manners, dear." She smiled at Anna. "Sorry."

"No matter," Anna said. "Those are my famous scotch cookies, with icing and the perfect amount of maraschino cherries and sprinkles."

"If you're a good girl, maybe we'll get you some," the mother said. The toddler cheered, arms in the air like a winning prizefighter.

Anna must have to wipe that glass down dozens of times each day, but it didn't seem to bother her. "Don't recognize her," Anna said, passing the photo back. "But by midmorning I'm so swamped the West Point Sea Serpent itself could slither in here and I'd never notice."

"What about you?" Raina asked the mother. "Have you seen this woman?"

The mother shook her head. "Sorry, no." She turned to Anna. "What's the West Point Sea Serpent?"

"The Island's version of the Loch Ness Monster, but better." Anna winked at Raina. "It has fur instead of scales, a head like a horse, and a snakelike body as long as Main Street."

Raina didn't agree with her definition of "better." She'd take Nessie—in a freshwater loch—over the ocean's Serpent, if she had any choice in the matter.

RAINA SPENT THE REST OF THE MORNING IN MUCH THE SAME WAY, ASKING about Simone and fending off questions about herself. It took longer than it should have, forced as she was to chat a bit. Store to store, shop to shop. Without one lead on Simone.

She headed towards the now bustling pier, filled with tourists and fishers. Seagulls squawked in their continual efforts to swipe a piece of unattended food. She stepped onto the slightly swaying docks and peered down at the water through the gaps between the wooden boards. Breathed deeply. The midday sun beat down on the glimmering ocean. She couldn't see the phantom ship, but it beckoned her nonetheless, from somewhere in the distance.

Raina, Raina, the ship and its spectres murmured.

Come aboard, Raina.

Swim to us, Raina.

Come aboard, come aboard …

"No," she whispered back, tapping her fingers on her thighs. Even in Rustico, the call had never been this powerful during the day. She needed to be gone long before the afternoon dipped into dusk, before the call intensified even further.

Raina manoeuvred her way from deep-sea fishing tours to waterskiing companies—finding nary a clue that would lead her to Simone—to, eventually, her family's tour boat, the *Spirit of Rustico*.

If no one had seen Simone, then she wasn't here. Raina would look elsewhere, and double-check the hospitals to see if a woman matching Simone's description had been admitted since the night before, when she'd last asked. Unfortunately, she'd have to inquire at the morgue again. But she couldn't leave without at least a brief visit to say hi to her parents, no matter how much she was itching to get on the road and away from Rustico.

After hugs, hellos, and admonitions about why she wouldn't just get in the damn boat, Raina grabbed a lawn chair off the deck and set it on the dock. Her dad tinkered with the motor while her mom chatted with her. Brian wouldn't arrive until later, after having dinner with the kids.

"So, any luck?" Her mom tucked a stray strand of hair into the elastic of her topknot, sending her good-luck charm bracelets tinkling.

"No. I'm leaving this evening," Raina said.

"So soon?"

"Nothing here to help me." She handed her mom the file with Simone's photograph inside. "Can you take a look, just in case?"

"What, you had to ask the rest of the town before us?"

"It made logistical sense, Mom. You sleep in. Better to start with others."

"We work late. Don't get to bed until midnight."

"It wasn't an insult, just an observation. Besides, you always used to be up at the crack of dawn no matter how late you stayed up."

"Yeah, well, I used to be younger." Her mom looked at the photo. Her eyes widened and she laughed.

"How can this be funny?" Raina asked.

Her mom snorted. "You're right. This is serious stuff. You been searching long?"

"Yesterday evening and today. Cavendish, on the road, and here." She didn't mention calling the hospitals or the morgue.

"Enjoy seeing everyone in town again?" Her mom opened the pale blue cooler and handed Raina an egg salad sandwich.

"As much as I ever do. They're not great at minding their own business." Raina took a bite, and gave silent thanks to her mother for never slathering butter on the bread. Horrid stuff.

"Isn't your work easier with nosy people?"

"Not the same thing." When it applied to herself, that is.

"Course not. Too bad you couldn't come by the house last night." A smile flickered across her mom's face.

Not this passive-aggressiveness again. Although her mom's comment was curiously good-natured. Raina realized she'd eaten half the sandwich and washed it down with a gulp of water.

"I know your work is more important than your mother." Her mom was in full-on grin mode now.

"Mom—"

"But whenever you're in town, come see your mother first." She climbed the ladder onto the boat. A wave bumped it against the dock and back again.

"What're you getting at?" Raina stood so her mom didn't tower over her quite so much.

"Your case."

"You've seen the missing woman?"

"She's not missing," her mom said.

"Lemme guess. The wind whispered it in your ear?"

"No, smartass." Her mom mimed a drum roll. "She's hiding in the spare room in the basement."

"You're shitting me."

"I am not. If you'd stayed at our place last night I coulda saved you a lot of time."

"What the ..." Raina shook her head. "How'd she end up there? Is she okay? What happened to her?" She'd ask outright about the smuggling but that was too much info to give a civilian about the case, even her mother.

"She's your third cousin once removed. Hand me the cooler, would you?"

Raina passed it over, resisting the urge to snag a beer. "How come I've never heard of her?"

"Her mother accepted a transfer to a bank in the Yukon years ago, just after Simone was born. She figured if she was going to do a boring job, she may as well do it in an adventurous place. Hasn't been back since, other than a few visits. Besides, you have more cousins than you can shake a stick at. Hard to keep track of them all. Especially when they move away."

"Why's she hiding?"

"Don't rightly know. Or care. When family asks for help, you give it."

CHAPTER 3

Raina

Raina tapped her fingers on the steering wheel. She turned her Jeep into the cul-de-sac that held her family's gabled home, perched high on a hill, its backyard overlooking the harbour. What did the smugglers and her third cousin have in common? Raina, evidently. If Simone was wrapped up with something illegal and had reached out to Raina's mom for help, then Simone was seriously in trouble. Raina could protect her, see if she had information that could help. Given confidentially. She'd keep Simone's name out of it and tread carefully. Informants needed to understand exactly how much danger they were in. Turning on criminals was risky, but it was usually more hazardous not to.

Raina and Liam were great at playing bad cop/good cop in situations like this, nudging people into agreeing to inform so they almost considered it their own idea. Raina was always bad cop. She'd have to channel Liam's good cop somehow. Or maybe her mother. At least Simone was safe for the moment, but she couldn't stay with Raina's parents. Too risky. If Simone was hiding, then someone else must be trying to find her, other than the cops.

Raina parked and marched up the steps of the wraparound veranda, where she'd once spent hours curled on the porch swing, reading book after book. She stood on the worn welcome mat and unlocked the front door with the spare she kept with her car keys, though she seldom had use for it. Caps and coats drooped off an antique hat stand. Behind them hung a framed painting of feux follets—will o' the wisps—flickering over a dark marsh. Her mom fancied it helped her connect to the otherworldly every time she entered and left the house. The whimsy made her happy, so what was the harm, though the legend that feux follets were souls from purgatory in need of prayers was rather unsettling, to say the least. A field hockey stick was tucked into the corner. Her mom played in a seniors' league, but a cobweb near the bottom of its handle indicated it might not have gotten much use lately.

Raina kept her boots on, something she'd never do if her mother was home, but she couldn't exactly be intimidating in stocking feet. Her plan was to start with bad cop. She opened the basement door, maximizing the effect of its squeaky hinges.

"Hello?" a voice said. "Aunt Kate, is that you?"

Raina thudded down the stairs. Boxing gear peppered with white sweat stains littered the concrete floor. A cot was propped against the far wall. Near the corner, the door of the spare room opened to reveal a woman with purple-streaked hair and a nose ring. The air fairly sizzled when their eyes met. Raina shrugged off the sensation and concentrated on her work. "Hello, Simone," she said.

"Um, hello." Simone gave her a tentative wave.

Raina held out her badge. "I'm a police detective. I need to speak with you."

"Raina, right?"

"Detective Cormier, yes. What do you think you're doing?"

"Hiding. I know it's wrong. I didn't know what else to do." She twisted her hands in front of her.

"Why are you hiding?"

Simone's eyes scrunched up. Ah jeesh. She was about to cry. Where was Liam when she needed a good cop? She tried to soften her tone. "I can help you, Simone."

Simone took a few steps towards Raina, wincing at the cold concrete, and avoided a set of boxing gloves that sat in her path. "Are you here to arrest me?" she asked.

"Should I?"

"Well, I don't want you to. So no, you shouldn't. Did your mother tell you I was here?"

"She did," Raina said.

"How much trouble am I in?"

"You tell me." It was a common police tactic, getting a suspect to implicate themselves, which was similar to the one her mother had used when Raina was a teenager. Raina had seen through it, kept her mouth shut when her mother had no proof that she'd smoked, or drunk, or did anything else she wasn't allowed to do. Not a long list. Raina preferred to follow the rules, not break them. But it looked like Simone might succumb to the approach.

"I don't usually do stuff like this. It's been so weird ever since I had that dream and hopped on the plane. I'm not sure what to do."

"Why are you hiding in my mother's basement?" Raina asked.

"Because she let me."

"What did you tell Mom?" Raina knew Simone hadn't told her much, but asking the question was worth it to see what Simone revealed in her answer. Sometimes it wasn't the words but the tone, the body language, the hesitations, that gave someone away.

"Just that I needed some time to think. She picked me up at the hotel in Cavendish and drove me here. Said I could stay as long as I wanted. That she'd keep me secret from the town. Guess that didn't include her daughter."

"Why?"

"You know why. You're here to arrest me."

"We don't generally arrest missing persons."

"I'm not missing."

"Not now that I've found you."

"I mean, I was never missing. Just ... hiding for a while." She ran her hand through her hair and chewed on her lower lip.

"The rental company called the police when you didn't return the car. They were worried, after renting to someone so young, which turned out to be against policy. A mistake by a new worker. The car was found deserted at the hotel. You stopped posting on social media. Your phone was turned off. We couldn't get hold of your mother to see if you'd checked in with her. Were you trying to mislead us?" Raina backed Simone towards the punching bag that hung from the ceiling.

"You aren't here because of what I ... borrowed?"

Raina sensed clear quotation marks around that last word. "What did you steal?" Was it something a smuggler had forced her to do? She didn't seem like a criminal type.

Simone dodged the bag and put it between them. "Do you mean that, if I'd just come here in the rental car, kept my phone on, no one would be looking for me?"

"Correct. But, maybe it's a good thing you didn't. We can help, if you're involved with something illegal. Any information you have would be much appreciated. You'd be compensated for it. Protected." Raina could requisition some cash, get Simone on a plane home. Cracking down on smugglers was good for the Island, good for Simone, and good for Raina. Whatever assistance Simone could give was Raina's way to stay off that Coast Guard vessel.

"It was just a little bit illegal." Simone held her thumb and forefinger close together and squinted through the almost non-existent gap.

"No such thing, Simone."

"I'm so glad you're here. But can you be not so … intense?"

Raina tilted her head and held her palms up. "I'm no threat to you. As long as you're honest with me."

"I really need to talk to you. Not as a cop, but as a Doiron descendant through the female line. Back eleven or so generations. My mother used to tell me stories about you, and our family."

"What does this have to do with smugglers?" Raina demanded.

"It wasn't smuggling, it was an expulsion. The Acadian deportation. When the British expelled the French from PEI. Didn't you learn that in history class?"

Raina crossed her arms over her chest. "You're talking in circles."

"It's all connected, don't you see? It's why I called Aunt Kate. I didn't have your info, and you're not on Facebook. Or Twitter. Or Snapchat, or Instagram. You're like a twenty-first-century hermit. Then I remembered you were a cop and, well, I didn't think you'd be thrilled with what I did. I couldn't risk making contact with anyone until I'd had enough time to …" She trailed off.

"To what?"

"I even stayed away from social media. I haven't so much as played a game on my phone. Shut it down as we got close to Rustico. I think I'm going through withdrawal. Look, my hands are shaking." She held them out. "But, now that you're here … some seriously wild shit has been happening. It reminded me of stories about you. When you were like, a teenager." She looked at Raina as if she couldn't imagine she'd ever been that young. "We can help each other."

"That's why I'm here, to help you. Start with when you were in the airport. Did anyone approach you, ask you to transport something for them?"

"What? No. I wanted to ask you about your nightmares."

"What nightmares?" Raina snapped the words out.

Simone backed away from the punching bag and into the corner. A speed bag hung a few inches over her head. "The ones that started when you were seventeen," she blurted. "About flaming ships and spectres."

Raina's skin prickled. "How do you know about those?"

"Your mom told my mom. When they first happened. I was almost seven and scared to death. Like I had nightmares vicariously through you. They stopped soon after and I forgot about them. Until I had that dream. And you." She peered at Raina. "You still have nightmares," Simone said. "I knew it. I can see it in your eyes."

"Don't be ridiculous."

"I've always— how would I describe it—seen things. Known things. Just general feelings, before. But lately ..." Simone shrugged. "Anyways, like I said, I can help you."

"I don't need help."

"That's not true," Simone said with an unsettling authority.

"You don't know me at all," Raina said.

"I know what you're going through. Sort of. I think I can figure out a way to stop your nightmares."

Maybe it wouldn't hurt for Raina to hear Simone out. At the very least, she'd made Raina curious about what she'd taken, why she'd hidden it, and how—if—it was connected to her nightmares. The lure of the phantom ship. And the smugglers. "I'm listening," Raina said.

Simone relaxed and leaned against the wall. "Let me start at the beginning," she said.

"Wait."

Simone tensed. "Aren't you going to let me explain? You're not going to arrest me now, are you?"

"Just hold on a minute." Raina took out her phone and texted an update to her chief, that Simone was found and safe, and Raina would file a full report in the morning. "Follow me." They climbed the stairs to the main floor, leaving the boxing ring behind. Raina entered the kitchen, opened the cabinet over the fridge, and pulled out a bottle of whisky. "This isn't standard interrogation procedure, but since you're family …"

"Um, interrogation? I thought you were letting me explain."

"Slip of the tongue." Raina poured herself a double, Simone a single, and motioned her out to the front porch to sit. "Not on the swing, over here, at the picnic table." Raina wanted to be across from Simone so she could see her face. Raina took a moment to listen for the ship's call, to test its strength, but all was quiet at the moment, as if it were letting her focus on Simone. She'd thank the ship, but its absence was as ominous as its presence. "Talk," she said to Simone, setting the whisky bottle beside the citronella candles.

Simone's words came out in a rush. "I came here on a lark. After a dream. Not a nightmare, but fiery flashes of the Island. Like it called me home. Kinda creepy, mostly cool. I mean, there's more to this world than we can explain, obvs, but I'd never gotten such a clear message. I'd just finished my first year of a Philosophy degree at McGill University, didn't have a job for the summer, so thought, why not visit."

Talking to this not-missing-philosopher was trying Raina's patience. She breathed in, reminding herself she was good cop now. She'd keep asking questions, slowly get to where Simone connected to the smugglers. "How'd you end up in Québec? I thought you lived in the Yukon."

"That's where I was brought up. Mom and Dad still live there. Dad's a francophone, so I was raised bilingual, but there's not much chance to speak French that far North, and I wanted to immerse myself in French culture. Montréal is the best city for that. Did you know—"

"Is that relevant to what's going on here?"

"I guess not. But the dream is. It seemed a mash-up of 'One is not born, but becomes a woman.'"

"Simone de Beauvoir."

"Yep. Mom named me for her. Anyway, in my dream, the phrase was 'One does not become, but is born an Islander,' and I thought, wow, I was born on PEI, but know almost nothing about it. Mom paid for my plane ticket, gave me contact info for Aunt Kate in case I needed it—turns out I did—and told me to have fun. Then she and Dad took off on a river cruise on the Danube. She thought me touring PEI was better than my plan to stay home and write philosophical prose poetry until fall term."

"Really? You could have made a fortune."

"Yeah, Mom said you were sarcastic. Listen, already. When I stepped foot on the Island, it grounded me. Like I was exactly where I should be. So, I hit all the tourist spots, posted photos, toured around. But … I don't know how to say this." She reached for the whisky bottle.

Raina pulled it away. "Just spit it out."

Wind chimes tinkled in the soft breeze as Simone stared at Raina. "Answer one question first?" Simone asked.

"No promises."

"Did you really have visions?"

"What do your philosophers say about it?"

"Well, John Locke—"

"Jesus. Rhetorical question." Raina leaned back on the bench.

"Right. So, did you?" Simone asked.

Raina figured she'd go for half-honesty. "As a kid I played a divination game with my best friend, Hattie."

"Mom said you were right more often than not."

"Only in the way horoscopes or fortune cookies are right: You will go on a journey, you will meet someone new, you will face a challenge," she fibbed.

"That's not the story I heard."

"The key word there is 'story.'"

Simone upended her whisky glass to catch the last few drops on her tongue. "Anyway…after a few days on the Island, when I looked at certain people, I got, I don't know, a sense of their future. At first I thought my imagination was playing tricks on me. I've always wanted powers, but if I could pick something it'd be telekinesis. How cool would it be to move shit with your mind? But, beggars can't be choosers, as they say."

"So ..."

"I saw this woman. She had on a long raincoat and her back turned towards me. The strangest thing popped into my head. That she's going into labour. A split second later, I swear to god, she grunted, gripped her stomach, turned to the woman beside her, her wife, I think—only then could I actually see the first woman was pregnant—and said her contractions had started."

"Lucky guess," Raina said. "Coincidence. You'd probably seen her earlier and unconsciously realized she was pregnant. Very pregnant, clearly."

"Maybe. Except that night, I dreamed about a baby girl, born at ten pounds, three ounces. I read a birth announcement in the paper the next day. Photo of the two women, beaming with a baby girl. Ten pounds, three ounces."

Two coincidences were not a coincidence. And there was a third. Raina's vision of Simone. Was it all connected, somehow? The lure of the phantom ship. Visions, abilities, dreams, and nightmares?

"Day after," Simone continued, "several women I saw, boom, flashes of babies in their near future. Nothing off you, though, by the way."

Hardly a surprise. Not only did Raina not plan on kids, but the having sex part was a key component for an unexpected pregnancy, and she'd been going through a rather dry spell.

"I figured, this is crazy even for me," Simone said. "I googled 'baby fortune telling.' Best way I could describe it. No results, other than gender reveal parties."

"Ugh, I hate those things."

"Yeah, but they usually have cake. Speaking of which, I'm starving," she said.

"Talk now. Eat later."

"Bossy much?"

Raina raised her eyebrows.

"Fine," she said. "I went for a walk to clear my head and noticed the Charlottetown Archives. Like they were calling to me to explore their shelves. I figured it was worth a shot to check them out. I had to do research at the Montréal Archives once. You could spend years there following document after document. The Charlottetown one was way smaller but super interesting."

Raina gestured for her to move on. Simone was the very definition of a tangent.

"I called up items on fortune tellers, psychics, superstitions and stumbled on the idea of a jeteuse de sorts—a wise woman or sorceress—depending on the translation. And the translator, I suppose. They were often midwives. And da-da-da-da …"

Finally, her spiel seemed to be going somewhere.

"I found Celeste."

"Who's she?" And how could she help with Raina's nightmares and the phantom ship? With the smugglers?

"Our great-great-and-a-few-more-greats-ancestor. Her journal was there. It tingled when I touched it. Like, I dunno, soda water spilling over my fingers. I didn't have time to read much because the archives were closing soon. Celeste's writing was super hard to make out, all small and scribbly, half in French and half in English. But she included a line about being able to see into the past and the future. About another ancestor, Madeleine, who could do the same. Maybe it's in our genes or something? Do you see things, in your nightmares? Can you tell the future? See the past?"

Raina held up her hand to stop Simone's questions.

"Do you?" Simone asked.

Raina pressed her lips together. She pushed away from the table, stood, and walked away from her cousin, towards the corner of the deck. The neighbour's cat twisted itself through the bushes that separated their properties, as if copying her movement.

"Where are you going?" Simone asked.

Raina kept walking, her boots echoing on the wooden deck, and turned behind the house, ignoring the ocean that sparkled beyond the maple trees in her family's backyard. She turned the next corner, and caught a glimpse of her nieces playing in their treehouse. The eldest, Maeve, glanced up, smiled, and waved, gesturing for Raina to join them. Raina waved back and shook her head. "Maybe later," she called, the adult-to-child equivalent of a polite *sorry, no.* Raina circled the house and returned to Simone.

"Are you okay?" Simone asked.

"I'm thinking." Raina made the lap again. And again. Each time, Maeve waved hi, watching her aunt with keen interest. Raina nodded at her niece, but her thoughts were focused on Simone. While she had been talking, Raina had kept a careful eye on her face. Simone didn't twitch, didn't stumble, didn't change her tone. Didn't make any tells that she was lying. At the very least, she believed everything she said. But did Raina? She needed a few minutes alone, without Simone staring at her, to figure out how to respond. She'd spent her entire adult life pushing this strangeness away. No one knew the depth of it. Not her best friend. Not her mother. Simone seemed awed by it, the fact that there might be something...special about certain Doiron women. Raina didn't share that wonder, but Simone was the closest anyone had come to being an ally in all this.

If Raina could find a way to handle the lure of the ocean—resist the phantom ship—she wouldn't need a big break in the smuggling case. She could simply board the Coast Guard vessel as expected. She almost laughed out loud. Simply board a vessel? Not so easy. How could she defeat the phantom ship? It wasn't as if she could punch it or shoot at it. Entirely ineffective. But, the timing of all this, with Simone arriving and offering a way—a possible way—to deal with the phantom ship, just when it would most benefit Raina? Not a coincidence. Raina preferred to follow science, clues, logic. But where had that gotten her with the phantom ship? Handcuffed and drunk, that's where. It was time to deal with the phantom ship, once and for all. Then nothing would stop her from advancing further and further up the chain of command.

Two days left.

On the next lap, she stopped in front of her cousin, pulled her phone from her back pocket, and checked the time. "Not sure we can get to the archives before they close. First thing tomorrow we'll drive there. Take a look at the journal."

"Um, about that," Simone said, looking away from Raina.

Raina texted Oceanwaves that she'd be staying another night. The journal was worth the risk and, this time, she'd start off with the handcuffs on. It'd be uncomfortable, but survivable.

"It's not in the archives," Simone said.

"What do you mean?"

"It's in my suitcase."

Raina poured herself another finger of whisky. Its malty scent mixed with the citronella candle that sat on the table beside her glass. "Why is it in your suitcase?"

"I returned it the first time I checked it out. I'm not a klepto or anything. But …" She nibbled on her fingernails, refused to make eye contact. "Turns out, it's only on loan to the archives. Whoever loaned it may want it back, who knows when. So…will you arrest me if I tell you? Could we maybe have a family confessional, swear to keep each other's secrets?"

"I don't have any secrets." That was a lie. Raina had never told anyone about the lure of the phantom ship. She'd mentioned the nightmares, once, to her mother, who had dismissed them as stress induced. "But let's call this off the record."

"Whew. Okay. I know you're going to say I could've just scanned it, but the journal itself has power. And it's our ancestor's property, not someone else's to hide away who knows where."

"If that's true, we could've asked for it back." Raina wasn't sure how that "we" slipped out.

"Too risky. If they said no, and then it went missing, we'd be prime suspects. So I took my chance. Went back the next day—with a different archivist on duty—and used a fake ID to sign in, with a different name."

"A fake ID?"

"I *may* have gotten one so I could drink when I was underage."

Raina shook her head.

"Like you never did anything wrong when you were young?" she said.

"Just tell me what you did." For the love of all that was good in this world, she didn't add. The more frustrated she got with Simone the longer her story grew.

"Most of the items come in big accordion file folders. It's easy to swipe something and hand the folder back just a little bit lighter. You have to use cotton gloves to protect the documents, which also means no fingerprints. But"—she bit her lip—"when I hid the journal under my shirt, I think the archivist saw me, so I bolted. Ran track in high school. Came in handy. Figured I was in the clear until I realized I didn't have gloves on when I signed in." Her eyes grew wide. "What if the journal is worth a lot of money? What if whoever loaned it demands an investigation? They could get fingerprints and match them to mine, the ones I got taken when I volunteered at a March Break day camp. Worse, what if they confiscated the journal before I could've read the whole thing? I had to disappear. Just for a few days. That's why I left the rental car in the hotel parking lot. So no one could find me when I returned it, or by tracing it. I needed to figure everything out. For our family."

"You have an excuse for everything, don't you?"

"The law isn't always right," Simone said. "When you read Celeste's journal, you'll see it that way too. And there's no way you'll want to give it back, either."

"Is that a prediction?"

"Interesting choice of words," Simone said. "I'll get the journal."

CHAPTER 4

Celeste, 1864

Celeste stuffed newspaper into the toe of her too-big work boots, wincing at the crackles and crinkles. Noelle, her fourteen-year-old sister, younger by five years, turned over in the narrow bed they shared. Celeste froze, waited for her sister's snores to begin again, then stood. She knocked over the Bible that sat on a chair and it thunked to the floor. Drat.

"Time to get up?" Noelle mumbled.

"No, go back to sleep." Celeste layered her half of their tattered woollen blanket over her sister, who pulled it over her head and curled into a tight ball. Celeste exhaled, her breath visible in the cold late-spring air. Their room in the attic where they lived, atop the Union Bank, was outfitted with a stove, but coal cost money. At least they had an arched window with a view of the harbour; it was best to keep an eye on its icy waters. One never knew if the ships it brought would be foe or friend, if the creatures it supported would be predator or prey. The ocean was bountiful, but it also enabled the transport of enemy sailors and hid serpent-like beasts. And harboured the phantom ship, with its cold flames, cruel tricks, and deathly traps. The vessel was out of sight at the moment, but she cursed it as she did every morning, for what it had done to her twin brother, Yvon.

"Are you going to the market?" Noelle asked.

"Yes, but you stay here."

"Just because you're older doesn't mean you can tell me what to do." Noelle threw off the blanket and sat up. "I want to go."

"Maman said, if we moved here on our own, you had to mind my instructions." It'd been four weeks since they'd arrived in Charlottetown, so dissimilar to Rustico where they'd been raised, a small village where no one was a stranger and everyone knew everyone else's business. That was dangerous for Celeste. Most people didn't see what she saw. Some had started to ask questions, to glance at her with suspicion. It was not good to be different.

She'd started anew here in the city, relishing her ability to be alone in a crowd. Something she decidedly would not be if her sister accompanied her. Noelle tended to gape at people in fine dress hurrying from shop to shop, boys hawking newspapers on every corner, horses and carriages jostling for space on the street, and steamships blasting their horns in the harbour. "Tomorrow, after we have our pay, perhaps we can go to the park together," Celeste said.

"Can we buy an entire cake?" Noelle asked. "With frosting?"

"No, we cannot, little goose." Celeste kissed Noelle on the forehead. "We need a cobbler to fix your boots and make me ones that fit, coal for the stove, and oats for our breakfast. We must repay the butcher for his kind credit. Anything extra we send to Maman." She kept her annoyance out of her tone, but couldn't resist adding, "You know this."

"It'd be nice to celebrate our first pay, wouldn't it?" Noelle asked.

"We can celebrate when we have means." Celeste piled her tawny hair into a bun and stabbed it with a wooden knitting needle, which served the dual function of keeping her hair up and providing her with a ready weapon. Though she wouldn't likely inflict much damage with it, it made her feel better.

"Look out for Mrs. Pierce. She'll put you to work early," Noelle said.

"If I leave now"—Celeste gave her sister a pointed look—"I'll manage to miss the old shrew."

"That's not very nice."

"Truth is truth. I'll return soon." Celeste left the attic, closed the door behind her, and descended the twisting staircase, past the cleaning closet where Mrs. Pierce, the head housekeeper, doled out cleaning supplies like they were precious gems. She exited the side door of the bank, which sat on a full city block like a king on a massive throne, three storeys plus an attic high. She breathed in the salty air, paused, set her shoulders back, and strode up the alley. She'd managed to carve out a routine over the past few days, and even experienced momentary flutterings of belonging, imagining herself as a regular at the market, a familiar face on the waterfront, even someone brave enough to walk into the ladies' section of Noonan's Tavern to drink a pint of ale.

Lifting the frayed hem of her brown woollen skirt, she avoided the worst of the stinking mud of Great George Street. Planked walks had been laid down for pedestrians in some parts of the city, but none here. Although, with the bank's well-heeled customers, improvements were sure to arrive soon. A horse-drawn carriage pulled in front of her and she jumped out of its way. She bit back a curse as a servant hopped out, placed a stool in the sludge, and helped the bank's director, Mr. Forbes, step out. Mr. Forbes's single-breasted waistcoat and ruffled cravat hid the worst of his bulk—the man clearly never missed a meal—while his polished shoes flaunted his ability to avoid the city's grime.

As he entered the bank's front door, Mrs. Pierce rounded the corner, her perpetual frown deepening. "Miss Haché, where are you going?"

"Just to the marché." Celeste grimaced. She had trouble with words that were similar in French and English. "The market. For a bite to eat." If breakfast were included with their room and board, as she'd expected, she wouldn't have to take the time to run out. Although the inconvenience allowed her an excuse to escape into the bustle of the city each morning.

"Mind you're not one second late." Mrs. Pierce placed her hands on her ample hips. "The advertisement specified 'women of moral means,' and you two show up. You're lucky Mr. Forbes wanted me to fill the positions so quickly. If I had it my way …"

For an English Protestant such as Mrs. Pierce, their being French, Acadian, and Roman Catholic were three strikes and you're out. Least, that's what Yvon would've said. He'd adored the game of baseball that one of the travelling teachers had taught them to play.

Before Yvon was killed.

Everyone else said it was an accident, but Celeste knew better. She wore his boots now, a constant reminder of her loss. She'd ground through the soles of hers, so his were the only option.

Once out of Mrs. Pierce's sight, Celeste's step lightened. The city was hers, if only for a few stolen moments. Several strides later, she faltered beside the whipping post, where a man had been flogged yesterday, thirty-nine lashes for highway robbery. His tortured screams had filled the city, serving as a deterrent to all who might contemplate breaking the law. Thick dirt had been laid to cover his blood. Unlike the others who walked by, Celeste's mind's eye perceived the event as if it were occurring now, with red splotches, fresh and slick, flying from the man's back, splattering on the ground, and threatening to land on her skirt. She stepped back, then shook her head at herself. Just a vision, nothing that could hurt her now.

Her often dreadful but sometimes useful ability had passed through their family line, from her great-great-grandmother Madeleine, to her great-grandmother Sébastienne, to her grandmother Lottie, and to her. It was a fickle gift—to perceive what had come before or what might come after—that seemed to have skipped her mother and her sister. Lyrics of a gloomy ballad sprang unbidden to mind: "Le monde est un séjour de malheur." The world is a sojourn of misfortunes. Though how bad the misfortune depended on which world you lived in. Her own, or one with clean shoes that fit and a supporting hand.

She continued on and entered the Round Market, a domed-roof, one-storey building that held more food than she'd seen during her entire life. The first time she'd been here, she'd counted twelve butcher-stall bays circled around the edges—such an unbelievable number that she'd counted again—yes, twelve butchers in one place. In the centre, farmers sold butter, eggs, oats, turnips, and potatoes. She approached the baker's section: biscuits, cakes, and pies. Her mouth watered and her stomach growled.

A ruckus brewing behind her drew her attention from the intense scents of cinnamon and cloves. She recognized the voice of the butcher, one of their neighbours from Rustico, who'd given them a credit. He made the trek to Charlottetown once a month to sell his wares. "My meat's not diseased," he argued with a police constable. "Anyone told ya so is a snollygoster liar."

"Save it for the Mayor's Court," the constable said. He turned to the uniformed man beside him. "Burn the meat outside. Let that be a warning to others."

"Don'tcha touch that meat," yelled the butcher as the constable dragged him away. "How'm I to feed my family? Ya yellow-livered bastards."

"Yuuh, yuuh, yuuh," the baker closest to Celeste said, her words more an intake of breath than anything. "Second time this year that man's been arrested. But as long as he pays the fine and his rent, they let him do it all again. The bloody gall of 'em, eh? Codgers."

"Yuuh, yuuh, yuuh." Celeste mimicked the sound in her ongoing effort to perfect her English accent. She sympathized with the butcher and made a conscious effort to avoid recalculating how many extra shillings she'd have if she could delay repaying their debt to him. She and Noelle hadn't gotten sick from his meat. "The bloody gall."

"Same order as usual?" the baker asked. "One day-old biscuit and one large apple scone?" the baker asked.

"Yes, please."

"Wouldn't you rather two fresh scones?"

"Tomorrow, perhaps I'll buy four," Celeste said.

The baker handed over the pastries and turned her attention to another customer, a Black woman who, based on their conversation, was a schoolteacher at the Bog School. Celeste wrapped her purchase in the cloth she'd brought with her, tucked it into her apron, and exited the market. As she passed the horses, the mass of flies she had to wave away dampened her appetite for a welcome moment. On her way back to the bank, she paused to stare in the display window of a portrait studio. The banner caught her attention: *With the new tintype, exposure is a mere 15–30 seconds. No posing tables required.* Such wonders to enjoy in the city. The ability to capture a moment, reproduce it, hold it in your hand, and share it with others was remarkable. A photograph wouldn't disappear like a fleeting memory or an elusive foretelling.

"Company," a loud voice soared, drawing out the last syllable. "Quick march!" Feet pounded in unison. "Left turn."

A group of volunteer soldiers appeared, in a mish-mash of uniforms, remnants of the now-disbanded City Guards. The officer-in-charge tipped his hat at her. She dropped a perfunctory curtsy and hurried in the other direction. Her mother had warned her to steer clear of soldiers. She'd cautioned her a great deal about many things, most of which Celeste ignored, but not this one. Her family had a damnable history when it came to uniformed men.

She swallowed her biscuit in two bites. With a glance back at her newfound city, she joined her sister in the attic and handed her the scone.

"You ate yours already?" Noelle asked.

"Sorry, I was too hungry to wait."

Noelle broke off a piece, popped it into her mouth, and savoured it. "Was your scone as sweet as this?"

"Sweeter, I bet." Celeste ignored the rumbles in her stomach.

"If we can't buy a cake tomorrow, what about meat pie?"

"Absolutely, little goose. You will have a full belly, that I promise." She ruffled her sister's hair. "But now we've work to do. Get dressed. I'll meet you downstairs."

Celeste hurried towards the bank's salon, where the executives met every morning before the bank opened. They lounged in comfortable chaises and deep-seated chairs while smoking pipes and drinking tea, the door propped open to allow some of the smoke to dissipate. The smell of rich tobacco wafted out of the room on the words of their conversation. Celeste wrinkled her nose at the scent but breathed in their discussion as they rubbed their palms together with glee at every deposit accepted, loan approved, official bribed.

She could always find something to scrub—or pretend to—to give her a reason to be nearby. Today, she scoured at a nonexistent stain on the floor while they chuckled about profiting from construction and railways. At first, she'd scampered away when one of the men left the room, but he paid her no attention, wasn't the least bit interested in what she was or wasn't cleaning. None of them were. So she listened. Day after day, week after week, she memorized their secrets, the deals they discussed, the men they named as supporters, the ones who were adversaries. If the executives didn't want to be heard, then they should've been more circumspect.

When Noelle appeared at the end of the hallway, Celeste mopped her way towards Mr. Forbes's office, which was the closest to the bank's lobby. The room was a fair enough size but cramped with too much furniture, as if each extra piece made him that much more important. He demanded that his stove be lit and burning all day. That man used more coal in a week than they had all month. A large portrait of Queen Victoria, jewels dripping from her ears and neck, hung above his desk. She looked down her regal nose at Celeste each time Celeste walked into the room. The desk was in its usual state, scattered with envelopes, documents, and unsigned bank notes. Celeste did her best to dust under and around them while Noelle laid the fire.

The bank notes were supposed to be locked in the tall steel safe that stood in the corner, but the director was lax with security. The gin in the bottom drawer might have had something to do with it. She'd considered taking a gulp herself—he'd never notice—but that would mean putting her lips where his had once been, and the slight gratification she would get was not worth it.

Without the signatures of the bank's president and cashier, the notes were useless, but the sight of them sitting out in the open was thrilling, nonetheless. These ones were in the amount of twenty dollars each. Celeste peered at them, amazed at what difference existed between them and the only ones she'd ever used, in shilling and pence amounts. Using the mix of British and American terms had been confusing at first, but people seemed to accept it quickly enough. She wondered how long this newfangled paper money would last. If it bought them food and shelter, that was all that mattered.

The notes were warm to the touch today, as if they'd laid in sunlight. Or gotten too close to flames. She trembled and they began to burn at her skin, sizzling almost, in her hands. Was this a warning of some sort or was it an inviting sign? She dropped them, stepped away from the desk, and her hands cooled. She put the notes to the back of her mind and bent to pick up a copy of yesterday's paper. *The Examiner* had fallen onto the floor next to a hip-high stack of local and international newspapers.

"Lis-moi quelque chose," Noelle said.

"English, Noelle. You have to practice." Celeste stared at the photographic etching on the front page—attributed to a Mr. David Campbell—of five of society's elite standing on the Government House lawn, the women showing off newly-fashionable crinoline skirts and the men with doffed top hats. She'd aim her evening walk there today, continuing her habit of using the front page as a horoscope of sorts, allowing it to take her in whatever direction it depicted. It was a good way to explore. One never knew when learning something about a place, a person, or an event would be to her advantage. She closed her eyes and pictured herself in the etching, important enough to be immortalized on the front page, then opened her eyes to her present reality.

"This is a good one," Celeste said to her sister, pointing at an article. "'To marriageable young ladies a word of advice: a man is better pleased when he has a good dinner upon the table than when his wife talks good French.'"

Noelle scoffed. "You won't let me speak French at all." She grabbed the paper and crumpled it.

"If I had an advice column," Celeste said, "I would write, 'To marriageable young women: don't listen to codgers.'"

Noelle frowned. "Codgers?"

"I heard someone use the word at the market. I think it means men, and not in a nice way."

"You trying to turn into an Englishwoman?" Noelle asked.

"Yes, and so should you. The more we appear as the others, the better."

Noelle tossed the ball onto the fire. Smoke wafted out of the stove.

Celeste rushed to open the flue and the window. "What're you doing?" Mrs. Pierce had lectured them about using the stoves properly. It wouldn't do for the bank's executives to smell like commoners. "If we're let go, we lose our work and our rooms," Celeste said. Eventually, her plan was to move out of the bank, get better jobs, more independence. But just like coal, that would take money.

"Désolée," Noelle said.

"Sorry won't do much good if we're out on the street." Celeste fanned the air with her apron.

"We could always go home."

"No, we cannot." Celeste tapped her fingers on the desk. Tap-tap-tappity-tap. It was exhausting trying to protect someone who refused to see threats. Part of her was glad of Noelle's innocent approach to life. The other part wanted to shake her sister silly. "I thought you were excited about getting paid," she said.

"I am, but … I miss Rustico. Don't you?" Noelle asked.

"Back to work, little goose." She scrubbed at the window so there'd be no telltale sign of soot on the glass.

"What do you miss most?"

"Can you think of nothing else?"

Noelle stared through the bottom of the windowpane as if she could see the north shore. "I miss our clam bakes. Except for the time Auntie and I drank too much of the juice they left behind after we boiled them. Racing her to the outhouse was not at all ladylike." She giggled, then turned serious and continued her list. "Tending the garden. Minding the stove. Churning butter with Maman. Step-dancing in the kitchen."

"What about gathering mussel mud? Do you miss that?" Celeste spat the words out.

Noelle jerked as if Celeste had hit her, tears springing to her eyes. "I miss Yvon as well," she said.

"I know, little goose. I know." But while Celeste and her sister might mourn their brother equally, only Celeste's grief was coupled with guilt. She wouldn't fail Noelle the way she'd failed Yvon.

CHAPTER 5

Celeste

Celeste searched out Mrs. Pierce, fairly sprinting down the hallway towards the freedom and security their pay would give her and her sister. As she passed a few executives, she bowed her head and slowed, picking up her speed once she was past them. Mrs. Pierce was in the cleaning closet at the back of the bank, with brooms, mops, and soap powders lining the walls.

"You're here for your pay, are you?" Mrs. Pierce asked. "Couldn't wait even five minutes for me to organize this mess?"

Celeste raised her eyebrows. The closet was as tidy as always. Mrs. Pierce could find fault with God, if she so chose to question Him. "Yes, Mrs. Pierce. Sorry, Mrs. Pierce." Celeste calculated their earnings and their expenses as she waited for the head housekeeper to turn her attention away from the supplies. She and Noelle each earned one dollar each week, which meant, for the month, together they'd made eight dollars. What an enormous sum. They could send half of it home to Maman. That left them four dollars, which was forty shillings. Scones were two shillings. A small meat pie, if she haggled, was seven. The cobbler would be eleven. So, if they each had one scone a day, shared a meat pie once a week, skimped a bit on coal, she might even be able to purchase the cake Noelle craved, buy a bottle of wine at Gahan Grocery to celebrate, save a bit for their future…

Mrs. Pierce knocked her out of her reverie when she handed her two slips of paper.

"One is for the room and board deducted from your pay. Four dollars."

"What?" Celeste blurted.

"The other is for your pay, two dollars, deposited in the bank. Held in trust, mind you, as you don't have a male guardian."

"I don't understand."

"I'll do the sums for you."

"That's not what I meant." Celeste shook her head. "Our pay was to be eight dollars, and room and board was to be included."

"Don't be absurd."

Celeste clenched her fists, her breathing ragged. She forced her hands open and pushed her shoulders into a relaxed posture. "Mrs. Pierce. Ma'am. There must be some mistake. The advertisement promised—"

"Whoever read it to you made a mistake. The wording was quite clear. Six dollars a month. With the expectation you would board here at the bank, eat lunch and dinner from our kitchen. Not that the cost was included."

Celeste's nostrils flared. "It is you who are mistaken, ma'am. I am quite literate. The advertisement is in our room. I'll fetch it." She turned to go.

"You will not." Mrs. Pierce grabbed her arm. "Talking like a lady doesn't make you one. Back to work."

Celeste shook her off. "We've finished for the day."

"Mr. Forbes allowed in a few customers after closing. They tracked in muddy prints. You're to scrub the floor." Mrs. Pierce crossed her arms over her chest, as if daring Celeste to defy her.

Celeste stared at the head housekeeper. "Fine then. I'll tell Noelle."

"I'll inform her. On your way, now."

"No need, Mrs. Pierce," Celeste sweetened her voice. "You have enough to do. I'll get my sister."

"You'll do your work as I assign it or you'll find another job. Which is it to be?" Mrs. Pierce planted her feet wide and stared at Celeste.

Finding another job meant finding another place to live. Impossible, with no pay. Which Mrs. Pierce well knew. Celeste ducked into the closet so the head housekeeper wouldn't see her anger, busying herself with gathering brushes and soap powder. If she pretended this was of no consequence, then Mrs. Pierce might think she was placated. A humble worker simply following orders. "I'm pleased to help as needed, Mrs. Pierce," she said when she could trust her voice.

"Be sure to rinse the floor twice. With clean water. I'll send Noelle to the pump," Mrs. Pierce said.

Celeste lugged the cleaning supplies to the bank's lobby, which was empty of customers. A few tellers tallied up deposits and withdrawals. She dropped the supplies to the floor. A teller glanced up from behind his wicket, frowned, and went back to work. She examined the floors. Dirt and grit dotted the wooden boards, but nothing that needed more than a quick sweep.

Noelle soon arrived lugging a bucket, water sloshing over its sides. "What's going on?" she asked. "Mrs. Pierce is acting quite odd. Chased me out of our rooms and then stayed behind, muttering something about cuts to the bank's housekeeping budget. I asked her what she was doing and she demanded I get water."

"She's punishing me, that's what's wrong."

"What do you mean?"

"Just mix in the soap powder," Celeste said.

"Are you upset with me? Did I do something wrong?"

Celeste let her breath out in a huff. "No, little goose. It'll be fine. We may as well mop." Worrying her sister would serve no purpose.

They spent the next hour on their hands and knees, scrubbing the floor until it sparkled. If Mrs. Pierce thought she could punish Celeste into accepting her lowly station at the bank, she was as wrong as a three-headed goat. Cleaning was easy.

Punishment was living through the winters in Rustico, at the end of which they had to cut away the long underwear they'd worn for months as protection against the hateful cold, painfully separating it from the flesh and hair that'd grown through the cloth.

Punishment was watching the food stores empty out, their daily meals rationed so they could survive until spring.

Punishment was those three sharp knocks the evening before her twin and father were to begin gathering the mussel mud that would fertilize their soil.

When Yvon had answered the door, the entryway had been empty. Not even any tracks in the slushy yard. That night, he woke screaming, babbling about a woman in white who'd hovered over his bed, her hair hanging down and sweeping across his face. Celeste shushed him back to sleep. "C'est un cauchemar." But it wasn't a nightmare. It was a forerunner of his own death.

Celeste shuddered through the memory. No, Mrs. Pierce couldn't punish her, but she was going to succeed in cheating her. The more Celeste scrubbed, the more the image of the advertisement faded in her mind, the words and letters blurring until they disappeared completely. When she returned to the attic, she wasn't surprised to find that the advertisement she'd so carefully folded into their Bible was gone. That snollygoster, yellow-livered, codger bastard of a woman had snatched it away. There would be no money for their mother, no scones, no coal. No cobbler. No cake. No wine. And certainly no savings.

The city wasn't turning into the haven she'd needed it to be. She had to find a way to better their situation. While wearing her brother's cursed boots.

Truth be told, she knew what to do. Had it all planned out, in case it was needed. She'd just needed a nudge. And Mrs. Pierce had given her a shove.

WITH THE BANK QUIET AND NOELLE FINALLY ASLEEP—AFTER ASKING QUESTION upon question about Mrs. Pierce, Celeste dodging each one—Celeste skulked downstairs, heading straight for Mr. Forbes's office. The moon shone through the window, casting shadows across the corridor. As she stepped forward, her own shadow mingled with them. She creaked open Mr. Forbes's door and approached the desk. The unsigned bank notes sat out in the open, ready for the taking. She took this as a sign to proceed and snatched up four of them. They tingled in her hands. She shoved them into her apron pocket. She added a dip pen and jar of ink, then left the office.

Once safely back in the attic, she dragged a chair close to the window, using the sill as a sort of desk. The moon's light bathed her in warmth and a calmness filled her. Using a one-shilling note as an example, the last of the diminishing funds they'd arrived with, she practiced the bank president's and cashier's signatures, copying them over and over on a scrap piece of newspaper. She struggled with the swoops and slopes, worrying she'd run out of ink before she'd managed a passable signature.

When satisfied with her ability to successfully forge them, she placed one of the notes in front of her. Her hand hovered over it. If she ruined it, she could always burn it, though it would be a shameful waste. She looked at Noelle, thin body beneath thin blankets, and dipped the pen. She signed with a flourish, repeated the signatures on the other notes, and admired her handiwork. The counterfeit signatures nearly matched the real ones, except for a faint blotch on one note, which was bound to escape notice. Such flaws weren't common, but they did occasionally occur.

While men might bust into banks with shotguns and shootouts, she'd found a way to bloodlessly take back what she was rightfully owed. Maybe a bit more. Once the notes were dry, she picked them up and held them in her palm. No tingles, no heat. Was that because she'd made her decision, and her fate was set? Or had she just imagined it before, and no omen or premonition warned her, or urged her on? No matter, she'd done it.

She crawled under the bed and removed a brick from the back wall. She'd loosened it right after Mrs. Pierce stole the advertisement, knowing she'd need the hiding place ready. She should have thought of it when they first arrived in the city, hidden the advertisement away. But she'd had no warning, no vision, that Mrs. Pierce would steal it. She placed the notes into the hole, replaced the brick, and brushed away the fallen mortar.

She lay down on the bed, her eyelids finally growing heavy enough to close. At a flash of light, her eyes flew open. Oranges and reds reflected on the attic ceiling. She tiptoed to the window. Flames in the distance. The phantom ship. Shivers tickled her spine. Cold sweat popped on her brow, as if the ship were in the room beside her. Wood crackled. Embers floated. She covered her eyes and groaned.

After the night the woman in white had visited, she'd never seen her brother alive again. He'd left with their father to gather the mussel mud while Celeste was still asleep. She yearned to change so many things about that day, not the least that she'd accompanied them. If she had been there, she would've seen the flaming ship as well. She could've stopped Yvon, when he'd called out to their father that he needed to help a ship in distress. She could've told him everyone on board was long dead. But she hadn't been there, and Yvon rowed out alone, while their father was tending to the horses. The boat overturned—the lop-sided piles of mud ruining its balance—and Yvon fell out. Their father splashed through the waves, finally managing to find and drag her brother back to shore. But too late. Yvon was gone.

Now, the flickering in the attic stopped and Celeste lay there, in the dark, unable to sleep. At dawn, the first of the sun's rays reached through the windows and shone onto the wooden trunk that contained everything she and Noelle had brought from home. It fairly gleamed in invitation. She stepped over to it, dropped to her knees, opened the lid, and rummaged through their clothes. Nothing. Not possible. There had to be something here. The sighting, the memory, the light … they were trying to tell her something.

She emptied the trunk entirely and softly rapped on the sides and the bottom. There. A faint echo. She felt around the seams and her fingernails caught on a gap. A false compartment. She levered up a slat of wood. A thin leather-bound book with frayed pages beckoned her to open it. She read the first words, written in French, recognizing the handwriting as her great-grandmaman Sébastienne's, relating the story of her own mother. Madeleine. It began with their family's deportation.

Celeste rifled through the book's pages.

CHAPTER 6

Madeleine, 1758

The further from their hometown of Rustico they sailed, the closer Madeleine pulled her family. Her stomach churned like the ocean below. She fixed her gaze on a cresting wave, following its whitecaps until it crashed into another, then another, and another. They were surrounded by friends and neighbours on the deck of this British ship, *Patience*, but none were safe. Soldiers dressed in blood-red peacoats and sailors in blue reefer jackets spoke an incomprehensible language as they swept the Acadian community up and out of their island home, deporting them to France. To a country her ancestors had left decades ago.

Her fingers twitched to hold the small wooden cross and crescent moon that hung from her thin roped necklace, hidden by her long and tangled hair. But to do so she would have to let go of her two youngest—Joseph, three years old, and Marie-Blanche, who was five—clutched on either side of her. Instead, she drummed her fingers on their shoulders. Tap-tap-tappity-tap. Tap-tap-tappity-tap. She started the game they often played. Can you copy the rhythm? But neither child joined in. Her chin trembled as she forced away her tears. They would do her no good.

The three older boys, inherited when she married Alexis, crowded behind her. She shifted her body against her husband, whose bowed legs from years of fishing compensated for the rolling deck. His eyes protruded in his reddened face as he struggled to control his rage, though what portion was directed at her, and what at the British, she was unsure. Grégoire, Alexis's eldest at fourteen years old, hitched his breath, the way he used to when trying not to cry. Théodore and Josaphat, practically twins at eleven and twelve years old, pushed closer to her. Until recently, they'd judged themselves too old for such attention, but now they'd reverted to the little boys she'd met after their mother died. She hummed their favourite lullaby, all the comfort she could give.

A sailor with a manifest called for each family. His English twisted their names into ugly garbles as he sent them below. The deck cleared as their fellow Acadians took their turns descending into the bowels of the vessel, where they would remain for the twelve-week journey.

The sun dipped towards the horizon with a flicker, disappearing behind the phantom ship, crewed with spectral passengers, set afire for eternity. If she mentioned her sighting, Alexis would dismiss it as a reflection, but she knew better. Her unborn baby's kicks punctuated her thoughts. A boy. She'd read it in the tea leaves patterned at the bottom of her earthenware mug soon after the baby had quickened. She hadn't told Alexis. He didn't approve of such notions, preferring her to restrict herself to the practicalities of midwifery and herb gardening.

"We made a mistake," Alexis said through gritted teeth.

They'd fought over their decision to board *Patience*. They'd had a terrible option: cooperate with the deportation or conceal themselves in the woods. She believed journeying to France was the lesser evil, while he argued the opposite. They'd wavered for days, until Madeleine dreamed of what winter would bring if they remained on the island. Her newborn dying before he could breathe more than a few gulps of air. The other children sick and starving. Their frozen bodies covered in snow, including her own. When she'd woken the next morning, in a sweaty pool of fear, she'd told him nothing of her premonition, but her decisiveness was enough for him to agree to leave.

But now, as they faced the reality of months in the hold of an enemy vessel, with the phantom ship in the distance, she questioned herself. Questioned how she'd set this fate in motion.

"Durin," the sailor called, to no response. "Durin!" He brandished his musket, the bayonet affixed to the tip a more imminent threat than a voyage in the hold.

"Doiron?" Her voice quavered as Alexis stood mute beside her.

"Ya, Durin." He pointed to the ladder that led into the darkness.

Into an unknown future.

MADELEINE HUDDLED WITH MARIE-BLANCHE AND JOSEPH ON THE FLEA-INFESTED bottom bunk. Alexis and the three other boys shared the two bunks above.

Dozens of such beds held the Acadians, stuffed and stacked into the dank hold like livestock in a barn buried under a mound of dirt. Sunless days and moonless nights passed one into the other.

Madeleine adjusted her cloak over the two children and shifted onto her back. She grimaced at the stench from the latrine buckets secured at each end of the hold: one set for the women and children, the other for the men. Judging from the rankness of the smell—something between fresh horse manure and fresher cow dung—a sailor would soon appear to unlock the small hatch above the water line, on the port side of the hull. A volunteer would accept the foul job, climbing up to dump the contents of the pails into the ocean below. Once the pails were empty, there'd be a blessed moment to gulp in the brackish air before the sailor slammed the hatch shut. The Acadians took turns, each person enduring the nasty to savour the sweet.

"Two weeks," whispered Alexis so as not to wake the children. Every morning, as the sun shimmered briefly through a crack high in the hull, where the tarred boards didn't quite meet each other, he announced the progress of their journey. Three days ago, he'd begun including the death count. "Four gone to God."

"We made this decision together, Alexis. Enough." She suffocated under the weight of his blame. She closed her eyes and replayed her dream of what would have happened if they had stayed on the island. Even with any potential assistance from the Wabanaki Confederacy, Madeleine's family would have suffered greatly through the winter, playing lethal hide-and-seek with the British as the temperature dropped and the snow fell. She took solace in what her future might hold if they journeyed to France. A woman—who somehow seemed like family—standing on a cliff. How Madeleine longed for a sister, someone to share her gifts with. To help raise her children, with a full appreciation of their abilities. She longed to meet that woman.

When Madeleine could breathe freely, she opened her eyes. This had been the right decision. Difficult, with much risk, but the better path. Alexis mumbled something. She didn't ask him to repeat it. Every word he spoke to her was filled with bitterness, his way of managing his own guilt for the family being in this situation.

Joseph and Marie-Blanche stirred awake. She wiped the fear off her face and replaced it with a smile.

"Good morning, my lovelies." She pushed their matted hair off their foreheads as they rubbed their eyes.

"There yet?" asked Joseph.

"Not yet."

"Soon?"

"It will be as God wills."

"Today, please," he replied.

"You can pray for it, but God …"

"… works in mysterious ways." He drew the words out in a lilting voice and waved his hands.

"Yes." Madeleine patted his turned-up nose with her finger. "Now, time for the toilet."

"Smelly, Maman." Marie-Blanche wrinkled her own nose.

"You know the routine." Madeleine had set them on a schedule, a warped reflection of the one on the island they'd been expelled from, to help them pass the time, taking advantage of the ship's roster of chores. "Today is wash day."

"Yippee." Marie-Blanche loved anything to do with water. She was too young to understand that they sailed on a creaking ship that was a mere speck on a massive, hostile ocean.

A sailor opened the hatch, allowing the men to draw up pails of briny water and pass them out, one bucketful per family. They only had two clean buckets, so it took quite a while before each family had their turn. Alexis had been first in line, though, so Marie-Blanche didn't have long to wait. He placed the bucket in front of them and Marie-Blanche launched herself at it. She splatted the water with her palms. It sprayed up and drenched the front of her shirt. She chuckled as Alexis frowned. He opened his mouth to reprimand her, but Madeleine shook her head. On this journey, with so little chance for fun, her children deserved any moment they could steal. He grimaced and turned away.

A few seconds later, Marie-Blanche shivered and her lower lip trembled. "Cold," she said.

Although Marie-Blanche wasn't happy about being wet, Madeleine was glad the water seemed to have landed only on her clothes. They were half-washed and the water wasn't wasted, with no slippery mess on the deck. "Seawater is frosty as snow, little one, especially way out here." She changed her daughter into her only other set of clothes, wrapped her in a blanket, and returned to the washing.

"I warm now," Marie-Blanche said after a few moments. She dropped the blanket and threw herself at the bucket again.

"Marie-Blanche," Madeleine scolded.

Théodore swung down from his bunk and caught his little sister in his arms. "Once there was a blackbird," he said.

Marie-Blanche and Joseph cawed at the opening line from their favourite story, which Madeleine had learned from her own mother. Madeleine added a "caw-caw-caw," drawing out the last caw in a way that always sent her children into fits of giggles, even now.

Théodore related how Roubi the Dog—here the children barked along with Madeleine— dug up Mrs. Blackbird's yard and destroyed her nest. When he stole her eggs, Mrs. Blackbird set a trap to stop him. Once captured, Roubi pleaded for his freedom by promising to replace the eggs. Mrs. Blackbird agreed, so Roubi stole from a nearby farmer. Encouraged by his success, Roubi returned to steal bacon. This time, the farmer was ready for him. Théodore skipped the part where Roubi was pulled apart by the farmer's oxen, ending the tale with Mrs. Blackbird living happily. Here, the whole family—even Alexis—chorused with caws and barks. For the briefest most wonderful moment, Madeleine let the joy lift her heart. When the last animal sound faded, the pain of their situation crept back inside her as if it had never left.

That afternoon, the seas rose as if in anger at their brief respite. She lashed her littlest ones to the bunk with her blanket to keep them from smashing their heads on the bunk above or hurtling to the wooden deck. Soon after, they fell asleep. She watched them breathe in and out, memorizing their every feature as she had when they were first born.

"JE ME SOUVIENS DE MA MÈRE. JE ME SOUVIENS DE CHEZ MOI. JE ME SOUVIENS de la sécurité." I remember my mother, home, safety. Madeleine repeated these phrases to herself, the rosary in her chilled hands, as she moved from bead to bead. She couldn't remember when she had shifted from the Our Fathers and Hail Marys to these three phrases. It must have been sometime after Joseph had vomited up the rotten biscuits and maggoty salted meat that had served as a miserable excuse for dinner. He'd fallen into an exhausted sleep soon after. Marie-Blanche, who had only nibbled at her food, at least kept her portion down, slipping into her dreams with frightening ease, she had so little energy.

With the decision to leave—to allow themselves to be taken from their home—firmly made, she had done everything within her power to protect her kin. She scrutinized her dreams for signs and portents. She baked seven loaves of bread, careful to place them right side up to cool, for good luck on the crossing. She packed all her dried herbs, which weren't as much as she liked because she'd had little time to prepare. Snakeroot to settle stomachs, nettles for minor wounds, purslane for fever. She warned the children to board *Patience* with their right foot first. She helped Joseph and Marie-Blanche practice, making them walk through the front door again and again, only relenting when Marie-Blanche stopped lifting her left leg altogether, dragging it behind her as she stepped forward with her right.

The night before the Acadians were due to leave, Madeleine trod towards the beach. Dense clouds covered the sky, but the flames of the phantom ship lit her way. She removed her shoes and stepped into the icy water. The waves lapped over her feet and pulled the sand out from underneath them, making her one with the sea. She kneeled and dipped her necklace in the ocean. "Keep us safe," she said.

The spectres reeled and whirled over the phantom ship, step-dancing to music only they could hear. The captain soared towards Madeleine, stopping a short distance away from her.

"We will help, if we can. If you promise," the captain said.

Visions filled Madeleine's mind, the price of their assistance. She closed her eyes, let herself live in the possibility. Weighed it against the lives of her children.

She opened her eyes. The captain wavered before her. "I will do anything for my children," she said.

"Do you promise?" he asked. The waves rose. Cold red flames slipped over whitecaps.

She swallowed. "I do." The necklace had grown hot in her hands, scorching them. But instead of dropping it, she held it tighter. When the necklace cooled, she placed it around her neck and turned away, leaving the phantom ship behind, though she was more tied to it now than ever.

A WOMAN'S WAIL SENT A CHILL RACING THROUGH HER OWN BODY. HÉLÈNE, HER widowed neighbour whose little boy—not yet a year—had been sick for days. Madeleine grasped onto Marie-Blanche and Joseph, for she knew what that cry indicated. Any mother would.

"Maman, I'm squished," Joseph said.

Marie-Blanche curled into her.

Hélène's sobbing continued.

Madeleine forced herself up. She staggered towards the grieving woman, holding onto the bunks for balance. She'd helped bring this babe into the world, and now she'd have to help him leave. She crouched down and brushed away her neighbour's tears. "He's with God now."

"He cannot have him!" Hélène's eyes flashed.

"There is nothing to be done." The calmness in Madeleine's voice belied her fear that she was looking into the eyes of her own future.

Hélène wrapped herself further around her baby. Madeleine sat on the bunk and embraced them both. She wasn't sure how long they remained that way, but eventually, Hélène allowed her to take the babe. She lifted him into her arms and cuddled him against her, praying that death would not pass from this babe to the one in her belly. The woman in white had not yet come thrice knocking on the hull, signalling the death of one of her own.

Someone handed her an almost-clean piece of cloth; it became a shroud as they wound it around the small body, moving upward from his tiny toes, to his knobby knees, to his thin chest. They paused when it reached his chin. Madeleine kissed his lifeless cheeks. They continued until he was entirely encased. A hush fell over the hold as she walked to the hatch. When a sailor unlocked and opened it, the clean chill of the evening air rushed over her. She raised her eyes to the moon, alone in the sky with only the stars for company.

With a deep breath, she prayed over the boy, lifted her arms out the hatch, opened her hands, and let him fall to the cruel sea below.

She returned to her bunk. "Je me souviens de ma mère. Je me souviens de chez moi. Je me souviens de la sécurité," she began again, louder this time, her voice rising with each phrase. She fought to keep panic out of her tone, finally drifting into the oblivion of sleep.

THE WORDS OF A LULLABY WELCOMED HER TO WAKEFULNESS. FOR THE SLIGHTest moment, she imagined herself in the home she had made with Alexis, listening to him soothe the children with a favourite melody, his voice deep and clear.

"Dors, dors, dors, ma petite," Alexis sang.

Her body relaxed for a moment, but the swaying of the ship shattered the illusion. As time and war had shattered their marriage. Madeleine sat up.

Marie-Blanche peered at her. "Maman, you're awake. Sing please."

Joseph bobbed up onto his knees. "Yes, Maman. Sing, sing, sing."

A jolt of energy surged through Madeleine. She may not have her home, or safety, but she had her children. They had their father. She joined her voice with Alexis's, their words stretching between them, forming a cocoon over their family. "Dors, dors, dors, ma petite."

Sailors chanted above. "The maiden oh, the bottle, oh." Their feet stomped on the deck, their shanty assisting them in moving aft in time with one another.

"Dors, dors, dors, ma petite."

"A pipe of good tobacco, oh." Stomp. The deck shuddered.

"Dors, dors, dors, ma petite."

"So early in the morning." Stomp.

"Dors, dors ..." The words of their lullaby faded.

"The sailor loves all these, heigh ho."

SEARING PAIN ENVELOPED HER. NOT HUNGER, OR SHIVERS FROM THE FRIGID AIR, but her third baby. She shouted once, then clenched her teeth with a groan. She focused on the small gap in the hull above. A patch of sunlight pushed through, streaming towards her. A sign from God, perhaps a blessing for her child who would be born too soon? A good omen, that there would be joy in their life? This birth would reveal the truth of her premonitions. If he were to live, please let him live, then she'd made the right decision for her children.

A surge of pain sped through her. If she were back on the island, she might have been able to stave off this birth, using herbs to keep her son within her for crucial days more—a week even—during which he'd continue to grow. But she was now helpless to her labour, as helpless as she was to the whims of kings who traded away Madeleine's homeland with the stroke of a pen, sentencing her family to this ghastly journey.

She closed her eyes and opened them to see Alexis holding her hand. He kissed her cheek. "Hélène is ready to help," he said.

"Thank you," Madeleine whispered, not for the assistance but for the tender attention.

"Marie-Blanche, Joseph, off the bed. Climb up to your brothers' bunk," Alexis said.

"Want to see new baby, please Papa." Joseph tiptoed around Madeleine, his hands clutching the bunk's edges for support.

Alexis picked Joseph up and plunked him on the bunk above. He started to cry but Marie-Blanche shushed him. She was adept at reading a situation, figuring out the best response. She took after Madeleine in that way. Life might not be fair, or just, but it was the one they had.

"Here, Papa." Grégoire pulled the blanket off his bunk and tucked the edge under the frame. It dropped down and formed a curtain, giving a small measure of privacy.

"Thank you," Madeleine said. Perhaps he'd finally forgiven her for replacing his mother.

Hélène nudged the sheet aside and crawled into the bunk at Madeleine's feet. Madeleine caught a glimpse of Josaphat and Théodore, worry plain on their faces. The blanket fell back into place.

"Madeleine, I'm here if you need me," Alexis said.

Along with all the island Acadians. A second later, she had no care for privacy as a horrible pressure built in her womb. The baby fought to get out. Sweat drenched her brow.

Contraction followed contraction.

Time stretched.

Moments and hours passed, merging one into the other.

Finally, she nestled her new baby boy, François-Xavier, against her breast. Her hands trembled as she held him and a shaky laugh escaped her. He was small but healthy.

Alexis was overjoyed, covering both of them with kisses. "Did you see it? Did you know he'd be safe?"

She nodded, unable to speak. He squeezed her hand and cuddled beside her. He had touched her more in the last few moments than he had since they'd boarded.

She ignored a neighbour's body being transported to the hatch as yet another family mourned. A few days ago, she'd heard a splash that was not caused by one of their own. The sailors were losing to the sea as well.

THEIR FAMILY'S DELIGHT WITH FRANÇOIS-XAVIER COULD ONLY SUSTAIN THEIR energy for so long. Madeleine tried to engage the children but found the only thing she could focus on was nursing the baby. He fussed and refused her more than he accepted any nourishment. She whispered encouragement to him, to little avail.

One day—she had lost track of time as it had been far too long since they'd seen the sun peek through the boards—Marie-Blanche stopped halfway through a game of cat's cradle. She'd yanked a strand of wool off her frayed blanket, which Madeleine had helped her detach. Anything to keep her occupied.

Madeleine leaned forward to check her daughter's forehead, which was hot and dry. "How's your belly?"

"Hurts," Marie-Blanche answered. "Maybe I ate too much."

Madeleine frowned. The only thing any of them had eaten that day was bits of dried apple. Was something wrong with her mind?

Marie-Blanche broke into a wan smile. "Teasing, Maman. You say to laugh." She held up an index finger. "One a day."

"You little scamp." Relief flooded over her as she kissed her daughter's nose. "So, is your belly truly bothering you?"

"Yes. Like string." Marie-Blanche yanked on her cat's cradle to demonstrate.

Madeleine's own stomach clutched at the description of the symptom that had decimated her neighbours and now threatened her family. Across the hold, Alexis helped Théodore from the bucket in the men's corner and then went back for Joseph. When Joseph's knees buckled, Alexis picked him up. She winced at his sluggishness—her boy who could never stay in one position for more than a few seconds, who bounced from place to place, who had once whispered in her ear that he'd build a boat to take them home—could barely walk a few short steps except to use the bucket. Maybe it was a good sign, that he somehow had something left inside him.

But she kept hope at a distance, for hope was too painful.

Alexis would not meet her gaze.

She tapped her fingers against her necklace. Tap-tap-tappity-tap.

Madeleine dreamed the woman in white knocked once, twice, three times. When she woke, gasping and choking, the woman lingered in her mind's eye, trailing her thin fingers over the children.

There were four weeks left in their journey.

Life continued in a ghastly rhythm.

Théodore was dying.

Alexis cradled his son's head on his lap. Closed his son's eyes after he died. Joseph, Marie-Blanche, and François-Xavier slept. The ship rocked through the waves. Grégoire and Josaphat picked up Théodore. The three brothers moved through the hold, two of their hearts beating and one, just turned eleven, stilled. Alexis accompanied them to the hatch. Madeleine held François-Xavier tight in her arms, unable to do anything but watch as they gave Théodore to the ocean.

"Did you trade one for the other?" Alexis grunted.

"What?" She didn't understand his words.

"You knew François-Xavier would live. Did you know Théodore would die?"

"No, absolutely not." She shook her head so hard her ears rang.

"Is it because he was not of your flesh? He loved you." Alexis's lips curled.

"I loved him. Fiercely. It would have been worse if we had stayed. Much worse."

"How can it get worse?" He slammed his mouth shut as if to take the question back. She hugged her baby close. Prayed to God.

Christmas passed and the days bled towards the new year.

There were three weeks left in their journey.

She poked and prodded her children constantly, plying them with questions about how they were feeling. She refused to let anyone else hold François-Xavier, fearing to lose even a second with him. She transferred him from one arm to the other, biting the nails of her free hand. If she had the room to pace she would have; instead, she crossed and criss-crossed her ankles, bent and straightened her legs, grasped at her necklace.

Days later, Joseph was dying. Madeleine cradled her son in her lap as he died. His eyes were closed so she kissed his lids. Marie-Blanche and François-Xavier slept. The ship rocked through the waves. Grégoire and Josaphat shook their heads, refusing to carry another sibling away. Alexis picked up Joseph. Her eyes followed their son, three years old. She would never see him again. God was punishing her.

There were two weeks left in their journey.

Her nails were bitten to the quick. She tried to focus on her surroundings but they blurred as if she were removed from them. All she could see was her children. She spent every moment concentrating on them, as if her attention alone would keep them alive.

To no avail. Marie-Blanche was dying. She and Alexis supported their daughter's head. Marie-Blanche died with her eyes open, staring at the cat's cradle hanging at the end of the bunk. François-Xavier slept. The ship rocked through the waves. Alexis looked at Madeleine with empty eyes. She picked up Marie-Blanche. Alexis and his sons watched. She carried her firstborn, her daughter, five years old, across the hold. God had abandoned her.

There was one week left in their journey.

They arrived in Saint-Malo, France.
François-Xavier lay dead in her arms.

CHAPTER 7

Madeleine

Madeleine kept living, in that she woke in the morning and closed her eyes at night. A blanket of guilt entombed her, knit together by Alexis's condemnation and the reproach she directed at herself, the strands intersecting until she couldn't tell one from the other.

She plodded beside Alexis, Grégoire, and Josaphat as they travelled, with several other families, away from Saint-Malo and towards Belle-Île-en-Mer. They'd learned that the French king had granted the Acadians land on the island—in the parish of Locmaria—as compensation for their expulsion, though they were to be charged an annual occupation fee. His generosity only stretched so far.

"Thyme for stomachache. Tarragon for nightmares. Savory for cramps. Marjoram for sadness. Chamomile for sleep," Madeleine muttered to herself. "Plant in the shade, situate in the sun. Keep moist, water often. Break into small pieces. Grind with a mortar and pestle. Bring to a boil. Thyme for stomachache..." Madeleine fell into the repetition to keep her mind occupied, away from thoughts that she had misread the signs. True, François-Xavier had lived weeks, instead of moments, but there was little consolation in that. She had lost all three children from her womb and one of her beloved step-children. What sense was there in her own survival? What good had there been in her preparations, in her abilities, in her deal with the phantom ship? It had all been for nothing.

Alexis ignored her, speaking only to Grégoire and Josaphat. His anger was like a living thing that emanated off him and coated her body. She tried to pierce through it, but he had built an impenetrable wall between them, with his sons firmly positioned on his side. Still, she took some comfort that they were alive to be angry at her.

"Marjoram for sadness, chamomile for sleep." Madeleine focused on these two herbs, mixing and brewing more than she should with every meal. She trod forward in a daze, refusing offers to ride in the cart until she was almost asleep on her feet.

Days later, when they reached the western coast of France, with blistered feet and weary limbs, a small sailing ship awaited them. The sight of the vessel—sails flapping as sailors climbed the rigging—dissipated the fog she had surrounded herself with. She shivered at the memory of their journey across the Atlantic, but these sailors were French and this voyage was merely a few hours long.

When they cast off, she moved away from the others and leaned against the bulwark. The cool spring wind slashed through her clothes but she ignored it, her gaze fixed on Belle-Île-en-Mer. The island shone in the distance as the sun washed its shores. Seagulls screeched across the cloudless sky, as if leading Madeleine towards the island. As the ship approached the island's harbour, she noticed a figure perched high on a cliff. Their eyes seemed to connect, even though the distance was too far for this possibility. For a brief moment, it was as if Madeleine herself stood on that cliff. Could smell the violets. Feel the ground beneath her feet. Was that the woman from her dream?

Alexis interrupted her thoughts. "Madeleine."

She jerked at his gravelly voice, strangely unfamiliar. Even though she had listened to him talking with others, it sounded odd for him to be addressing her.

"We are married," he said.

"I am aware," she said, her voice rasping. She couldn't remember the last time she had spoken to someone else.

He handed her a waterskin. She accepted, swirling the water in her mouth before she swallowed.

"We cannot change the past," he said, "so we must move forward. As man and wife. But you must agree to stop talking about, or taking action on, any dreams or premonitions. I cannot have it."

She considered his offer, though it was not an offer at all, but an ultimatum. She nodded and turned back to the island. The figure on the cliff had disappeared.

AT FIRST GLANCE, THE PARTIALLY-CLEARED PLOT THEY HAD BEEN ASSIGNED was more than satisfactory. The ocean arced in the front, a forest lay behind, and meadows reached out on the sides. But the ground itself was a rocky mess. Preparing it for planting would be an arduous task, though Madeleine welcomed it. It would allow her to keep her hands busy and fall into an exhausted sleep each night.

They'd been given a small supply of tools, seeds, and food staples. Within a few months, Alexis and the boys had managed to chop enough trees to build a one-room cabin, with a stone hearth and dirt floor, and Madeleine had prepared enough land to plant a small garden. They had regained a semblance of being a family, a wounded one, as rough and raw as their bleeding and chapped hands.

Summer flourished around her. She relished the warm air and the colourful foliage. She roamed farther afield in search of kindling and edible plants while the others cleared ever more land and stockpiled firewood. She spent hours—all day sometimes—without another human in sight. She hummed lullabies no one heard. Played cat's cradle with long pieces of grass. Stared at the ocean, watching for the phantom ship, come to mock her. Lost more and more weight until she wondered if she would simply disappear.

One day, as she sniffed at violets, peered at crimson berries, dug out pale green leeks, and examined brown-capped mushrooms, a shadow fell over her. A strange sense of déjà vu overtook her. She looked up. A person stood beside her. She jerked and stepped away.

"Poisonous, or no?" The woman's words were French but the accent odd.

Madeleine peered at the tall and slender woman. Wavy hair the colour of the full moon tumbled over her shoulders.

"Hello?" Madeleine stuttered.

"Hello," the woman said in a clear voice.

Madeleine surveyed the area, trying to understand where she'd come from. Surely she had not simply appeared out of nowhere. A path just beyond led into a wooded area, trees clustered together as if supporting one another over the long years of their lives. She must have approached from there. Madeleine brushed her hands on her apron and tucked her hair behind her ears.

"Welcome to the island." The woman leaned in as if imparting a secret. "Though don't refer to yourself as an islander if there's a local within hearing. You don't warrant that label unless you're born here."

Madeleine lifted her chin. "I am an islander. Just not from this island."

"Interesting," the woman said. "As am I. Though mine was a much larger one. My name is Elinor." The wind shushed through the long grass and set Elinor's hair flying.

"I'm Madeleine." She fiddled with her cross and crescent moon necklace. She noticed now that the woman's silvery-white hair was misleading; they were about the same age.

"You're one of the Acadians?" Elinor asked.

"Yes."

"It's fateful you've arrived here. You left an island occupied by the British only to land on one freshly relinquished by them."

When Madeleine had learned that the British had once occupied Belle-Île-en-Mer, then left it again to its French inhabitants, a tiny corner of her mind opened to the possibility of someday returning to her own island home. "I had once thought it was not possible to escape them," she said. "But now ..."

Elinor nodded. "Indeed. This island escaped. I escaped."

"What do you mean?" Madeleine waved away a buzzing mosquito.

"It's a rather long story. Shall we walk a bit? I'm sure you could use a break from your work."

Madeleine considered. She craved the chance for conversation, for company, but still, she considered declining. Maybe she was better off alone. What was the point of it all, anyway?

Elinor touched Madeleine's arm and an image flashed in her mind. The figure on the cliff, solitary, high above the ocean, yet somehow grounded. For a moment, Madeleine's view shifted to the figure's perspective. She could see herself on the ship, almost transparent in the blinding sun. As if she were fading away. Elinor's view of her. Madeleine had begun to think the woman had simply been a wish, not a possibility.

Elinor let go, her eyes on Madeleine's face.

Madeleine gazed back. She covered her eyes with her hand to block the sun and scanned the meadow. Just an empty field and lonely cabin in the far distance. No sign of Alexis and the boys. "To answer your question," she said, "not poisonous." She picked the mushroom and placed it into her apron.

"Impressive, for someone new to this island."

"Plants are much the same everywhere. Avoid anything with milky sap, shiny leaves, or yellow berries. If all else fails, watch to see what the animals eat." As if on cue, a chipmunk raced underfoot, disturbed by their steps.

"You're well taught," Elinor said.

"My mother. Though she died before she could impart all her ..." What word should she use to describe it? "... wisdom."

"No one can ever impart all their wisdom. There's always something else. May I ask, did she die on the voyage to France?"

"No, years before." Madeleine's voice wavered. So much loss.

"I'll tell you about myself, then, shall I?" Elinor said.

They'd reached the edge of the cliff. Elinor pointed to where the island curved in the northern distance and jutted into the sea. "If you squint, you can almost see the watchtowers of the fortified town, Le Palais. Though it was rather ineffective at holding off the British soldiers who took it over."

"Were you there when they attacked?" Memories of the British landing on Île Saint-Jean shuffled through her mind.

"Oh no, they brought me with them kicking and screaming. But it did me no good in the end."

"You're British?" Madeleine asked, though the woman's accent was different from the officer on board *Patience*.

"I am not."

"Where are you from? What happened?" The invasive questions slipped out of Madeleine's mouth. But Elinor had offered her story and it seemed she was a survivor. Madeleine needed to hear of a hard-won triumph.

"Swansea. In Wales. Until soldiers snatched me away and threw me on a ship. I suppose they were worried there wouldn't be enough locals to terrorize here in France." Elinor stared into the distance.

Madeleine nodded. It had been a fear on their ocean journey, though one that was buried beneath so many others. But the sailors had stayed above and the prisoners below. The decks that separated them had some advantage. "Were there many of you?"

"A dozen or so, although our numbers were starting to dwindle."

Madeleine could guess at the reasons. Death by disease, childbirth, despair ... Different from her own journey, but similar in the end.

"Anyway," Elinor continued, the word allowing her to skip over the details of her experience. They continued their stroll, far enough back from the cliff for safety but close enough to hear the crashing of the waves far below. "When rumours started that the British were leaving, sailing off to one place or the other, I determined I would not go with them. I would flee into the countryside. Or out the watchtower's window."

Madeleine murmured her understanding. After Joseph and Marie-Blanche died, she'd fantasized about jumping out the hatch. Every time it opened, it called to her, a possible release from her pain. Though God forbade it, it wasn't Him but François-Xavier who anchored her to life. Once her baby was gone, she bent into the pain. Deserved it, even, for allowing him to die.

"I'd tried to escape once before, though the punishment was ... unpleasant." Elinor raised her hands and turned them over. Her palms were covered in welts. "My chances of success were higher with their preparations to leave. Little time to chase a runaway. I managed to procure oleander leaf, dried it, ground it up, mixed it into ale, and offered it to the last damned soldier that night. He drank it like a glutton." Elinor paused in her story.

Madeleine nodded. Poison.

"I slipped out of the city and ran until I reached the end of the island." Elinor spread her arms wide. "I positioned myself on the cliff, right here, where I now often sit to watch the ships," she glanced sidelong at Madeleine, "and waited until the British flags disappeared into the distance."

"How did the villagers greet you?"

"My limited French did me no favours. But the town crier's wife was in early labour with a difficult birth and the midwife had decided to travel to Le Palais to visit the apothecary."

Madeleine assumed the timing was something other than a coincidence.

"I offered to help," Elinor said, "knowing that if they survived, I might be accepted."

"If they died, you'd be cast out. Or worse."

"Exactly," said Elinor.

"It went well, then?"

"It did. Afterward, I traded for French lessons by assisting with women's work. Settled on a piece of land at the edge of town. It's back that way"—she pointed to the woods—"nestled in a vale. As it hadn't been cleared, I was allowed to claim it as my own. Eventually, I built a small hut. Women find their way to me when they need me, ignore me most other times. The midwife here is rather traditional, so I'm able to offer women something ... different. It has allowed me to live a comfortable life. Do you understand what I am saying?"

"Why are you telling me this?" Madeleine asked.

"You must answer my question first."

"You're the woman on the cliff," Madeleine said in response.

"I'm a woman, and I'm standing on the cliff. As are you." Elinor grinned.

"You're teasing." A smile tugged at the corners of Madeleine's mouth. She breathed deep and plunged into their friendship. "Fortune showed us to each other. Brought you here today."

"Indeed. We are alike, you see. It's why I've told you my story. Taken from our homes, concealing who we are. I knew it as soon as your ship came into sight. But I wasn't yet sure of you."

Madeleine barked out a laugh. She snapped her hands up to cover her face.

"Are you quite all right?" Elinor asked.

Madeleine shook her head, snorted.

"I think you should sit down." Elinor led her to a large mossy rock.

"I'm fine," Madeleine said, but she sat anyway. She tapped her fingertips on her knees. "How is it possible that we have so little control over our lives?"

"Even for those more powerful than we," Elinor said, "there's always a man with a sword, or a gun, or a decree, who is stronger. But we have our ways to take back control, don't we? To live our own lives. If we're brave enough to claim who we are."

They lingered in silence for some time. The wind eddied through the grass, their hair, the trees.

"It is not your fault, Madeleine." Elinor squeezed her hand. "Whatever happened. You did what you could. You must forgive yourself. Then you can trust."

"I do trust you, even though we've only just met," Madeleine said. Elinor seemed an old friend, not a new one.

"That's not what I meant," Elinor said. "You must trust yourself. Be true to who you are. Your abilities. It is how you can honour your mother. All those who came before and will come after."

Madeleine closed her eyes and traced the outline of her necklace, cross and crescent moon. She would have more children, she saw. She and Elinor would help her girls learn about their abilities. So her daughters could teach their own daughters, on and on through their family line.

Perhaps the phantom ship had kept its end of the bargain after all.

CHAPTER 8

Celeste

Celeste was so immersed in Madeleine's story that it took a few moments to realize Noelle was perched on the end of the bed, reading over her shoulder. "C'est tellement triste."

"Oui. Quatre enfants morts." Celeste shook her head. Reading the story in French had her thinking in that language as well. She switched to English. "Four dead children on one voyage."

"Who is it about?"

"Our great-great-grandmaman Madeleine."

"Where did you get it?"

"I found it at the bottom of our trunk." She left out the part about it being hidden. Had her mother put it there for her to find? Or had it been tucked away for years, forgotten and lost? Waiting for Celeste to find it.

"How did it get there? I didn't see it when we unpacked."

"Must've been wrapped in a blanket," Celeste said.

"But we took every blanket out when it was so cold—"

"Breakfast and work, little goose." She placed the book in the trunk with a sigh.

"I want to read it now," Noelle said.

"You cannot." Celeste slammed the lid of the trunk. She'd share some elements of Madeleine's story with her sister, but the whole of it was for her alone. Noelle had a strong connection with their mother. Celeste's had been…less so. She wanted one relative—Madeleine—to herself. "I have a surprise for you this afternoon," she said.

"Truly? What is it?"

"Let's buy a cake and go for a picnic in the park. We'll wear our Sunday best."

Noelle squealed and clapped her hands. "You received our pay."

"I did," Celeste said. The twenty-dollar notes stashed under the bed weren't their pay so much as recompense for getting cheated by the bank, but they amounted to the same thing in the end. "Don't mention anything to Mrs. Pierce. She doesn't like to talk about the financial side of things."

"If you think it's best," Noelle agreed.

"I do," Celeste said, as they descended from the attic to the bank's main floor.

When they entered Mr. Forbes's office, she slipped the pen she'd taken back onto the desk and poured some of the ink from a full bottle into the one she'd almost emptied. Her hands trembled and she dropped a blob on what looked like a contract. She rubbed it with her thumb, only grinding it in worse and staining herself. She licked at her skin, then dug in her teeth to scratch some of it away. It seemed it would always be there, a reminder of what she'd done. A mark of sin.

"Celeste. Noelle," shouted Mrs. Pierce from down the hall. "You're needed in the kitchen."

"Yes, ma'am." Noelle walked into the hallway.

Celeste stopped trying to remove the mark. She should be pleased with what she'd done, not ashamed. She was protecting her sister.

Mr. Forbes entered his office. As usual, he ignored her. She stepped out and stood just outside his doorway as he plopped onto his long-suffering chair. He dropped his hat onto a pile of papers and leaned down towards his bottom drawer. The clinking of glass told her he had more than one bottle of gin now. Good. She was an invisible servant, his desk was a mess, and he was a day-drinker. He shouldn't notice the notes were gone.

Even so, she risked a peek back at him to check. His head was bent over one document or another. He wasn't cursing or searching. She'd gotten away with it. She forced herself to stride away at a steady pace.

LATER THAT DAY, CELESTE AND NOELLE CHANGED INTO FLORAL-PATTERED dresses with plain trim and strolled down Great George Street, arm-in-arm. The closer they got to the baker's shop the more Celeste's hands shook. She'd convinced Noelle they should dress up to celebrate, but her hidden aim was so that using a twenty-dollar note for such a small purchase wouldn't arouse suspicion.

"What's wrong?" Noelle asked.

Celeste withdrew her arm from her sister's and willed herself to steady. "Just eager for our picnic." The late afternoon sun shone through thin clouds while a cool breeze shivered over Celeste's skin.

Noelle inhaled the scent from a basket of pink lady's slipper flowers decorating a tearoom's outdoor seating area. "Perhaps we could come here someday for lunch."

"Perhaps." Celeste's limbs twitched and tingled as the note scorched through her small, crocheted travelling bag. Was it her imagination or a sign? Her future with respect to the stolen counterfeit notes appeared to be uncertain, wavering between good tidings and bad.

Maybe this was a mistake. If she could get another job, perhaps as a washerwoman, she could work in the evenings to supplement their paltry pay at the bank. Her hands were already raw from mopping the bank's floors and clearing ash from the stoves, but with enough money, some lotion could fix that. Noelle could live without cake. Celeste opened her mouth to tell her sister she was sorry, she'd miscalculated, they couldn't afford a fancy cake from the bakery, or anything from a tearoom, but they could still have their picnic with biscuits from the market. A sense of relief settled on her shoulders, with the decision made. Noelle would understand.

Noelle reached out and squeezed Celeste's hand. "Thank you for bringing me to the city."

Celeste stopped. "You like it here?"

"I think I do." She spun in an impromptu twirl, bumping into a frowning man who dodged her skirts. "My apologies," she said. She made a face at Celeste and giggled. "Oops."

"You are quite lighthearted." Celeste's resolve slipped.

"I see the opportunity now, here with you. It just took some time to get used to it, that we would have the resources to belong in the city. Maybe, one day, we could move into an apartment." She turned the word over as if truly understanding it for the first time.

"Look at you, speaking like a city girl." Celeste hugged her sister close. She would do anything to keep that smile on her face. She patted her bag, as if to damn the fates, as they passed by the portrait studio. An advertisement for a special introductory sale caught her eye. A camera, with film and plates, cost just over five dollars. Surely paying with twenty dollars would be reasonable. That would leave her with smaller notes she could use elsewhere. "Let's go in," she said.

"Why?" Noelle asked.

"To buy a camera, silly."

"Can we afford that?"

"Of course we can. Just today, thanks to our industriousness, Mrs. Pierce increased our pay by a few shillings." The lie slipped out without a thought.

"Wonderful," Noelle said.

"Indeed." They would make a life for themselves in Charlottetown. Celeste would ensure her sister was safe here, happy, with a future.

As she opened the door, the bell jangled, announcing their arrival and setting Celeste's nerves afire once more. She calmed as a slim man with thinning hair welcomed them with a French accent. The words danced in the air, beckoning her towards them.

"Well, hello there." He tucked his thumbs into his suspenders. "You'll forgive me." He pointed to his waistcoat hanging on hook. "The way the sun shines through the window cooks me like a turkey."

"Mais oui." Celeste tested the words, letting her breath out when he smiled.

"Bienvenue. A French customer. What a treat. Je m'appelle Monsieur Biset."

"Mademoiselle Celeste Haché." She offered her hand and he clasped it gently for a moment. "And my sister Noelle."

"Welcome, welcome," he said.

"You don't try to hide that you're French?" Noelle asked.

"Not much use with a name like Biset." He shrugged. "I could anglicize it, pronounce the 't' at the end, but I'd prefer not. I'm old enough and successful enough to get away with it. Only portrait studio on the island." He gestured to the far wall, which had a white background with several carved wooden chairs in front of it. "And the first one in the Maritimes to sell cameras to the general public. All styles, sizes, and prices. One for every budget." He waved his hand at the contraptions of boxes, bellows, and lenses sitting on his shelves. The wall behind the cashier counter was covered in framed photographs of people and landscapes. Celeste could travel to other times and places by simply moving her gaze from one to the next.

"I'm interested in that one." Celeste pointed to a small accordion-like box, with a circular lens affixed to its front.

M. Biset picked it up. "It's small and portable. Almost magical, one might say."

"Capturing images for all time," Celeste said.

"It works the same as a daguerreotype, with a wet collodion process."

She nodded as if she understood. He continued for some time, using strange terms, his motions become more animated and his voice rising as he spoke. "And so," he eventually concluded, "the image appears upside down to the photographer."

"Merveilleux," Noelle said.

"It is marvellous," he said. "What a charming pair you two are. You should come to dinner sometime. My wife would love to meet you. Both our children have moved off island. It'd be positively cheering for her to have some life in the kitchen. It's small, mind you, but laughter exceeds small spaces, non?"

"That is most kind." Celeste hesitated. Passing the note would mean cheating M. Biset, branding him a criminal if he were caught with it. Why hadn't she considered this before? She'd been so swept up in the benefits of her actions she hadn't properly considered the consequences for anyone else. She managed to shake off the thoughts. No one would get caught. Her note would mix with the others, then he'd spend it somewhere, and it would get lost in a sea of dollars, shillings, and pence, with no way to trace it to him or her.

He piled equipment on the counter. "You'll need a case, a light tester, a—"

"My goodness, do you think I'm a Vanderbilt?" she said, in imitation of one of the bank's customers who'd complained about fees that week. "Just the tintype camera and the plates." It wouldn't do to have him think she had too much money.

He laughed. "Fair enough, Mademoiselle Haché-not-Vanderbilt. I'll include the developing if you buy more plates now."

"Agreed." A higher price would make it even more natural to use a twenty-dollar note.

Her fingers quivered as she removed the note—now quite cool to the touch—from her bag. She hoped M. Biset would think she was excited over her purchase, not terrified at being led away in shackles. M. Biset deposited the note in his cash drawer, handing over the precious change that would allow her to buy her sister that cake—such a simple thing, but the ability to pay for something that wasn't a strict necessity was intoxicating—and start saving for an apartment.

As she and Noelle exited the shop, they dodged a newsboy on the corner who was waving the latest newspaper at passers-by. "Schooner *St. Cecilia* quarantined. Possible smallpox. Get your paper here," the boy called. Celeste focused on the flapping paper. No image on the front page. Odd. She squinted towards the harbour, searching for the ship. There it sat, anchored at the end of Peakes Wharf. She could just make out the yellow flag of quarantine on its mast.

At the bakery shop, Noelle stood in front of a long display table, peering at several cakes, each under its own glass dome, dillydallying over which to choose. Apple was her favourite, but she'd never tasted lemon. At first, Celeste was delighted at her sister's indecision, brought on by such delicious choice. But soon she tapped her foot, with one eye on the light outside, eager to try her camera before dark. Finally, Noelle chose lemon. The cashier placed the cake in a round tin box decorated with red and pink flowers. Noelle proudly carried the cake while Celeste carried the camera, and they were off to the park.

They turned towards the harbour, crossing the road after a horse and buggy thundered by. Celeste ushered Noelle to a bench near a flower garden, far enough away from the docks to avoid the noise and the smells, but close enough to enjoy the ocean view, which stretched in front of them like a future filled with possibility.

"We've forgotten to bring utensils," Noelle said.

Celeste settled the camera on her lap and removed two silver-plated dessert forks from her bag.

"You've thought of everything. But aren't those from the bank executives' salon?"

"Yes, but they won't mind us borrowing them. We're the ones who wash them every day. Shouldn't we be able to use them?"

"No, actually. They aren't ours," Noelle said.

"Don't be so prim. There's no harm in this." Celeste held out a fork, danced it in front of Noelle's face. "You deserve a treat."

"I suppose." Noelle swallowed. No doubt her mouth was watering.

"Are you ready, little goose?" Celeste lifted the tin's lid. An entire lemon cake, topped with yellow frosted furls, sat before them.

Noelle took the fork and poised it in the air. "We're not going to slice it into pieces?"

"No, it's all for us. Go on."

Noelle dug into the very centre, lifted out a mound of cake and frosting, and swallowed the bite whole. "It's divine." Her lips puckered. "Sour but sweet. My new favourite."

"So this is what they mean by tangy," Celeste said as she took a bite.

Women with parasols up against the sun strolled by as the sisters reduced the cake by half.

When sated, Celeste jumped up. "You'll be my first subject."

"Truly?" Noelle straightened her back, pinched her cheeks, and tucked a few stray curls behind her ears.

"Who better?" Celeste thought back to the images she'd seen in the newspaper, to how the subject was arranged, how the viewer's eye was guided. "Smile," she said. "And don't move." She positioned herself so the harbour was in the background, looked through the viewfinder, adjusted the bellows, and paused at the disconcerting upside-down image. "I forgot you'd be upside down."

"I can fix that." Noelle leaned her head towards the ground.

"Silly. Sit back up." When she did, Celeste removed the lens cap to expose the film and counted to twenty. She hoped a flash in the distance—the setting sun, only the setting sun— wouldn't ruin the photograph. She replaced the cap.

"I can't wait to see it," Noelle said.

"Nor I." Celeste forced away the misgivings that now swirled around her. "You hold the cake and I the camera, and we can explore the city some more."

At the end of the evening, pleasantly exhausted, they returned to the attic. Celeste concealed the camera behind a blanket under the bed, pushing it back against the wall where she'd hidden the notes.

"Why put it there?" Noelle asked.

"Just to keep it safe. It's an attractive item for a thief." The word caught in Celeste's throat. That's what she was now. A thief. She shook the word off. Not a thief, she thought. A survivor.

ON HER LUNCH BREAK, CELESTE REMOVED HER APRON, THREW ON HER COAT TO cover her work clothes, and hurried to the portrait studio. "I finished my set of plates."

"A whole set since yesterday?" replied M. Biset. "Careful, that's a costly habit."

She waved off the comment. "Not if you have free developing."

"Only the first set, remember. Otherwise you'd bankrupt me." He smiled. "Did you enjoy it?"

"I'm amazed. Such a different way to look at the world, through only a narrow view, upside down."

"Yes, but the beauty of it is," he replied, "by narrowing in on a subject, you open yourself up to the experience of others."

"What a fine sentiment."

"I have a poet's mind or so Madame Biset tells me." He gestured to the portrait of him and his wife that hung behind the cash register. Mme. Biset's sharp eyes pierced towards Celeste, as if in warning to keep her husband out of any tomfoolery. "Leave your camera here," he said. "Come back later. I'll have your photos for you and reload your plates."

Celeste tore her gaze from the portrait, thanked M. Biset, and left the shop.

When she returned after work, an unfamiliar man in a black suit and black cap was speaking to M. Biset. They leaned against the counter, the man in front of it, M. Biset behind, sorting through photographs. They looked up as she entered.

"Finally, you're here," M. Biset said.

The stranger held one of her photographs, the first she'd taken, of Noelle in the park. Celeste wavered between rushing over to examine her results and running away. Who was this man? Had she been caught? She rubbed her sweaty palms on her apron which, unlike her visit earlier that day, she'd forgotten to remove or even cover with a coat. She looked like a poor cleaner, not a woman who could afford a camera. She'd prepared a story, if needed, that she'd found the note on the street. Another idea came to her now. Perhaps it would be better to claim that a man—she could easily make up a vague description—had given it to her. That she'd refused but he'd pressed it on her, with the explanation that he'd received good fortune and wanted to share it. For the grace of God. That was better. But once they discovered she worked at the bank, they'd be suspicious.

"I ... I'm sorry. I've forgotten something. I'll return later." Of course, she would not. Could not. With a sigh, she turned away.

But before she could exit, M. Biset introduced the man. "This is Mr. Morrison, the editor of *The Examiner.*"

Celeste breathed out. The newspaper, not the police. She forced a smile on her face and said hello.

Mr. Morrison nodded at her. "A pleasure to meet you. Mr. Biset showed me your photographs. You have a modicum of talent."

"Thank you."

"This one here." He waved the photograph he held. "The *St. Cecilia* in the background. It's well-framed, with the woman in the foreground providing scale and contrast."

"That's my sister." Her fingers itched to grab the photograph, to see the result of her shot, but Mr. Morrison slipped it into his suit pocket.

"It's not her I'm interested in," he said. "It's the ship. The newspaper's photographer, Mr. David Campbell, boarded her to do a story on its voyage. Bad luck all around, though. He was quarantined with the passengers and the crew when it was discovered that a few people had broken out in smallpox symptoms. Damned inconvenient. I came here to ask my good friend Mr. Biset to help, but he recommended you."

"What do you mean?" Celeste stammered.

"I'd just developed your photographs," M. Biset said. "Right there in front of me was the ship with the quarantine flag. No need to send someone out to photograph the ship when you've already done it. Admirably, I might add."

"I had a good teacher," Celeste said. "M. Biset was quite patient with me. Showed me how to—"

"Don't much care about the hows or whys, just the results," Mr. Morrison said. "You'll sell it to me, of course. It'll be the basis of the wood engraving we set for the paper."

"The front page," added M. Biset.

"I'll pay you half our current photographer's rate for it," Mr. Morrison said. "You'll agree that's fair."

M. Biset, standing behind Mr. Morrison, gave a small shake of his head and pointed his finger upwards.

Celeste straightened herself to her full height. "I'm sure I'm worth the whole rate. Especially if it's to be on the front page."

"Yes, well, we didn't have to give out that information did we?" Mr. Morrison said with a glance over his shoulder.

M. Biset shrugged. "Come on, old man." He grinned. "You've the funds for it."

"Three-quarters. That's as high as I'll go."

Celeste agreed, not knowing how much three-quarters would amount to, though it was more than nothing. Maybe she herself would never be on the front page, but one of her photographs would. Wait until she told Noelle.

"Now, in the matter of a replacement photographer ..." M. Biset said.

"Right," Mr. Morrison said. "It's highly irregular to hire a woman, and an amateur at that. But I haven't the time to mess about. Don't usually do this legwork myself, but I figured Mr. Biset couldn't refuse me in person. Now he's endorsed you. If you bring any newsworthy photographs, I'll pay you at your same rate. Just until Mr. Campbell is back, mind you."

"I accept," Celeste blurted. She'd figure out a way to work at the bank and the newspaper. This opportunity was not one she could refuse. Perhaps she wouldn't have to cash any more of the notes. This was a blessing, a way forward for her and her sister.

The editor outlined how she would be paid, shook M. Biset's hand, tipped his cap at her, and left.

Celeste said goodbye and thank you to M. Biset and rushed to the bank. By the time she reached the top of the attic stairs, she'd formulated a plan.

"So every time you see Mrs. Pierce," she told Noelle, "just tell her I'm fetching water, or cleaning supplies, or anything, really, so she doesn't suspect I'm gone. I'll dash off on quick breaks, at lunch, and leave early at the end of the day. Surely you can handle the last mopping."

Noelle stirred the stew she'd brought up from the kitchen for their dinner, the stove now well-stocked with coal. "You want to sneak out and leave me with all the work? And what if we get caught lying?"

"I'm trying to secure that apartment you mentioned. This is a chance at something better for us." Celeste held her sister's hands in her own. "Nothing will go wrong."

"How do you know? Have you had a vision?"

"Of sorts," Celeste answered.

"But, working for a newspaper? Can women could do that?"

"Why not? Apparently there are photography studios in Europe that are run by women, or so M. Biset says. Imagine that."

"Are there any newspaperwomen on the island?"

"I don't think so, but someone has to be first. Why shouldn't it be me?"

"You're sure about this?"

"Absolutely."

"All right then." Noelle held up her spoon. "Are you hungry?"

Celeste nodded as she walked towards the window. She leaned on the sill and peered towards the darkening harbour. The flag of the quarantined ship flapped in the wind. She tamped down a ghoulish wish that the quarantine would last long enough for her to prove herself at the newspaper. A flash in the distance caught her eye. Not the phantom ship, she told herself. It wouldn't dare touch their family again. She forbade it.

She'd received mixed signals about the future from those damned and yet hopeful notes. Was her desire to make this life of theirs work interfering with her interpretations? Her grandmaman Lottie had died when Celeste was just a few years old, so Celeste had no one to guide her in her abilities.

After dinner, she huddled in the candlelight with Madeleine's story, eager to learn more. The shadows grew as night claimed the city. As she read, falling into the French words, with the occasional odd phrasing or spelling she couldn't quite understand, she slipped into her great-great-grandmother's world. Imagined crossing the ocean, shadowed by the phantom ship, haunted by the woman in white. Grappling with her abilities. As Celeste grappled with hers.

CHAPTER 9

Madeleine

Seven years after she'd arrived on Belle-Île-en-Mer, Madeleine lay in bed, Alexis beside her, waiting for the household to fall asleep. Her family—which had grown again—was practically within reach of each other in the small cabin. Tow-headed Sébastienne was six years old, with slowly developing abilities in hindsight and foretelling. Before and after, that was how she interpreted them, though she couldn't always tell one from the other. Sébastienne cuddled next to four-year-old Charles, all light and laughter. They shared the straw mattress with their older brother Josaphat, whose head lay at the other end. Rose, her littlest, only a few months old, was snug in her crib.

Grégoire had left years before, searching for work. He'd sent word he'd been hired as crew on a sailing ship in Saint-Malo. Alexis worried his eldest had become a pirate corsair, out to exact revenge on any British vessel that dared approach French waters. Grégoire had never gotten over the deaths of his siblings. How could any of them? Every day was filled with grief, especially this time of year, when the veil between this world and the next was at its thinnest.

Tomorrow, October 31st, Catholics would celebrate La Toussaint by placing wreaths on family members' graves. Except her children had no graves.

Which was why Madeleine had finally accepted Elinor's offer to take part in Samhain. With Rose's recent birth, yet another new life in contrast to those Madeleine had lost, she felt a renewed need to discover if her deceased children were at peace.

She focused on cracks in the ceiling's wooden beams, calming herself until snorts and snores indicated the time had arrived to slip out of bed. She turned back the blanket, sat up, and placed her feet on the floor. A lightheadedness overcame her, such that she almost lay back down. What if the ceremony Elinor had planned didn't work, and the possibility of conversing with Madeleine's lost loved ones slipped from her grasp? What if it did work, and she learned something horrible about their afterlife? Surely Théodore, Marie-Blanche, and Joseph wouldn't be punished for resting in the ocean instead of consecrated ground. She pushed away the image of her children forever shifting on the currents instead of with God. And poor François-Xavier.

As Madeleine donned her cloak, Sébastienne stirred. "Maman," she whispered. "Please take me with you."

"My dear, I cannot." Madeleine could risk herself, but she would not risk her daughter—not to the ceremony, and not to Alexis, should he learn about her participation.

"But I want to meet my brothers and sister." She mumbled her words, still half-asleep.

Madeleine regretted letting Sébastienne listen to her discussion of Samhain with Elinor. Teaching her daughter about her abilities, their ancestors, and Madeleine's own story was tricky to balance with hiding their legacy from Alexis and the village. She often wavered between what to share and what to withhold.

"Not tonight, little one. Perhaps you will dream of something wonderful." Madeleine kissed Sébastienne, who lay down and thankfully closed her eyes.

Madeleine removed the bucket from the indoor privy and approached the door. If Alexis discovered her gone, she would have the excuse that she was emptying it. It would suffice as a reason—she had done so on a few other occasions if the smell got too strong. She creaked open the door, stepped out, and closed it behind her.

The night enveloped her. Three bats flew across the full moon. Small creatures rustled through the underbrush. An owl hooted, as if bidding her forward. Something flitted past her, too quick to focus on. Her skin tingled. There was more alive in the darkness than animals and birds. She emptied the bucket in the outhouse, placed it by the door, and walked from her home.

Several steps away, she turned, confirming nothing moved within the house. But even if Alexis burst out and demanded she return, she would not. Nothing could deter her from her path now. She waited a few more seconds, to be certain Sébastienne did not try to follow, then glanced towards the ocean. No phantom ship. She hadn't seen it since *Patience* left the Charlottetown harbour, but she kept watch for it all the same. Satisfied she was alone, Madeleine set off.

Elinor waited where the field met forest.

"Hello, Elinor," Madeleine whispered.

"Why are you whispering?"

"I don't know," she whispered again.

"There's nothing to fear. Anyone who's out is doing the same as we are." Elinor motioned for her to follow. Elinor had explained that, where she was from, Samhain was an honoured festival celebrated by the whole community. They lit bonfires to cleanse the air and invited the spirits to visit, setting places for them at feast tables. Then they dressed as the dead and called on their neighbours, who gave them cider for singing a verse.

As Madeleine pondered over the strange traditions, they walked deeper into the forest, following an old hunting trail. A cloud glided in front of the moon. She stumbled over a fallen branch, catching her balance just before she sprawled on the ground. "Can all your people speak with spirits?"

"No, only a chosen few."

"What if it doesn't work for me?" A murmuring babbled through the trees, calling to Madeleine.

"It will. You can feel them already, can't you?"

"Yes, I think so." The night shimmered with possibility.

"Spirits are all around us. All you need is my guidance to find the right ones, draw them into conversation. Sometimes they resist. If it's not done correctly, they can get frustrated."

Madeleine stopped. "Can they be dangerous?" She hadn't thought to ask this before, assuming Elinor would never put her in harm's way.

"No. But the experience can be disconcerting, as I've warned."

Madeleine nodded in the darkness. How could it not be?

They reached a clearing. "Here we are," Elinor said.

In the centre, a pile of wood and corn husks sat in a shallow pit encircled by stones. Elinor walked towards it, removed a flint and steel from her pocket, and bent. With one strike, the fire caught, growing until the flames crackled and flickered. Madeleine stared at the dancing sparks.

"See how the fire mimics the light of day?" Elinor asked. "By combining the moon and the sun, we can draw power from the earth."

With those words, the clearing glowed. The surrounding trees snapped into focus. With every piece of rough bark and bit of veiny leaf in fine detail, the earth and sky were at one with her.

"Are you ready?" Elinor asked.

"Y-yes," Madeleine said.

"Your intention must be strong."

"Yes." Madeleine's voice rang out. Her stomach fluttered and her hands shook. Heat seared the air. She removed her cloak and set it aside.

"Walk with me around the fire. Think of those you want to visit." Elinor placed her arm on Madeleine's shoulders and steered her to the edge of a wide arc that appeared, glowing in the grass. "It will take time. Do not rush. You must work through your emotions. When you can, focus on one unique thing about each of your children."

Madeleine trembled.

"You can do this," Elinor said. "If you truly want to."

"I do. More than anything. But … I'm scared." The words escaped her lips before she could stop them. She hadn't admitted this fear to Elinor. To do so would be to make it real, that she might discover something horrible tonight.

"Of course you are, my dear." Elinor held Madeleine's gaze but said nothing more.

Madeleine inhaled. She stepped forward on the arc. One step, then another, until her pace quickened and she could no longer feel Elinor guiding her. Smoke filled her nose and stung her eyes. Sparks flew. Images of her children flashed before her. Her breath quickened. Each step became a stomp. The memory of the sailors' song rose in her memory but she dashed it away, replacing it with the sound of the sweet lullaby. *Dors, dors, dors*. The soft words rose into a roar.

"Dors!" she shouted. "Dors! Dors! Dors!" She stamped around the fire. Why were her children eternally sleeping, when they should be tucked in their beds with their brothers and sisters? Why were they not by her side? Hot ash inflamed her nostrils. Anger and grief matched the flames, rising higher and higher towards the moon. She circled the fire, again and again. The night wore on.

Eventually, the fire and her rage waned. Her speed slowed.

She had had such little time with François-Xavier but remembered how he tucked his head against her breast. He found her now, and she held him in her arms, listened to his babbles.

Théodore's favourite pastime was telling stories. He collected them like rocks, reciting them to anyone who would listen, always gathering more. Stories were the reason he raced towards the church whenever word spread that one of the two island priests had arrived. He claimed he wanted to be the first to greet whichever priest had travelled to their town, to ask for a Bible story, but he preferred Father Moreau. He'd once confided that Father Bernard smelled of onions, Théodore's least favourite food. Now she recited a passage about Moses and the Ten Commandments, smiling as his voice joined hers.

Joseph was a climber. He'd jump to touch every tree branch within his reach when they walked to their blackberry patch. If he found one low enough, he pulled himself up, giggling and hiding behind the leaves. She played hide-and-seek with him now. As he dashed behind logs, she pointed to where he'd hidden, so he'd reveal himself.

Marie-Blanche. Her little one who loved water. She was the most difficult, for to reflect on what brought her joy also evoked the memory of her death. Her daughter's face shimmered in the firelight, as if viewed through liquid. Marie-Blanche was agitated, unable to settle into conversation with her mother. Madeleine continued walking though her legs foundered, but she was never able to reach Marie-Blanche, or see her clearly.

When the fire died down, a spark remained, flitting around Madeleine. A feux follet. A spirit trapped in purgatory.

Her daughter was disoriented and in torment. She wanted something Madeleine knew not how to give.

She wanted to return to L'Acadie.

MADELEINE PLIED ELINOR WITH QUESTIONS. "WHAT DID MARIE-BLANCHE mean? How could I possibly take her home? Can I talk to her again? Will her feux follet disappear?" Elinor responded that Madeleine needed to reflect on her experience and refused to answer any questions until after sunrise. They walked towards Madeleine's home in silence, though horrible thoughts raced through Madeleine's mind, of Marie-Blanche suffering. At the tree line, Elinor embraced Madeleine, giving her a sad but somewhat reassuring smile as they separated. Madeleine crossed the clearing on her own, but felt Elinor watching her, ensuring she continued on, back to her living family.

Madeleine snuck into the house and collapsed at the kitchen table. She traced the growth lines from the large tree they had felled to build it. Circles within circles. As dawn somehow arrived, Rose's cries pulled her back to herself. She stood to tend to her, but Alexis came out of the bedroom, the baby in his arms.

"Difficult night?" he said.

Madeleine peered at him. There was no trace of anger or confusion in his voice. He was simply asking a question.

"Just woke early," she said.

He handed her Rose.

Madeleine patted her bum. "She's dry?"

"I changed her. Thought you might need a bit of a break."

"Thank you." She had worried their already-tenuous relationship would tear itself apart after the deaths of so many children, but it had stretched thin instead, like a sheet washed too many times, tattered but still usable.

He sniffed. "You smell like smoke. Was the stove not venting properly?" He poked the embers of yesterday's fire, then stuck his head above the iron pot that hung from the stone hearth to peer up the chimney.

She licked her fingers and wiped her face to clear away any soot before he turned back to her. "It's fine. I stoked it up last night when I couldn't sleep and sat too close."

Alexis built the fire for their breakfast while Madeleine nursed the baby. Rose grabbed Madeleine's fingers and held tight. A rare moment of quiet. Peaceful, almost. But all Madeleine could think of was Marie-Blanche. The joy of connecting with her other children was tempered with worry over her. "Do you ever wonder … Do you think …"

"What is it, Madeleine?" Alexis sat beside her and took her hand. "You seem troubled this morning."

"It's La Toussaint," she responded, which was close enough to the truth. "We can't visit the graves of our children."

"It pains me as well."

She struggled with a way to ask him about Marie-Blanche. Maybe he would understand what she needed. "I had a ... a dream last night. A normal one. About the children. They were all at rest."

"That's a comfort." He gave her a warning look.

She hadn't made any mention about her abilities in years. Because of this, she'd even managed to assuage his concerns about rumours of Elinor being more than a midwife. But now, her grief was too heavy. Elinor was a great comfort, but she didn't understand losing a child. Madeleine and Alexis shared a communal pain, so she reached across the divide between them in hope that he would help put their daughter at ease. "Except Marie-Blanche."

His face reddened. He pushed up from the table, knocking his chair over. It banged on the floor. Rose wailed. Alexis leaned towards her. "How can you say such a thing?"

She hushed Rose, whose cries waned but simmered as if waiting for a full-on boil, like a kettle on the hob. "Marie-Blanche was upset. Said she wanted to go home. How can we do that? We have abandoned her. She is stuck." Tears streamed down her face. She had almost learned to manage the deaths, but this she could not bear.

"Madeleine. Enough."

"We need to help her. She's suffering."

Alexis lowered his voice. "I have ignored your nonsense for long enough. Let you pretend you were engaging in ..." He searched for the right words and spat them out: "Women's customs. Simply delivering babies with Elinor, caring for women's health. Do you think I am stupid? That you haven't been acting on premonitions or foretellings, despite our agreement that you wouldn't? I allowed it, when you kept it to yourself. But this, telling me of this supposed 'normal dream,' you called it? No more. I forbid it."

The others stirred in the bedroom. Likely waiting out the fight before making an appearance. She willed them to stay hidden, so she could have the time to convince Alexis he was wrong.

"Elinor is no longer welcome here," he continued. "That woman is no good, putting ideas in your head. I should never have allowed you to befriend her in the first place. An unmarried woman living alone. It's unnatural."

"Alexis. I've just had a difficult night. Forget I said anything." She could not lose Elinor.

"Do you think you are the only one who suffers? I feel as if someone is stabbing me with a pitchfork every waking moment." He rubbed the back of his neck. "God is merciful. Our children are with Him." His words were a plea for Madeleine to believe as he did.

"Yes, certainly, that is true," she said, rushing to agree. "I was only experiencing a moment of doubt. I have barely slept since Rose was born. Please forgive me. Do not take Elinor from me. This has nothing to do with her. It was a silly dream." Why had she said anything? Her desire to connect with him over concern for their children had blinded her to his likely reaction.

"I am sorry," he said, sounding as if he meant it. "I know she is important to you. But she's bad for our family. Surely you see that?"

"I do not," Madeleine said.

"You will obey me on this." His voice hardened.

"I will not."

Alexis grabbed Madeleine's arms and lifted her so her feet barely touched the floor. Rose whimpered and Madeleine clutched her tight.

He spoke slowly, as if every word required great concentration. "You will obey me, or you will leave this house, without the children."

"You wouldn't separate us."

"I will do whatever is needed to protect them, even if I must protect them from you," he said.

She scrabbled out of his grasp and stepped away, almost stumbling over a chair. Alexis steadied her, then pried Rose out of her arms. "Sébastienne," he called. "Come take your sister."

"Yes, Papa." She crept out of the bedroom. "Maman, are you feeling well?" Sébastienne was experienced at articulating one particular question while meaning quite another. Madeleine nodded. Sébastienne snuggled Rose against herself and backed out of the kitchen. *I'm sorry*, Sébastienne mouthed to her mother, her eyes flicking to her father.

"It's all right, my love," Madeleine said. Sébastienne hadn't chosen her father's side, just could not come to her mother's aid.

Charles peeked out the door, stepping back as Sébastienne closed it while cooing to the baby. Josaphat whispered that everything would be fine.

But it would not, for Alexis's face was set. "Think about how it would feel to have empty arms once again," he said. "If you go against me, you will be alone." He guided her into a seat and leaned down so he was level with her. "This is what is best. I have defended you—and Elinor—to the men in the village, because of how you assist their wives. But no more. You will not risk our home. Our family. You will make us outcasts. Then who would help us in the fields? Who would we sell our extra vegetables to? Elinor can afford to be excluded. We cannot."

The truth of his words tore a hole in her.

"You obey me on this, or you leave. Without the children. Josaphat and I can work the fields. Sébastienne can manage the household."

"She's only six."

"She's more than capable. You did the same to help your father, after your mother died."

Madeleine closed her eyes. She felt her necklace against her skin but dared not reach to touch it, for Alexis would be certain to slap her hand away, or even toss it on the fire, as he had threatened to do soon after François-Xavier had died. She focused on it. A flash of a possible future played out inside her eyelids. A lonely existence without her children. She was not sure how Alexis would keep her away from them, but he was a resourceful man. Sébastienne confined to the kitchen, not able to run and play as a child should. Confused about her own abilities as they developed, forced to tamp them down in her father's presence, with no one to share them with. Part of her daughter, the essence of who she was, destroyed.

Madeleine could not allow it. She could not leave her children. Would not leave them. She was trapped.

CHAPTER 10

Madeleine

That winter was their harshest yet. The bitter wind whipped the ever-falling snow into impassable drifts. The family had dragged their beds within reach of the hearth's heat. Alexis and Josaphat braved the cold only to feed the livestock; if it weren't for the barn, they'd surely have lost all their animals.

For the first few weeks after Alexis's ultimatum, Madeleine was able to function as a wife and mother. She cooked, she mended, she looked after her children. With no joy in her work, she found what solace she could from a tidy house and her family's full bellies. But with every chop of carrot and piece of kindling laid on the fire, she was further plagued by how she was failing Marie-Blanche. Sébastienne, Charles, and Rose were fine. Safe. Marie-Blanche was not. Madeleine began to push her tasks off onto the children, overseeing them with a distracted eye. Then she lost interest in doing even that. She murmured to herself and paced around their small home, rarely stopping for more than a few seconds during daylight hours.

Every night, as the sun set and darkness fell, a feux follet flitted over Madeleine's head. Marie-Blanche's spirit haunted her. While the others slept, Madeleine experimented with different combinations of herbs and silent invocations to communicate with Marie-Blanche, but nothing opened the veil between worlds. She fashioned a cat's cradle, but the feux follet only circled it. She started the tap-tap-tappity-tap game, but the feux follet would not flash in time to the rhythm. A transparent barrier grew between Madeleine and the rest of her family. They were right there—she could see them, hear them, touch them, even interact with them—but they were separated from her, nonetheless. Was this what it felt like for Marie-Blanche? Nearby but so far away. Separated and alone.

Madeleine's clothes began to hang on her like a scarecrow, her nails were once again bitten to the quick, and no matter how high the fire roared, she couldn't warm herself. Her thoughts centred only on Marie-Blanche. And L'Acadie. Was Marie-Blanche's longing simply a childish wish to return to their previous life, one that had disappeared at the hands of soldiers and sailors? Or something graver?

The seasons changed. Snow melted. Shoots poked out of the ground. Birds chirped. One day, Sébastienne coaxed Madeleine out as soon as the sun rose and the feux follet faded. They bundled up Rose, gathered their market baskets, and plodded along the muddy road. Madeleine walked in a daze. Even the arriving spring couldn't shake off her melancholy. After several moments, she realized they were on a winding path. "We have gone the wrong way," she said, turning in a circle. "Where are we? Are we lost?"

Sébastienne steered her back onto their route. "We are not going to market."

"Why not?" Madeleine asked, though she did not much care what the answer was. If Sébastienne had a destination in mind, she was content to let her daughter lead.

"We are visiting Elinor."

"I don't understand."

"You need Elinor. No matter what Papa says. I've seen it. Before, and after."

Madeleine stared at her daughter. Arguing would take too much energy. They continued in silence.

"Besides, he's gone fishing for two days. Josaphat's caring for Charles."

Madeleine stopped as if she'd bashed into an invisible wall. She had left their house with no thought of her son. Actually forgotten about him. Her thoughts were so muddled.

"This way, Maman." Sébastienne took her hand and led her into a small clearing.

Elinor's hut sat on a mound surrounded by chestnut trees. Squirrels chased each other up and around them. A doe stood under an oak. A dog barked and the doe raced away. The place looked so odd, as though she'd never been there. She swayed on her feet.

The front door opened with a squeak. Elinor rushed out. "Madeleine. Sébastienne. I'm so relieved to see you. I have missed you both."

Madeleine tilted her head at her friend, too weak to speak.

"You did the right thing, bringing her here," Elinor said to Sébastienne. Elinor ushered them inside and sat Madeleine down on the end of her bed.

"How long has she been like this?" Elinor asked.

"Since La Toussaint." Sébastienne took Rose from Madeleine and cuddled the baby on her lap.

Elinor and Sébastienne continued to speak but the words washed over Madeleine, as if she wasn't there. It should feel wonderful to be with Elinor again, but she didn't feel anything at all.

Someone thrust a mug of hot liquid in her hands and helped her drink. She sipped, then gulped, finding herself strangely hungry. After another serving, her eyelids grew too heavy to keep open. She lay down. Fell into a blissful dreamless sleep. With no feux follets.

THE LATE AFTERNOON SUN SLANTED ACROSS THE MUD-LINED WALLS OF THE small room. Murmuring conversation floated towards her. A baby prattled. She blinked at dried herbs hanging from the ceiling. Was cheered by their purple, green, and orange flowers. She shifted her focus. Sébastienne sat straight in a chair. Her feet almost reached the floor. She had grown. How could Madeleine not have noticed that until now? Rose played on Sébastienne's lap. Her baby had a full head of hair. When had that happened?

Their words took on form. "I had to change the recipe a bit, once we ran out of carrots, but the vegetable stew was still delicious. Papa and Josaphat ate every bite," Sébastienne said.

"Well done."

Madeleine recognized the voice. Elinor. She sat up. Her head pounded.

"Maman." With one step Sébastienne threw herself at her mother, mushing Rose between them. "Are you better? Did it work? You look better. We missed you."

Madeleine squeezed her daughters to her. Kissed the tops of their heads.

"Your colour is back," Elinor said. "How do you feel?"

"I...I don't know. What's wrong with me?"

"Hard to say. You seem to be on the mend now. But if your daughter hadn't brought you to me, I fear for what might have happened." Elinor beamed at Sébastienne. "I'm proud of you."

Sébastienne grinned. "I tried to help you myself, Maman. Whenever Papa and Josaphat were in the barn. I used mortar and pestle to grind herbs, made tea, but only remembered how to fix a tummy ache. You didn't have a tummy ache, did you?"

"No, sweetness, I didn't." Madeleine's voice cracked. How could she have been so selfish, to withdraw like that, away from her children who needed her? "Thank you. And I'm sorry."

"It's all right, Maman."

Madeleine averted her gaze from Sébastienne's. She didn't deserve forgiveness. She had gotten so wrapped up with a dead child that she had abandoned her living ones.

"Why don't you give Rose to me and see if the fiddleheads are growing?" Elinor said. "You know the spot."

Sébastienne looked at her mother.

"I'm fine," Madeleine said. "Truly." Her limbs were heavy but she forced herself to gesture towards the door. "Go ahead."

Sébastienne nodded, handed the baby over, and skipped out.

"You must accept my apologies," Elinor said. "I should have been more forceful with Alexis. I tried to visit, many times, before we were snowed in, and then again when the worst of winter passed, but he refused to let me see you."

"It's not your fault, Elinor."

"What happened between you?" Elinor asked.

"I asked him about Marie-Blanche. If he thought she was at peace. Told him I had a dream about her. He didn't react well."

"I see."

"What do I do now? I have so many questions. About Marie-Blanche. How can I help her? Is she suffering? If she wants to go home, how do I get her there?" Madeleine's pulse raced with every question that had haunted her over the winter. "Is that even what she really needs?"

"I feared this was what consumed you."

"I can't stop thinking about her. Is this what's made me ill?"

"Perhaps. Grief, disappointment, fear. They are sicknesses just as any other." Elinor laid Rose on the bed and gathered Madeleine into her arms. "I failed you. I should have foreseen this outcome."

Madeleine leaned into her, felt their heartbeats merge. Her own pulse slowed.

Elinor pulled back so she could look into Madeleine's eyes. "Have you noticed a difference in Sébastienne?" she asked.

Madeleine grimaced. "Clearly, I've noticed very little. But she seems quite capable, not that it's my doing."

"That's not entirely true. Yes, you may have been…absent for the last few months, but you prepared her well. She's learned much from you."

"And you."

Elinor nodded her head in thanks. "She is a wonder." Elinor glanced out the window at Sébastienne, who was playing fetch with the dog. "As she grows, it will become more difficult for her to hide her abilities from Alexis. Suppressing them may change who she's meant to be. Which could have harmful consequences. For her. For you. For your descendants."

Madeleine traced her fingers over the necklace she kept hidden from her husband, with its cross and crescent moon. If he didn't see it, he could pretend he'd forgotten about it. "He's not a bad man," she said. "And not much different from other men when it comes to women's work."

"Perhaps. But he's not particularly good for you, is he? For your health? Will you survive being cut off from who you truly are? Will Sébastienne? What about Rose, in a few years?"

Madeleine groaned as she ran her hands over Rose's forehead. The baby giggled and grabbed her fingers. If she were made to choose between her husband and her children, she would choose her children, every time. Both living and dead. Perhaps this was what fuelled Marie-Blanche's desire to return to L'Acadie—to free her mother and her siblings from a restricted life. To help them start a new one. With Elinor.

MADELEINE FELL BACK INTO THE PATTERN OF HER FAMILY. IF ALEXIS NOTICED a difference in her, he made no comment. She forced herself to eat even though she had no appetite. Stilled her limbs at night to feign sleep, though she could not rest. Ignored Marie-Blanche's feux follet that flickered around her once dark fell, praying her daughter would forgive the apparent treachery. She ran through plans and possibilities, scouring for signs that one decision was preferable over another.

Sébastienne passed verbal messages between Madeleine and Elinor, stealing away on the pretense of gathering mushrooms or berries. Alexis and Josaphat, busy with farming and fishing, paid little attention to the girl.

Madeleine managed to send word to Grégoire through several travellers, using funds from Elinor to pay for their discretion, asking if her stepson could arrange passage for their family across the Atlantic. Weeks later, a response came back, that Grégoire believed it was possible. With his message, he sent a wooden carving of a dog, for Josaphat, as a reminder of Théodore's love of stories. Of Roubi. Madeleine shaved off a sliver of the tail and dropped it into her tea. When she finished her cup, she spoke a few words and read the leaves. A faint and wavering image of a woman appeared in her mind, standing on the deck of a ship, with long hair loose in the wind. Madeleine was convinced the woman would be a worthwhile ally.

As dusk fell on the night Madeleine was ready to depart, she mixed a valerian root elixir into Alexis's tea to ensure he slept well and heavily. When he laid his head down, the children long since asleep, she kissed his cheek, remembering the first days of their marriage, when they had hope and affection for each other. She left him with that memory and he smiled as he drifted off.

"I am sorry," she whispered. "But if you cannot accept me, cannot accept our daughters, will not help me put Marie-Blanche to rest, then we must leave." She turned to the sleeping Josaphat and set the carving of Roubi beside his pillow. "I wish you well, my boy," she whispered. "I regret taking your sisters and brother away. But you will find happiness. Have children of your own." He was courting their closest neighbour's daughter. Madeleine had foreseen that they would wed before next winter and would gift Alexis with grandchildren, which would be a salve to Alexis's heart. He cared for his children, of that Madeleine was certain, but his love was of a different kind than hers, more distant, and on his terms instead of their own. So was that truly love? It did not matter now.

She wished to leave him some explanation of her decision, but there was no way to do so. She could not write, he could not read. She couldn't risk telling any neighbours of her plan. The women may have kept their secret, but if any of the men learned of it, they would doubtless have warned Alexis.

No, there was nothing to do but disappear. She crafted a cat's cradle and placed it on the kitchen table. Alexis would understand that what she was doing was for their children. He would not agree, and he would be furious, but he would understand.

She swaddled Rose and went to nudge Sébastienne awake. Before she could touch the girl, she opened her eyes. "Ready, Maman?"

"Yes, my dear. Tend to Charles, please."

Sébastienne picked up her younger brother. His head lolled on her shoulder. He would sleep all night, regardless how many times he was moved. Madeleine envied his peacefulness. They crept out of the house. Madeleine closed the door, turned, and rested her forehead against the wood. "Be well," she whispered. She ignored the tears that sprang to her eyes and focused on staying strong for her children as they walked off their land, towards the main path. The feux follet followed.

As she considered all that had happened over the last several years, she could almost visualize the lines of events, actions, and reactions that had led to this point. Not fate, so much as an unavoidable decision.

Elinor waited some distance away, in a patch of moonlight, with horse, cart, and supplies. The nickering of the horses was the only sound among them. It would be profane to speak at this moment of one life ending and another beginning.

Elinor jumped out of the cart to help Sébastienne place Charles into the back, while Madeleine climbed up onto the bench with Rose. Once Elinor and Sébastienne were beside her, Elinor grasped the reins and clicked to the horses to move ahead. Madeleine cuddled Rose while the feux follet flickered around Sébastienne, then flew in front of them, leading their new family forward.

CHAPTER 11

Madeleine

The stone ramparts of Saint-Malo rose in front of Madeleine, blocking her view of the inner town and the harbour beyond, though seagulls squawking reminded her of the ocean's presence. She had left Elinor and the children at a small auberge, run by a widow, in a village not far from Saint-Malo. Grégoire had suggested it as a safe place to arrange lodging, though he was under the assumption that Alexis would be with them. The aubergiste seemed pleasant enough, welcoming Madeleine and her children, and Elinor, who Madeleine introduced as her sister. Perhaps they were not related by blood, but they were family all the same. Madeleine's feet ached and her muscles cried from the long journey, but she had little time to spare, so she hurried herself along despite her exhaustion. Her sleep over their travelling weeks had been erratic. While most of her attention was always on Rose, Charles, and Sébastienne, she was preoccupied with watching for evidence of pursuit, for Alexis to appear and demand his children back. This split focus was made worse by thoughts of Marie-Blanche. The feux follet flashed agitatedly every night, as if urging them on.

Now, Madeleine blended into other women with baskets on their arms, perhaps on their way to or from the town market. She passed outside the Grande Porte, a massive entry point into town. A guard stood beside a set of wooden doors reinforced with iron, which looked as if they would need several men to close. She kept her head down, avoiding eye contact. Nothing about her was likely to attract undue attention, but she could take no risks, being so close to escaping France.

She approached the southwestern corner of the wall and turned around it, to her right, finding the pier directly in front of her. The sea stretched beyond, waves lapping at the edge of the city, the high tide covering every bit of sand. The summer sun glinted off Fort du Petit Bé, a fortress that sat in the middle of the harbour, guarding the town as well as France itself. The fort's nickname was Corsair City, as the pirates had taken it over years before. Grégoire lived there when he wasn't sailing. It seemed a lonely place, isolated from the town, the country. At low tide, the fort was entirely surrounded by sand—Madeleine had never heard of tidal ranges so great, even in the legendary Bay of Fundy, but the aubergiste had sworn it was true—so the corsairs could not dock their ships there. Typically, they remained at sea, ferrying passengers in tender rowboats. But preparing one for an ocean crossing required docking at the town's pier, situated over a deep channel, which was where Gregoire's ship would be now.

The pier bustled with sailors loading supplies, hammering planks, and shouting orders, eager to push off on their journeys so they would arrive at their destinations before the dangerous autumn winds whipped the sea into a frenzy. Vendors hawked salted meat and tots of rum. She pushed through them.

She shaded her eyes against the bright sky. A blackbird—a good omen that suggested safe passage and protection—swooped across the figurehead that decorated the bow of a four-masted schooner. The carving was a quinotaur, a five-horned bull with a tail in the form of a trident. Another chimera, like the sea snake with a horse's head that the original inhabitants of Île Saint-Jean warned the Acadian settlers not to harm. This was Grégoire's ship, then. *La Terreur*. The ship her family had been deported on, *Patience,* had not been kind to them, so perhaps terror would serve them better.

She stepped towards the gangplank and a boy nestled in the rigging whistled, catching the attention of a corsair who blocked her way.

"What do we have here?" he asked, turning to face her, a pipe in his hand. "What business does a woman have with pirates?"

"Don't let the captain's wife catch you asking a question like that," said another. "She'll have you flogged." It was Grégoire. "That's my stepmother," he said.

"Then you deal with her," the other corsair said. "Interrupted my pipe anyway."

Grégoire clomped towards Madeleine, greeting her with a quick embrace. His calloused hands scraped through her thin blouse as his long beard, tied at the level of his neck with a leather strap, swept over her shoulder. She wrinkled her nose but squeezed him tight, despite the rankness of his clothing.

"It's good to see you," she said, though she was shocked at his scrawny body and gaunt face. The travellers they had sent their messages through had assured Madeleine he was doing well. Clearly, they had embellished the truth. She was about to do something similar, though it would bring pain, not relief.

"Where's Papa?" His breath stank of rum.

"I have bad news." She took a steadying breath. "He has taken ill. He had to stay behind."

"Ill? What's wrong?"

"Consumption."

"Will he recover? Why didn't you delay your departure?"

"It's not certain he'll survive."

Grégoire stared at Madeleine for a long moment. She kept her eyes steady on his face. Hated herself for bringing him more to mourn. But he nodded his head as if he expected little else. Death had taken so many of his siblings, it seemed no surprise to him that it would take his father as well.

"Thank you for making the trip to tell me in person. I wish you well." He kissed her on the cheek and turned to board the ship.

"Wait, Grégoire." She grabbed his arm. "This doesn't change our plans. The children are here with me, except Josaphat, who's engaged to be married." A slight exaggeration, but it would explain his absence. "A family friend, Elinor, is assisting us."

"Don't be ridiculous. You can't travel across the ocean without Papa."

Madeleine set her jaw. "We can and we will."

"On a pirate ship? With no male relative?"

"You're a relative."

"I have sworn my allegiance to my captain. My crew is my kin."

"You can't turn your back on your family," she said.

"I'm doing you a kindness, advising you against this journey. Besides, part of the price of your passage was Papa's help with fishing and sailing."

"I have something else to offer, if I may speak with the captain's wife." Rumours of the woman had reached the auberge, which matched the vision she'd manifested from the sliver of Grégoire's carving.

"What do you mean, something else?" Grégoire shook her arm off. His eyes flashed. "Papa forbade you using your cursed abilities."

"Cursed?" Madeleine dropped her demure comportment, advanced on him so he stepped back. Her necklace fell out of her neckline as she did so. "You dare call me cursed? You became a corsair. Embraced a vicious life." The cross and crescent moon swung with her accusations.

"And yet you seek our help?" a woman's husky voice boomed above them.

Grégoire bowed his head. "Madame Dieu-le-veut."

"Bring her aboard," the woman said.

"There's been a mistake," Grégoire said.

"The only mistake I see is you disobeying an order."

"You've done it now, Madeleine," Grégoire said.

Madeleine forced the tremors from her hands as he led her up the gangplank. A woman in a long black tunic and bare feet stood on the forward deck. A purple skull cap perched atop her head, doing nothing to restrain her waist-length hair from thrashing in the wind. "Follow me," Madame Dieu-le-veut said as she strode through a group of corsairs who parted like she was a killer whale plunging through a pack of sharks. Madeleine gulped and trailed her, glad that Grégoire was at her back. Now that she was here, her plan seemed mad indeed. Two women and three children asking for passage on a pirate ship. But she couldn't turn around now. Even if she wanted to flee, she wouldn't be able to push back through the corsairs without Madame Dieu-le-veut leading the way.

As they passed the main mast, three pewter mugs hanging from a stanchion rope caught her attention. She reached out to touch the closest, its handle cool on her fingers. The mug was a reminder these corsairs were human, that they needed water to survive, that maybe some of them were quite like Grégoire. Hard men surely, though perhaps not bad. But the wind delivered a message to her, sending the corsairs' flag—red-and-blue background with a white ermine weasel—flapping. Madeleine would do well to keep up her guard.

Madame Dieu-le-veut, Grégoire, and Madeleine ducked through a hatch into a companionway that led down a few steps into a chartroom scattered with maps. They turned, continued down again, and entered a cabin that smelled of tobacco and sweat. Madame Dieu-le-veut ushered Madeleine in. Grégoire stopped at the entrance, his eyes on a piece of parchment tacked to the door.

Madame Dieu-le-veut motioned for Madeleine to sit at a small wooden table near the cabin's entryway. Madeleine complied, gawking at a hanging blue, orange, and green rug depicting strange creatures, which divided the quarters in two. Just beyond was a four-poster bed, covered in pillows. The inside of the bulkhead was lined with shelves of masks, animal horns, and books. A sailor arrived, was granted access, and carefully placed a tea set onto the table. The dainty cups were at odds with the man serving them.

"Madeleine Doiron, welcome to *La Terreur*. I'm Charlotte Dieu-le-veut, the captain's wife and the most important crew member." She sat across from Madeleine and poured them both tea. "All these louts call me Madame, but you, you can call me Charlotte."

"Happy to meet you, Charlotte." Madeleine took a cup, swirling the liquid to allow the tea leaves to settle at the bottom for a proper reading.

Charlotte tilted her head at Madeleine, copied her movements, and set her cup down. "Grégoire told me your story. The British." She spat towards a spittoon. Half of the globule hit the target while the other half fell to the deck and glistened in the light that streamed from the four portholes. "We've slowed them down on this side of the ocean, but that's left your part of the world on its own. Opportunity for us corsairs. Plunder and skirmishes, that's what gets our boys' arses out of their hammocks in the morning. Ain't it, Grégoire?"

"Yes, Madame," he answered.

Madeleine blinked.

"Ah, don't worry, the legends about pirates serve us well, but it's really more searching than attacking. At least nowadays. Rumour is, Captain Kidd buried a treasure somewhere south of Île Saint-Jean, on Oak Island. I've always wanted to go there. My grandmother, Marianne Dieu-le-veut, was there before Kidd. She was a fierce pirate herself. Had the gift of luck, she did. That's why she got the name Dieu-le-veut. Whatever she wanted, God gave her. Though that's a bit of a tall tale. But my mother and me, we kept her name, all the same. Anyway, we're off to hunt for Kidd's treasure before word gets out." She turned to Grégoire. "Your island's got its own share of booty, don't it?"

"Yes, Madame. Legends that lead to West Cape, North Cape ..."

"All the Capes. We'll get rich on this trip, we will," Charlotte said.

"We have a city with your name," Madeleine said. "Charlottetown."

"Do ya now? Quite the coincidence. But you don't believe in those, do you?" Charlotte narrowed her eyes at Madeleine. "To other things, for now, then. It seems you're missing a husband. Wasn't he part of the deal?"

"Yes, but he became ill and couldn't make the trip. Unfortunately."

Charlotte leaned towards Madeleine. Peered into her eyes. Madeleine met her gaze.

"Unfortunately," Charlotte repeated, as if she knew that was not at all how Madeleine felt. "You've the agreed-on price, otherwise?"

"Yes." Madeleine had brought half the money with her. Elinor had the rest.

"Returning you to British-occupied lands won't put us on the good side of the French king. Is it worth the coin, I wonder?" She continued on, as if not really expecting an answer. "Thing is, I don't much care for any king, French or British, and I don't much care for them telling me what to do. Neither does my handsome husband. So maybe we'll take ya just for the fun. The captain's a man of few words. I want someone to talk to. Might be nice to have another woman around. Particularly one as interesting as you."

Madeleine nodded.

"How about we do a test?"

Grégoire gaped, his eyes bulging.

"Don't worry, ya lout," Charlotte said. "It's not a corsair test, but a woman's one."

Madeleine decided she didn't want to know what the corsair test was.

"You tell me a story. If I like it, we'll give you passage and you'll be under my protection. We may be pirates, but we have honour. Sworn to the chasse-partie." Charlotte pointed to the document posted on the cabin door. Writing lined the top, with what looked like several signatures and many X's at the bottom. "Pirate code, about booty shares and votes, but what matters to you is the one about how any civilian taken on by the captain—or his wife, I added those words meself—has safe passage and will suffer no harm. I suspect that's why Grégoire here suggested you join us. Just keep your kids out from underfoot. Can't guarantee they won't get stepped on if they're where they shouldn't be."

Madeleine wouldn't let them out of her sight, code or no code.

"Grégoire, you're dismissed." She waved him away. He left, with an uneasy glance over his shoulder.

"Your stepson says you're a midwife."

"Yes."

"Not much use for one of those on board a pirate ship." She guffawed. "But you're more than a midwife, ain't you? I can tell. Why don't you explain your unique, how shall I say it, skills?"

"I thought you wanted a story," Madeleine said.

"Come now," Charlotte said. "No time for games." She pulled a knife from a holster on her leg and picked her fingernails with it. "Your husband ain't sick, is he?"

"He is. He … he has … It's consump …" Madeleine stuttered. Stopped under Charlotte's steely gaze.

"You'll not lie to me. I'll throw you off this ship, leak word that you poisoned your husband."

"I have done no such thing." Though she had helped him sleep through the night when they left, she did not give him poison.

"Truth may not be respected ashore. But on my ship, it's the damned law. Now, I believe I've asked you a question."

Madeleine considered. All her information, all her divination, even the tea leaves in her cup at this very moment, told her she must get Charlotte on her side. So she shook her head. "No. He is not sick. I snuck away in the middle of the night."

"You lie to your stepson about something so serious?"

"I had to choose my children or my husband. I chose my children." Madeleine held up a hand. "Before you mention Grégoire, he's a grown man, makes his own choices." And he's already lost, she didn't add.

"What's that around your neck?"

"This?" Madeleine's hand flew to her necklace. "Just a trinket."

"Oh, you're lying now. I'll not warn you again." Charlotte thrust the knife's point into the table. She leaned forward so they were almost nose-to-nose. "You're a soothsayer, I can see it in the way you swirled the tea, the way you look into my eyes. You also have skills with herbs, I would guess. Me," she said as she sat back, "I've an ability to see the truth in any statement. Useful skill on a ship full of thieves and liars."

Madeleine sighed, resigning herself to telling this woman everything. She had better accept her only option. "It's a family heirloom. A talisman."

"Give it to me," Charlotte said, her hand out.

"What? Why?"

"Because I want it."

"I cannot."

"Damnit, Madeleine, I thought we were coming to an agreement here. It's clear you'll do anything for your children, so let's get this over with, shall we?"

Charlotte was correct. If this was the price for her children's safety, she would pay it. Madeleine gripped the necklace in one hand, lifted it over her head with her other. Willed that it would come back to her family, eventually. Heat soared from the necklace, scalded her palm with the imprint of a cross and crescent moon. She dropped it onto the table.

Charlotte snatched at Madeleine's hand, turned it over, traced the symbols with her fingers. Then she poked the necklace with a finger, picked it up, and placed it around her own neck. "Will it work for me?" she asked.

"I don't know. As far as I can tell, it's always been worn by a Doiron woman," Madeleine said. "But, if I had to guess, I'd say it might enhance your own ability."

"Not give me yours?"

"No," Madeleine answered truthfully.

"We could use your soothsayer powers. We'll be traversing new waters, riding new currents, finding new winds. We need a guide."

"I must clarify," Madeleine said, not wanting this woman to think she had been misled. "I can't see the future, exactly, but I can read omens, get glimpses of which path to take."

"And ..." Charlotte prompted her to continue.

"I can make invocations. For healing, good fortune, good weather."

"Can you trust these abilities?"

Madeleine considered. Remembered Elinor's words from the long-ago day when they met on that cliff. "Yes, I can."

A tall, bearded man stooped through the hatch, standing to his full height when he entered. His broad shoulders filled the door. A gold ring was pierced through one ear. "This her, then?" He pointed a filthy finger at Madeleine.

"Captain, luv. It is indeed."

"Your assessment?" he asked.

"I'd like to grant her and her family passage. They might prove useful," Charlotte said.

He nodded his head, "Passage granted." He turned and left.

"Thank you, Charlotte," Madeleine said.

"Ah, don't be thanking me yet. It'll be a rough voyage."

Madeleine had no doubt of that. She was journeying back to the domain where the phantom ship was strongest. She raised her hand to gain strength from her necklace, but her fingers found only empty air.

CHAPTER 12

Celeste

The sun had barely risen when Celeste dashed into the street.

"Newspapers," called a singsong voice. "Get your newspapers here. Newspapers."

She followed the cries at a pace just below a jog. A newsboy stood near the whipping corner, but she ignored the splotches of red only she could see and strode straight towards him. He held a stack of newspapers tucked under an arm and waved one copy in the air with his other. She snatched the paper from him, eager to see the photograph she'd sold to Mr. Morrison the day before.

"Hey!" he said. "That's one shilling!"

"I don't want to buy it, just look at it." Above the fold, Noelle smiled at her, with the *St. Cecilia* in the background, its quarantine flag clear as anything. She hugged the boy, accidentally knocking off his smelly cap.

"You mad?" He struggled to get out of her grasp. "Let go. Gimme my paper."

She released him, picked up his cap, and placed it back on his head. "Sorry about that." She peered at the image more carefully. In the upper left-hand corner, farther out to sea, was another ship. Mr. Morrison had held her photograph by that edge when he'd waved it at her, which must've been why she hadn't noticed until now. The out-of-focus ship was blurred, but seemed to be in flames. She shivered. The flashing light when she took the photo—the phantom ship. Caught for all time in a photograph with her sister. Her hands grew cold and clammy. The ship had been some sort of friend to Madeleine—maybe—but it had caused Yvon's death. What did it mean for Celeste and Noelle?

A short article at the bottom of the page drew her attention away from the phantom ship, about a woman passing off a counterfeit twenty-dollar note at a dress shop. She was reported to be an upstanding citizen, the wife of a prominent businessman, so was not under suspicion. What were the odds someone else was passing off counterfeit notes? Not high. The notes must have been one of Celeste's. But they couldn't trace it back to her. Could they? Celeste grabbed at the knitting needle in her hair and adjusted it, taking a moment to steady herself.

"Lady, do ya hear me? Give it back."

She jerked her attention to the newsboy. "My apologies." She handed him the paper and one pence. "For your troubles."

He snatched the money and it disappeared into his pocket. "Newspapers!" he began again. "Get your newspapers here."

Celeste shook off the sighting and the article, reorienting her attention to the opportunities her camera, and the quarantine, would bring. More work at the newspaper meant less at the bank. They could eventually leave it behind and get that apartment Noelle dreamed about. They would be truly independent. And safe. She mulled over what she'd read of Madeleine's story, about her premonitions. If God gave her a gift, she should use it to the best of her abilities, shouldn't she? But how? She'd read of no spells, no instructions, not even a recipe. She should have flipped through the rest but had been too wrapped up in every word of her great-great-grandmother's story to do so before she'd fallen asleep. Maybe tonight. She did learn something though: to trust herself. Capturing the *St. Cecilia* on film, phantom ship or no, wasn't an accident, but fate. Fate would take her to another opportunity. It had to.

BUT CELESTE'S LUCK STALLED. SHE ROAMED THE STREETS FOR DAYS, FALLING into bed exhausted at night. Despite her attempts to sell several photographs to Mr. Morrison, he'd refused them all. What had she been thinking? That she'd get a front-page photograph every day? She needed to prove herself, as fast as possible.

One evening, after hours of walking, her feet swelling in her boots, arms aching from lugging the camera, she realized she'd been travelling in something of a spiral, with Pownal Square Jail at the centre. She stopped. Was this a warning or an opportunity? How very brazen for someone who had counterfeited notes to get too close to the very place she wanted to avoid. But she wasn't advertising her actions to anyone. She was just a woman with a camera. And her walk was heading towards the jail, not away from it. A sign, then, surely, that was where she could go. She strode straight for it as twilight descended.

The large brick building—similar in size to the Union Bank—was undergoing renovations to make it more secure. A planked wall surrounded the building, obscuring it, while scaffolding jutted from the floors below towards the roof. She stood beside a heap of discarded building materials and regarded the area. Two police constables shared a smoke near the front entrance, talking and gesturing as if telling a story about their latest arrest, or maybe conquest, but the area was otherwise quiet. Until shouts from inside the jail drew their attention. She was about to follow them when something clattered on the other side of the wall.

A hand reached over the top. The image sent a chill down her spine, but she shook it off. A man popped up, breathing heavily. The moon shot out from its cloudy veil and the lamp above her flared. She raised her camera, exposing a shot as he paused, one leg over the wall, scanning the ground. Then he leapt down. He ran towards her and she dodged out of his way. She struck the dirt with a cry as her camera flew from her grasp.

He turned to her and held his hand out to help. Running feet smacked towards them. "Sorry, miss." He raced away.

Two policemen thundered past, ignoring her. She wished the escaped prisoner good luck and slowly stood.

Another policeman approached as the first two turned the corner in pursuit of their quarry. He huffed and doubled over, his hefty stomach squishing his thighs. "They'll get him," he muttered.

Celeste started to back away into the shadows but her foot caught a can of nails and kicked it over with a clanking rattle.

The policeman straightened. "You there. Did you see what happened?"

"Y-yes." She considered lying but he wouldn't believe that she'd missed it. She was in a prime location to be a witness.

"Inside with me then. You'll need to make a statement."

"I should get home. My … husband will be worried about me."

"Won't take long." He took her by the elbow and guided her towards the front door.

She glanced behind for her camera. It had landed against the wall but was somewhat concealed by a few trampled bushes. She was glad it had fallen from her hands. Otherwise, the policeman would likely have confiscated it.

"Some idiot worker left a ladder inside the wall," he said. "But you didn't hear that from me. Stay away from the press once those vultures show up."

"Of course. Horrible people."

As they climbed the stoop and entered the building, she shuddered so violently that the policeman stopped.

"Are you all right? Must've been a frightening experience for you."

She nodded, though the fear was not from the escape, but from the foreboding that crashed into her. "All I saw was a man climbing over the wall," she sobbed, the tears not entirely fake. "That's not much use to you."

"We got him," called a triumphant voice from just outside. The two policeman who had chased the prisoner dragged him in. His eyes locked with Celeste as he passed by. She saw an inkling of a possible future reflected at her. She blinked to dispel the thought.

"No need for me, now, constable, is there?" she asked.

"S'pose not." He tipped his hat at her. "Have a lie-down when you get home. You'll feel better. Tea, maybe?"

"Yes, thank you." She hurried out of the building onto the now deserted street and towards her camera. She bent to retrieve it. The lens was broken and the bellows torn. She picked the camera up with a sigh. She had three notes left that weren't doing any good for her hidden away. Dare she pass another to fix the camera? She would let her photograph of the escaping prisoner decide. If it had been properly exposed, lit, and framed, if she were able to sell it to the newspaper, she would have the camera repaired immediately. If not, she would consider waiting until she had legitimately earned enough to do so.

The next morning, her byline was once again on the front page. The prisoner's face was somewhat obscured, but she had trapped him with half his body above the wall and half hidden below, before he had found temporary freedom. She was to be paid at the beginning of next week. She interpreted this as meaning she was safe to pass the note.

The day passed slowly, clouds blotting out the sun and sprinkling showers on the city. When she left the bank, with a small umbrella to keep the worst of the rain off, she glanced towards the harbour. The yellow quarantine flag was gone from the *St. Cecilia*. She was competing with the newspaper's regular photographer now. Mr. Morrison wasn't likely to print a woman's photographs when a perfectly good man was available.

She had no time to waste. She had to do this for Noelle. For their future. She squared her shoulders, shook out her umbrella, walked into the studio, greeted M. Biset, and gave him the camera.

"Did this damage happen when you captured the jailbreak on film?" he asked. Concern mixed with interest on his face.

"Yes. You saw the newspaper then?" She leaned her umbrella against the counter.

"Mighty fine work. You have quite the eye."

She beamed. "Thank you. You have been a most patient instructor."

"What transpired?"

"I got knocked over. It was a disturbing experience. But I drank some chamomile tea last night that helped calm my nerves."

"If you come by tomorrow I'll bring in some of Mme. Biset's strawberry jam. The sweetness will warm your heart."

She pressed her fingers to her smiling lips. "That is most kind." She gestured at the camera. "Can you fix it?"

He turned it over. "Should be able to. It will take a few days."

She passed him the twenty-dollar note, her hand shaking, avoiding his eyes.

"Are you sure you're fine?"

"Quite so."

"You don't carry anything smaller?" He tilted his head at the note.

Shivers ran through Celeste. He hadn't so much as paused when she had given him the first one. Were two notes in one place overdoing it? "Maman gave them to us when we left. In case of emergency. We're settled at the bank now so I have no worries about using them."

"Hmmm. I thought your parents didn't have much extra."

"They didn't. Gave everything to us. To assure our success here in Charlottetown." She forced confidence into her voice.

He peered at the note, rather more carefully than usual. "This is odd."

"What's that?" She shifted from foot-to-foot and grasped her hands to keep them steady.

His eyes narrowed. "This blob of ink. I've never seen one mar a note before."

"Must have been a bad day for signatures." She forced a chortle, fixing her gaze on a landscape photograph, following the lines of the hills in an attempt to keep her nerves under control.

He pointed a finger at her and she backed away. "A woman was briefly detained yesterday for passing a fake note. I read it in the newspaper. Turns out it didn't originate with her. Mayhap you've somehow ended up with one as well. But from Rustico? That doesn't make sense."

"Oh, I must have been mistaken, then. This note is from the bank. I must have mixed it up with Maman's."

"That's quite a lot of twenty-dollar notes you have."

"Not at all. But, I must be going. I have an appointment to see a doctor. For my nerves. Forgot about it until just now." She grabbed her umbrella.

"Mademoiselle Haché. Did you know about this? That the note was counterfeit?"

"Of course not," she retorted.

"Well, I must report this to the police."

She stopped, heart beating so loudly she swore he could hear it. "Can you keep me out of it? I'm just a victim in all this, like you." She pasted a demure look on her face and backed towards the door.

"Have you cheated me?" His words shattered her outward calm.

"M. Biset, I would never do that." And yet, she had.

"Now you're lying to me. You and your sister—"

"Noelle had nothing to do with it," she blurted.

"But you did?"

"No, I misspoke."

"How could you betray me? If I passed this off, I could have been arrested." His eyes darkened. "Was the last one you used counterfeit as well?"

Celeste didn't know what to do. She ran.

CELESTE WANDERED THE STREETS, HIDDEN UNDER HER UMBRELLA, AVOIDING pedestrians attempting to flee the now sheeting rain. She berated herself for passing another note, considered the best way out of this. Perhaps M. Biset wouldn't go to the police. Should she let him calm down, then explain everything to him? No, that was too risky. He wouldn't understand. Worse, she had betrayed him, which was as clear as the fact that she had only one path. She and Noelle had to leave. She would go to the newspaper offices, argue for getting her pay early. They would board the last coach out of the city, regardless of its destination. They could change their names, find a new place to live, secure work. She would need to give Noelle a reason for leaving but would think of one later. Tell her sister it was an emergency and she would explain once they were gone. Her plan settled, she marched to the bank and straight to their attic.

Noelle wasn't there. A sense of foreboding hit Celeste, of the walls closing in, but she shook it off. She dove under the bed, grabbed the loose brick, seized the last two notes, and cast them onto the embers of their stove. She poked at them and the coals flickered. She raced to pack their things. Only what they could carry. The trunk would have to stay behind. As she ruffled through it, something sizzled underneath her fingertips. She removed her hands and the feeling stopped. She reached back in and felt around the bottom. The false compartment where Madeleine's story had been hidden was scorching hot. She opened it, stretched her arm in as far as possible, and found something in the far corner. She pulled it out. A roped necklace with a wooden cross and crescent moon. Madeleine's. Was this what the gleaming sun had been trying to show her, when she'd first found Madeleine's story?

She placed the necklace over her head. It tingled against her skin. Her great-great-grandmother would guide her. Help her.

"Celeste," Mrs. Pierce yelled from the bottom of the stairs. "I saw you come in. The police were here. Don't you hide from me." She started up towards the attic.

Celeste panicked. Clutched Madeleine's book. Before this, it could have been explained as fanciful fiction. But now, it would be used against them. She and Noelle would be branded as godless mystics. Celeste crawled under the bed and stashed the book in the gap in the wall, where the notes had been, covering it with the brick. As she squiggled out, she sensed someone standing on the other side of the room. She flinched, but it wasn't Mrs. Pierce. A vision, not of the past. A flash of the future. Three women. Then they disappeared. She barely managed to stand before Mrs. Pierce entered the room.

"They arrested Noelle for counterfeiting," Mrs. Pierce said.

"What? No, that's not possible," Celeste shook her head. Her poor little goose. She must be so scared. Celeste had to get to her.

"They intended to arrest you as well."

"I'm sure it's just a misunderstanding." She pushed past Mrs. Pierce.

"Yer fired. Women of moral means don't get arrested."

Celeste ignored her words. It didn't much matter. They were leaving anyway. She could bail Noelle out. She had sewn several notes—real, not counterfeit—into her skirt, from her change and her pay from the newspaper. They had their savings in the bank. She would find a way to withdraw it before the bank closed, get some man to say he was their guardian, and then they would say goodbye to the city, never to return.

"Your pay will be confiscated, naturally."

She paused at the top of the stairs, eyes wide. "You can't do that."

"No, but Mr. Forbes can. He's furious. How do you think this looks for the bank? To have employees stealing. Counterfeiting?"

"I ... I didn't ..."

"I'm summoning the police." She smirked as if nothing would give her more pleasure. "They said to alert them as soon as you returned."

For the second time that day, Celeste ran.

She pounded down the steps and crashed out the side door of the bank, into the rain. She was soon drenched. She slowed a block away from the jail as a terrible thought occurred to her. What if she didn't have enough money to bail them both out? If she were arrested, she wouldn't be able to help Noelle. She steered herself away from the jail and towards the coach station. She couldn't allow herself to be taken into custody. And truly, Noelle would never be convicted. She was completely innocent and utterly believable. Celeste would leave, make a new start, then send for her sister. Yes, that was it. This way, they would only be separated for a short period of time. The best option for both of them.

She plodded through puddles in the almost empty streets. Shivers overtook her, not entirely from the cold. How had it come to this? She had managed to create the possibility of a grand future, and it had been snatched away. She had misread the signs and foretellings. To Noelle's detriment.

As she approached the coach station, the necklace grew hotter. Her steps slowed. Flashes of Madeleine's life leapt through her mind. Suddenly, she understood. The reason she had misinterpreted the signs was because she wasn't protecting anyone. Just being selfish. The signs weren't telling her to buy the camera with the first note, or get it fixed with the second, they were telling her not to. To make the moral decisions. Trusting oneself doesn't work if you are blind to the havoc you're creating. She hadn't done anything for Noelle; Celeste's decisions, her actions, were for herself alone. She turned towards the jail. She would not abandon her sister. She would bail her sister out so Noelle at least could have her freedom.

But when she arrived at the jail, a policeman arrested her and refused to accept bail for Noelle. He entered Celeste's name in a ledger, beside Noelle's, scheduling them both to go before the magistrate. He would decide their fate.

CHAPTER 13

Celeste

Celeste shuffled forward, head down, hands cuffed, towards the jail cells in the rear. A constable held her by the elbow, which she tucked as close to herself and away from him as possible. She wiped her clammy hands on her apron, which was too wet from the rain to do much good.

"Got the other one," the constable said to the guard at the entrance to the cell block.

"Found her already?" the guard asked, scratching his red scruffy beard.

"Turned herself in, can ya believe it?" The constable pushed her forward, knocking her off balance. Her wrists wrenched in the cuffs as she stuck out her arms to steady herself.

The guard caught her. "Whaddya doing?" he said to the constable.

"My job. Don't much care if it's a man or a woman." He turned and strode away.

The guard pulled a ring of keys from his pocket. They jingled and jangled, each one a symbol of what she'd lost. Her sister's trust; their employment; their place in the city; the one chance she had at a hopeful future. The guard found the right key, opened the main door, and motioned her in. "Right then, this way."

She followed him into a dim narrow room that was lined with cells filled with grubby prisoners. The smell of piss and vomit permeated the air. She gagged.

"Sorry 'bout that," the guard said. "Ye'll get used to it, though." He had a slight Irish brogue that tinged his English, similar to the way her French did hers.

"Hey, lady," one man said. "Two of you now? My lucky day." He grabbed at her through the bars, managing to touch her shoulder.

Celeste jerked away as the guard whacked the prisoner's hand with his baton.

"Hey now, I'm not doing any harm." The prisoner rubbed his knuckles. "There's no need for that."

"Where's your manners?" the guard asked. He raised his voice. "None of that from any of ye. Hear me?"

The prisoners muttered agreement.

"Keep to the centre, Miss Haché."

"Thank you." Celeste had already positioned herself so she couldn't be reached from either side, chiding herself for not doing so in the first place. She needed to pay attention. Learn the rules of survival here. "Mr. …?"

"Murphy," he supplied. "You're down at the end. Don't get many women in here. There's a few empty cells to give ye a bit of a buffer and a curtain for privacy."

As they passed the threadbare drapes hanging from the ceiling, Celeste saw Noelle, huddled in the corner on a thin mattress, which sat on a wooden bench. The guard selected another key, creaked open the cell door, and gestured for Celeste to enter.

She complied and rushed to her sister as the door clanged shut. "Are you all right?"

Noelle glared at her. "What did you do?" she whispered.

"I'm sorry, little goose, this has just all gotten out of hand. I thought I had everything under control. You weren't meant to be involved in this." She reached for the ratty blanket folded at the bottom of the bed and wrapped it around herself for warmth, dropping it when she noticed a particularly nasty stain. She had no wish to contemplate what had caused it.

"They said I was being arrested as a co-conspirator for stealing, counterfeiting, and passing notes. I thought they'd made a mistake until I thought about that camera. Did you do all this so you could work at the newspaper? Was cleaning the bank, doing an honest day's work, below you?" Her eyes flashed with the lightning outside.

Celeste looked up at three small windows high overhead, rain leaking from their frames. How did that escapee get out? Not from here, with no way up. It must have been during some sort of transfer. Did they let prisoners out to use the facilities? The bucket in the corner quickly disabused her of such a notion.

"Are you listening?" Noelle shook Celeste, who gave no resistance. "Did you do this? Why take such a risk? We were doing fine, even had our pay, with enough to save a bit."

Celeste took her sister's hands in her own. She drew in a deep breath. Time to tell her sister everything. She switched to French so, if they were overheard, no one could use their conversation against them. Sound carried in here, if one of the other prisoner's low whistling was any indication. "Our pay was garnished," she said. "After they charged room and board, not much was left. The bank wouldn't let me withdraw even that without a male guardian."

"But, you told me ..."

"I had to lie to keep you safe."

"You had to do no such thing. You just wanted to. To become a lady photographer, leaving me alone and traipsing around the city."

"That's not the way it happened. I needed the smaller notes to buy food and coal. Get you your scones. Cake. So I used the first note for the camera."

"The first?" Noelle asked. "There were others?"

"Just one more, that's what got me caught."

"How could you do that to M. Biset? Shame on you. He was so nice to us."

"I regret that. I did have second thoughts, had even decided not to cash that note. But then, on our way to the portrait studio, you said you were loving the city, looking forward to getting an apartment." Celeste shrugged.

"Don't you dare blame this on me, Celeste Marie Haché."

"But—"

"You should have confided in me. We could have figured something out. Just because you're older doesn't mean you can make all the decisions. Especially when they're horrid." Her hand flew to her mouth. "What if ... Do you think we'll be sentenced to thirty-nine lashes? Would they do that to women?" Her face crumpled.

"It wasn't a violent crime," Celeste said. "I'm sure the most we'll get is a prison sentence." She affected a certainty she didn't quite feel. It all depended on the formal charges.

"You say that as if it's nothing. We'll rot in jail, for how long? When we get out, we'll be unemployable. Or we'll end up in debtors' prison. They'll never let us enter the bank, much less work there. We can't return home as criminals. What will Maman say? You have ruined us, Celeste. Our life was difficult, yes, but we were surviving. Now, because of your …" She paused. "Greediness—there, I've said it—we're in a jail cell."

"Little goose—"

"Don't call me that."

Up until this point, Celeste had held herself together remarkably well, but now she fought against unravelling. She closed her eyes, told herself to keep calm, and opened them again. "I tried to tell them you had nothing to do with it. Begged them to release you. But they didn't believe me."

"Why would they believe you? A thief and a liar."

The words hurt all the more because of their accuracy. "I'm so sorry, Noelle. I'll think of something."

Noelle turned her face towards the wall. She didn't speak for the rest of the night despite Celeste's efforts to engage her. Celeste sat in the dark, listening to the grunts and moans of other prisoners, to the guard complaining to his replacement that if his wife didn't get pregnant soon, he would never hear the end of it.

She toyed with the cross and crescent on Madeleine's necklace. She replayed all her actions, all her premonitions, in her mind. Willed herself to make other choices. If only that snollygoster prisoner hadn't banged into her, then her camera wouldn't have busted and she wouldn't have passed off that second note. Her *if onlys* led far, far back, along a trail of events and decisions, many of which she had no control over. If only they weren't poor, if only the bank didn't cheat them. The necklace grew fiery hot on her chest in a warning so clear it seemed Madeleine herself was giving it in person. Stop blaming others.

She finally fell asleep, her dreams a mess of death and despair. Mixed in, though, were the beginnings of a plan. She grasped onto an idea like one of the spider webs that crisscrossed their cell, allowing it to keep her tenuously tethered throughout the night.

THE NEXT MORNING, AS DAWN ANNOUNCED ITSELF WITH A GLIMMER OF LIGHT through the high windows, a guard traipsed down the hall towards them, stopped just before the curtain, and cleared his throat. "Ye women decent?" Mr. Murphy's voice. A good sign.

"Yes, sir." Celeste said as she and Noelle stood.

He peered past the curtain, seemed satisfied, and stepped fully into view. His blue wool uniform was wrinkled and bags sat heavy under his eyes. "Time for the magistrate. You're first on the docket."

"Did you not sleep well?" Celeste asked, in a soothing tone.

The guard raised his eyebrows at her. "Never had a prisoner ask that before. Least not seriously."

"You look tired," she said.

"My wife's feelin' poorly," he said. "She's got a bit of a short temper nowadays."

"Oh dear. If you ever need any advice…"

"From a prisoner?" he scoffed.

"From a woman."

"Hmpf. Don't know about that. Let's go now." He cuffed them and walked them out of the cell. No one tried to grab at them, but Celeste could feel stares following their progress. Noelle kept her eyes on her cuffs, wincing as they rubbed against her wrists. Celeste's own wrists chafed where the cuffs bit into her skin.

As they exited the jail Celeste turned her face to the sun. It'd only been several hours that they'd been locked up, but the mere fact that they couldn't leave made it seem longer. What might it be like for days, weeks, or months, without seeing anything but a glimpse of the sun or the moon? Without feeling the breeze on her face? She couldn't imagine it. Prayed she wouldn't have to experience it.

She tensed as they crossed the street to the courthouse, which was an imposing building with high columns, as if demonstrating they were mere ants on which justice could stomp if it so wished. But ants were resilient, could carry many times their weight.

"It'll be all right, little goose," Celeste said. She linked her pinky finger with her sister's, was relieved when Noelle didn't pull away. Mr. Murphy ushered them into a large room. He led them down an aisle, with chairs on either side, scattered with people. The closest thing Celeste could compare it to was a funeral. Mostly men with grim faces, a few in uniform, a few in cuffs, one or two with notepads on their knees. One man, dressed in a tailcoat, stared at her as if she'd personally affronted him. At the front, low benches faced an elevated dais where the magistrate, dressed in a dark suit, loomed before them. Celeste tightened her grip on her sister, fighting to keep her legs from shaking.

The magistrate read their charge sheet. "You are accused of illegally obtaining and passing off illegitimate currency. Do you understand these charges?" They nodded. "I need a verbal response," he droned.

"Yes, sir," they chorused with uneven voices.

"How do you plead?"

Celeste paused, looked at Noelle, who stared straight ahead. Celeste pursed her lips and swallowed in an effort to get her dry mouth working. She dropped Noelle's hand and touched the necklace but felt only coolness, as if Madeleine had left her on her own for this decision, so she placed her hands over her heart instead. "Not guilty."

"And you?" the magistrate asked Noelle.

Noelle turned her head towards her sister. Celeste tried to link pinky fingers again but Noelle moved hers out of reach.

"Don't have all day," the magistrate said.

"Not guilty," Noelle said.

Celeste let her breath out in a quiet whoosh. Noelle wasn't likely to say Celeste was indeed guilty, but it had been a possibility. At least her sister could take comfort in the fact that she herself hadn't lied.

The judge pointed to the charge sheet. "It says here you have no family ties, no resources. No reason to stay in town, so you're at risk of fleeing. No bail."

Celeste's stomach dropped. "Sir, please. We're simply two young women on hard times. Innocent of the charges. We want to clear our names. We've no money and nowhere to go. There's no need to lock us up."

The magistrate's beady eyes fixed her in her place. "You dare question my ruling?"

"I … I just wanted to explain."

Noelle elbowed her. "You're making it worse," she whispered.

"My apologies, sir," Celeste said. "But—"

The magistrate interrupted her. "I'm not quite finished with you." A slow smile spread on his lips, as if he were now enjoying this. "There's another charge for Miss Celeste Haché."

"What?" Celeste's mind raced. What could it be? What had she done? Maybe a related charge, like fraud?

"Assisting with a jailbreak."

The words cut through Celeste. They didn't make any sense. "I did no such thing."

"Seems you were the witness who disappeared after photographing the incident. Got you the front page, didn't it?" His teeth glistened with spit. "It's right here in black and white." He waved a copy of the newspaper at her.

Celeste longed to snatch the knitting needle out of her hair and stab the paper to his desk. All the better if she scratched his fingers while doing so.

"I … I was there, yes, but … it was simply … a matter of circumstance," she stammered, heart pounding. "I'd nothing to do with the escape."

"That'll be determined at trial. What's your plea?"

She wavered on her feet and blanched. "My plea?"

"Yes, to the charge. Let's hear it now."

"Not guilty, of course," she managed.

"Of course," he repeated with a smirk. "Trial to take place at the next sitting of the Supreme Court. Take them away."

Her head spun. Had the magistrate added that charge out of spite? Did they think she'd orchestrated an escape for a photograph? Ridiculous. She needed a lawyer. But the notes sewn into her skirt were insufficient for that. And what lawyer would take payment from a known counterfeiter? Not only had she not gained bail, so they could run in anonymity—even if she had to bully Noelle into it—there would be even more attention on Celeste. Well, she had a backup plan. Would have to use it.

As they were led away from the magistrate, she slowed her feet, stopped. "I'm feeling dizzy," she said, which wasn't entirely a lie. "I need just a moment, please, Mr. Murphy. If I may."

He agreed and she scanned the room, eyes skipping over lawyers and observers as the magistrate issued an arrest warrant for a no-show who'd been out on bail. Another prisoner was walked through the doors by a guard. The man who'd grabbed at her grinned as he passed. She ignored him, saw what she wanted on a small table near the entrance.

"I think I can continue. I'm a bit unsteady though," she said.

Noelle narrowed her eyes at Celeste. Shook her head. She wouldn't know what Celeste was planning, but she clearly suspected something. Celeste avoided her gaze and started walking again. As she approached the table, she staggered into it, snatching up a thick book and hiding it in her apron, easy enough to do even with cuffed hands.She hoped the book's bulky spine meant it concealed something with which to write.

Noelle helped Celeste up.

"Are you ill?" Mr. Murphy asked.

"I'll be fine now."

"Bad news about the bail." Mr. Murphy said. "And the additional charge." He tilted his head at her.

"It's preposterous," Celeste said. If he believed she'd assisted with an escape, she'd lose the relationship she'd begun to build with him.

"Agreed," he said. "Imagine, a woman doin' that."

For once, Celeste welcomed being thought of as the weaker, dumber sex. They exited the courthouse onto a street that was much busier than when they'd arrived. Celeste resisted the urge to glare at the passersby going about their business as they wished. Most avoided her, though a few stared at the handcuffs that marked her as a prisoner. She supposed there'd be an article in the newspaper about their arrest. Thank goodness their mother couldn't read, on the off chance a copy somehow made it to Rustico.

"Mr. Murphy, see that shop over there?" she gestured to a tearoom with her elbow.

"What about it?" He led them into the jail.

"They have the most marvellous lemon balm and ginger tea concoction. It might help your wife, if she's feeling poorly. Calms the nerves. And the temper."

"Hmpf," he said.

"No harm in trying," Celeste said. "You've been more than kind to us. I want to repay you."

"Perhaps," he said.

Back in their cell, Noelle rounded on Celeste.

"Assisting with an escape? And what did you take? Haven't you gotten me in enough trouble already?"

"The charge is ridiculous. No one's going to believe it."

"So you had nothing to do with it?"

"Nothing. It was a simple coincidence."

"Why would they charge you, then?"

Celeste didn't answer, but she was beginning to suspect that the bank might be behind it. If Mrs. Pierce's anger was any indication, the executives would be furious. But Celeste wasn't helpless against them. She fiddled with Madeleine's necklace. She'd miss it when it was gone.

ONCE IT SEEMED THE NIGHT GUARD WAS SETTLED AT HIS POST, CELESTE removed the stolen book from her apron. It'd been a risk, but the theft was only minor. Noelle frowned at her, but said nothing.

Celeste turned the book—a journal, as she'd hoped—over in her hands, peering at it in the quiet dimness. The cloth cover was blue, the edges decorated with a broad border of gold flowers. Inside, only the first few pages were written in, with someone's name and address, comments about the weather and the shopping. She tore them out, sneezing softly to cover the noise, and dropped them into their commode bucket. They sank in the icky contents. Now no one could prove the journal wasn't her own, tucked quite properly into her apron when she'd been arrested.

There was indeed a pen—a newfangled fountain pen—in the spine and it appeared to be half full. She poised it over a page. First, she would write the letter she hoped Mr. Murphy would deliver. Then, she would write about her own experiences, hinting around anything that might implicate her, until she could include a more fulsome account. She'd never get back to the book that held Madeleine's story. It was secure, perhaps, but unreachable. So she'd write her own.

WHEN MR. MURPHY CAME ON DUTY, SHE CALLED HIM OVER.

"Did you try the tea?" Celeste asked him.

"I did." He nodded. "Don't quite know why. Tea shops are sure not my place. Prefer the pub."

"How was it?" She inclined her head. "Did it suit your wife?"

"Worked like a charm, thank ye. We even slept the night through."

"You do look better, I must say." She stepped close to the bars so they were almost nose-to-nose. "I could help you even more."

"Oh, hey now, don't get the wrong idea." He backed away. "I honour my marriage vows."

"You mistake my meaning." Celeste cast her eyes downward. "But it is a delicate matter. I overheard your conversation the other evening. About ..." She looked up and let him fill in the meaning.

He flushed a deep red.

"There's nothing to be embarrassed about," she said. "It's quite normal. Naturally, I won't breathe a word."

His eyes bulged and his mouth worked like a fish. He turned to go.

"Wait, please. As I've said, you've been so kind to us. I want to return the favour."

He hesitated.

"I can guarantee you a baby."

"You sellin' one?" He chuckled awkwardly.

"It's just a bit of women's work."

His face screwed up in confusion. "What're you talkin' about?"

She scrutinized him. His desire for a baby fairly screamed its presence in him. A son.

"It's quite simple," she said. "Just give your wife this." She opened her collar to show him Madeleine's necklace. "If she wears this for a few months, you'll have your child."

He scoffed. "You think I'm an idiot?"

"What do you have to lose?" Celeste said.

A constable called from the main door. "Got a transfer here."

"In a minute," Mr. Murphy hollered over his shoulder. He tapped his foot. Shook his head. "This is outlandish." But he hadn't yet left, hadn't told her to keep her ideas to herself. His fingers twitched. "Fine, give it to me," he said.

"I need something first."

"Shoulda known this was a trick," he grumbled. "Serves me right for talkin' to prisoners. Even female ones."

"No trick, just trade. I proved I could help with the tea, didn't I?"

"That was tea. Just tea."

"But I knew the exact kind for the exact problem."

He stepped away from her. "What's your angle?"

"I'm simply giving you the benefit of generations of my family's knowledge." She didn't say abilities. That would scare him off.

"I could just come in there and take that from you." He jingled his keys.

"It won't work if it's taken by force." She had no idea if that were true, but she figured he wasn't the kind of man who would do that anyway.

He glared. "Name it, then. But that necklace better work."

"It will." Celeste was almost certain it would. If it didn't ... well, she planned to be out of his reach by then. "I need a message delivered to a Mr. David Campbell." She held up the letter she had written the night before, carefully phrased in case Mr. Murphy decided to read it.

"Who's he?"

"Just a man. You can find him at *The Examiner*."

"Not talkin' to a newspaperman." He crossed his arms in front of his thick belly. "That'll get me fired."

"He's just a photographer. And we'll keep you out of it. No one will know."

"Whaddye want a photographer for?"

"That's my business. Do we have a trade or no?"

"I can't just walk into the newspaper offices, no matter who I'm seeing."

"Wait outside the building. When a man with a camera leaves, follow him for a bit. Once you're out of sight of the offices, talk to him. Please."

"Hey," the constable called again. "I'm not setting foot in this godforsaken stinking cesspool. Not my job. Come get your prisoner."

"Do you want a son or no?" she asked. That word, *son*, as if by magic, seemed to make up his mind.

"Fine," he said. "A trade."

She touched the necklace. Wished it well, imagined it in the hands of a descendant sometime in the future. Removed it from her neck and mourned its loss. She couldn't figure out a way to keep it and get out of jail, so say goodbye to it she must. For Noelle.

When she handed it to him, the cross and crescent catching the light, Noelle gasped and he flinched, almost dropping it. He recovered, shoved it in his pocket with a parting glance at Celeste, and walked away.

"Was that Madeleine's necklace?" Noelle yanked on Celeste's arm. "The one described in her story?"

"Yes."

"How could you give it away?" Noelle asked. "Why didn't you tell me about it?"

"I just found it, in our trunk. Maman must have put it there for me to find, when I needed it." Or Grandmaman Lottie did, but claiming their mother had was a simpler version of the truth.

"Like Madeleine's story?" Noelle asked.

"It's possible. You know Maman doesn't like talk of abilities other than God's. But she must have reconsidered. Decided we needed to know about our past."

"You mean *you* needed to know."

"Perhaps. Regardless, I had to give it away. It'll find its way back to our family when it's needed most." She hoped.

"You gave away an heirloom for a falsehood," Noelle said. "You're cheating Mr. Murphy."

"You think so little of me?" Celeste was taken aback. Yes, her sister's accusations she was a thief and liar were hurtful, though somewhat accurate. But to think Celeste would cheat a man who was sympathetic to them? She stumbled over the thought. She had done the same with M. Biset. She sank onto the mattress, put her head in her hands. Watched two rats in the cell across from them fight over a long-forgotten crumb.

"It seems there's nothing you won't do," Noelle said.

Celeste looked up. "I really am helping him." The necklace assisted her in sorting through her thoughts, finding her way, making better decisions. Even if the necklace had no power when not worn by a Doiron woman, its goodwill was sure to be of benefit to Mrs. Murphy. "Which will help our situation."

Noelle turned away.

Celeste opened the journal and continued writing, the fountain pen scratching out her words, as day turned slowly to night.

CHAPTER 14

Raina

Raina clasped her hands onto Celeste's journal as soon as Simone handed it to her. It hummed with an energy so startling, despite Simone's earlier mention of it, that Raina nearly dropped it. She braced herself for the ocean to pull at her, as it did whenever she experienced a premonition or a vision or anything out of the ordinary, but instead, touching the journal grounded her. The phantom ship didn't call, didn't reach out for her, didn't do anything at all. The humming of the journal and the sizzle on her fingertips were matched with only quiet, like a crime scene once the sirens had been turned off and the police tape removed. Not peaceful, but almost settled. She traced the flowers that decorated the edges and the spine of the cloth book.

With a deep breath, she opened the journal. A yellow slip of paper fell out—the carbon copy of the archival retrieval request. She scanned through the journal's pages, skimming over the French parts, refusing Simone's offer to translate. Her high school French was sufficient for the moment. To tell the truth, she didn't want to hand it back. Raina would never admit it, but she understood why Simone had stolen the journal.

When Raina read the part where Celeste pilfered the bank notes, she fought the urge to yell into the past that of course the phantom ship was a warning. But that would be as futile as shouting at the characters of a horror movie not to go upstairs, to stay away from the basement, just get out of the house already. Not that Raina watched those types of films. Life was frightening enough. Besides, if she thought she could change the past, she'd check into an institution. Instead, she looked at Simone. "Clearly you take after Celeste."

"I had my reasons. So did she. She needed to survive."

"There's always another way."

"Says a woman who never had to choose between food on the table and a roof over her head," Simone said.

"You've had it so hard?"

"Just keep reading."

Raina supposed it was easy enough—and perhaps unfair—to judge Celeste's actions, detached as Raina was from her ancestor's situation. Future Doirons might judge Raina herself. With that uncomfortable thought, she bent back over the journal, squinting to read in the waning light. Soon, crickets chirped and the automatic front porch light clicked on. Shit. The sun had set. She braced for the compelling call of the phantom ship. Now, even with the journal, it burbled and murmured, though its words were muffled. "Do you hear that?" Raina asked.

"I hear the wind. The ocean. Is that what you mean?"

"No." Raina set the journal down and took her hands away from it.

Raina, Raina. The ship's call lifted into the air until it roared. *Come aboard, come aboard...*

Raina clamped her hands back onto the journal. Their voices faded. Incredible. She skipped through more pages. "There's nothing here about nightmares."

"About that ..."

"You said you could help me with them." Though softening the ship's lure was an even better result, she didn't appreciate being lied to. Plus, softening wasn't enough. She needed to eradicate it.

"Not exactly. If you recall, my exact words were that I thought we could figure out a way to deal with them."

"Jesus, Simone. Do you always have to twist things?"

"Mom says I'm the loophole queen." She looked proud about it. "I needed to get your attention. And, you have to admit, there's potential here. More than you've found on your own."

Raina had to give her that.

"Your mother never taught you anything about predictions?" Simone asked.

"Not much." As far as Raina could figure, her mom didn't much understand her abilities. "Though the idea of predictions fascinated her, fairies, folklore, legends, and superstitions were more her bailiwick."

"She's so cool."

"Who?"

"Your mother, of course. She took me in, baked me hermit cookies, told wild and crazy stories about supernatural shit."

"Yeah, that's Mom, all right."

"Did she maybe think it was better to keep the whole premonition thing from you? Like maybe it was something you needed a rite of passage for, or a summer solstice, or a blue moon—"

"Definitely not." Raina interrupted before Simone could list off every day with some sort of supernatural connection. Her cousin was as fond of run-on sentences as her mother. No wonder they liked each other so much. Though how either of them got a word in edgewise was a mystery. "If Mom had abilities, she wouldn't have hidden them." Raina couldn't believe they were talking about premonitions as if they were normal, though she welcomed the chance to be somewhat honest about this part of her life. "Mom wanted them more than anything. Even resorted to the Ouija board when my best friend slept over, which was the only time she could get me to use the darn thing. Hattie loved it. Anyway, I kept my hands off it, and Hattie said Mom clearly moved the pointer herself."

"Maybe not every generation inherits the abilities, like Celeste wrote, especially if there's no one to teach you."

"Maybe."

"Tell me everything about when your premonitions started." Simone fairly bounced in her chair waiting for the answer. "What were they like?"

Raina didn't give her much. "Fun, at first."

Before she'd turned thirteen, she searched out hidden doors to fantastical worlds. She checked every wardrobe, every tree trunk, every shadow, desperate to find magic. Like mother like daughter, she supposed. Then, when she reached her teens and everything that came with them for a girl—hormones, bodily changes, and, eventually, menstruation—the ability to tell the future slammed into her, most often through images from novels, like when she found her favourite red sneakers mistakenly placed in a donation bin thanks to a vision of *The Wonderful Wizard of Oz* sitting in a cardboard box. It was as if photographs only she could see appeared in the air, showing snippets of the future and making her giddy. She shared the premonitions with Hattie, who believed her immediately, demanding

Raina read books about glamourous women so she would divine up a boyfriend and cooler hair for each of them. Of course, that's not how it worked. Far as Raina could figure, the books were a way for her to initially process the foretellings; they didn't cause them. Then she told her mother, which was the beginning of the end for them. Her mom didn't believe her initially, until Raina correctly predicted the neighbour's lost cat being found in a garage down the street, thanks to an image of the Cheshire Cat from *Alice in Wonderland* mixed with Josie and the Pussycats practicing in Archie's garage.

"Then awkward," Raina added.

Her mom peppered her with questions every day, asking where she went, what she ate, if anything precipitated the visions. She surreptitiously copied Raina's actions, trying to create a context that would allow her to experience premonitions as well. When Raina came home early from school one day to find her mom eating a peanut-butter-and-bacon sandwich—Raina's favourite meal, which her mom always shuddered at—Raina stopped talking to her mom about premonitions, or about anything else.

"Then terrifying," Raina finished, shaking her head and refusing to even think about that moment on the water, when she was seventeen. She'd barely even picked up a novel since, preferring non-fiction books that had no connection to her own life.

Dark had fallen. Hooting owls replaced the crickets. A dog howled in the distance.

"You have no idea how to tell a story, do you?" Simone asked. "You're supposed to give detail. That was what, seven words?"

Raina turned her attention back to the journal. If it could help…

"Fine then, don't tell me." Simone pointed to the journal. "Just skip to the last page, already. Celeste mentions her great-great-grandmother Madeleine. She was kickass."

"What does it say about her?"

"Apparently, Sébastienne—Madeleine's daughter, and Celeste's great-grandmother—wrote out Madeleine's story in a book. Celeste briefly mentions it. We need to find it. Sébastienne died before Celeste was born, and her grandmother

Lottie when Celeste was only young. Celeste's mother didn't know much about wise woman stuff. I don't think she liked it."

"Jesus, I need a genealogical chart to keep all this straight," Raina said.

"Celeste had to learn from Madeleine's story," Simone continued. "And so do we. Maybe that'll help your nightmares."

"Where is the book?" Raina asked. If Celeste's journal dimmed the call of the phantom ship, what powers might Madeleine's book have?

"I'm not sure. You're a detective. You can detect. Just flash that badge."

Raina slapped at a mosquito and waved her hand over the smoke of the citronella candle they'd lit to chase the biters away. Her stomach sank with the crunch of wheels on gravel as her parents' car pulled into the driveway. Raina tucked the journal into the back of her waistband and pulled her shirt down over it.

"Hey Aunt Kate, Uncle Warren," Simone said as Raina's mom opened her door. "You're earlier than usual. How was the tour? Any luck seeing the phantom ship?"

"A few glimpses at sunset," she said as she climbed out. "But then one of the kids was so seasick, we turned around early." She walked towards the veranda, a smile on her face, as Raina's dad unpacked the trunk. "Which turned out to be good luck. How wonderful to see the two of you here together."

"Can I go with you tomorrow?" Simone asked. "Now that I'm not, you know, hiding?"

"Worked everything out, have you? Absolutely you can come," Raina's mom said. "Maybe you can convince Raina to join us. Get reacquainted with the family business and all."

"Ooh, yes please," Simone said.

Raina shook her head. Even if she managed to get on the water again—which was a big *if*—she would never board the *Spirit of Rustico*.

"Well, you're here now," her mom said. "This calls for a feast. I'll make us a late dinner."

Simone opened her mouth, as if to spill out everything they'd learned—although Raina assumed she'd leave the stolen journal part out of it—but Raina shook her head. Sharing all this with Simone was one thing. With the rest of her family, quite another.

A devious smile crossed Simone's face. "I'll help you, Aunt Kate. You can tell me more about the Doiron women. My mom said something about ancestral abilities?"

"Simone …" Raina warned as they followed her mom into the house.

Simone turned and winked. "No worries, just asking innocent non-relevant questions, for no reason at all."

"Keep it that way," Raina said as Simone and her mom disappeared around the corner, on their way to the kitchen. She held the front door open for her dad.

"How're you doing, kiddo?" He stepped onto the veranda and into the house. "You're staying?"

Her parents were acting as if it were a once-in-a-lifetime occurrence, like seeing the Aurora Borealis at low latitude.

"What do you think of Simone?" He tossed his softball cap onto one of the hat rack's top hooks. It landed askew, making it seem as if it were floating on one of the feux follets in the painting behind it. His nickname was Stretch, not for his height—he was five foot ten—but for the way he could jump into the air and elongate his body to snag a ball that was sure to have been a home run.

"She's something else," Raina said.

"Your mum's been happy to have her here. Nice to be able to talk to her, cook for a relative." He was also fantastic at stretching out a guilt trip. "Be back in a sec. Just going to take a quick shower." He walked up the stairs to the second floor, favouring his right foot as he limped from one riser to the next.

"Maybe you should just go to bed, Dad."

"I'm fine," he said, picking up his steps.

Raina watched until he got to the top and then strode into the kitchen. Oil sizzled in a pan. Her mom broke off dried oregano from a batch of herbs that hung in the window over the sink. She tossed it into the pan with a generous scoop of minced garlic.

"Is Dad okay?" Raina asked.

"What do you mean?"

"He looked tired."

"He's always tired by this time of night. We both are. He's having some problems with his hip. Brian's been a great help." She was not too bad at guilt herself. "I texted him. He's on his way over." And she was an efficient multitasker. "Simone, can you chop the onions? Raina, gather tomatoes from the garden?"

Raina pulled an empty yoghurt container from a drawer, left the house, and opened the garden gate to the well-lit side yard. Brian appeared out of the shadows. Sneaking up on her had been one of his favourite pastimes when they were kids. Then she'd chase him until she caught him or collapsed in laughter at his dodges and sidesteps.

"Sis, great to see you," he said, in an almost believable tone.

"Hi, big bro." She gave him a quick hug and patted his stomach bulge. "You never should've let Mom share her secret lasagna recipe with Claire."

"It's not like she makes it every night. Besides, she likes a man with meat on his bones."

"Keep telling yourself that, Casanova."

"How does your boyfriend like your skeletal physique?" He smirked.

"Wise ass," she said, though the insult was fair play for her crack about his girth.

"Still no one to keep around, eh?"

She shrugged and walked down the tilled rows, past the carrot tops poking out of the ground and the pea shoots rising over the lattice, towards the staked tomato vines. "Help me pick, would you?"

"It's hardly a two-person job." He watched as Raina selected several, releasing their viney smell as she pulled them from their stems.

"How are Claire and the girls?" Raina asked.

"Good. Claire heads to Nova Scotia for a few days tomorrow to spend time with her university friends. They're doing a wine tour in the valley and then hitting Halifax's nightlife."

"What are you doing with the girls?"

"Same thing we do whenever Claire's away. Eat pizza and watch videos. Claire pretends to be upset about it so Nora thinks she's getting away with something. Maeve seems to have figured it out."

"She's wise beyond her years, that one."

"What's this about a cousin? Simone?" he asked.

"Just here for a visit," Raina said. "She's inside."

"Mom's text said something about hiding her."

"How fast can Mom text these days?"

"She used 'that gal in the phone,'" he laughed.

"What?"

"That's what Dad's been calling Siri. I suppose a better question is, why are you here?"

"I'm working a case. It's resolved now." At least, Simone's case had been. The smugglers were never-ending.

He waggled his fingers in the air. "Use anything special to figure it out?"

Raina ignored the question and headed back towards the house, her container loaded with tomatoes.

"What would your cop friends say if I told them you thought you were a supernatural prodigy?"

They had a version of this fight every time she came home. He still hadn't forgiven her for leaving the family business. He'd been working two jobs since high school. Full-time year-round as a realtor, and part-time during tourist season with their parents. He'd been the realtor who'd negotiated the deal for Hattie's café.

"If anyone held their teen years against them," Raina said, "there'd be no one on the force." Sometimes those years were even helpful. Liam grew up in Wellington, so he knew where all the high school kids had their drinking parties from personal experience. They didn't bust them all the time—just enough so the kids didn't get too carried away.

"Yeah, but it's not teenage wild oats, is it? You actually believed you had powers," Brian said. If he couldn't see or touch something himself, he assumed it didn't exist. Leveraging myths about a phantom ship for tourists was one thing. But accepting premonitions or anything remotely supernatural? Not Brian. "Maybe you still do," he continued. "What, you think Rustico's the source of all that?" For someone who dismissed the supernatural, he sure seemed to understand it. "That's why you don't come around," he said. "Don't want to deal with it."

"Maybe I just don't want to deal with you," Raina said.

"Right, so you leave me to take care of the business, take care of Mom and Dad. I do have a family of my own. And Claire's mother and father aren't getting any younger, either. Unlike you, she helps her parents when she can."

"Mom and Dad hardly need much from me."

"How would you know? It's not so easy for them anymore. Long hours on the water, working in the sun, lugging around all that gear. Every year I have to spend more and more time helping them. And you, you just traipse in like you're doing us all a favour with a quick visit here and there."

Raina's chest tightened. The journal offered some protection against the phantom ship. Too bad it didn't do the same against brothers. "What is that supposed to mean?"

"I think I was rather clear. You're either a member of the family or you're not. It's not freelance, you don't get to pick your jobs."

"You're not the final arbiter on family. You have no idea what my life is like. I don't have to answer to you." Jesus, who the hell did he think he was, judging her like that? Besides, Mom and Dad were fine. Tired, but fine.

Their mom popped her head out the front door. "What's taking so long? I need those tomatoes."

They pasted smiles on their faces and entered the kitchen. In the bright light, Raina took a long look at her mom, assessing every wrinkle on her forehead, the slight bags under her eyes.

Her mom stepped back. "What're you staring at?"

"I like your earrings."

The golden stars flickered as her mom reached forward to take the tomatoes. "Since when do you care about earrings?"

"Jeesh, just being nice," Raina said as her mom introduced Brian to Simone.

"How do you blow your nose with that ring in there?" he asked.

"Same as you do," Simone said. "So, Aunt Kate, you were going to tell me about the Doirons."

"Pour me some of that red wine, would you?" Raina's mom took a sip once Simone handed a glass to her. "What do you want to know?"

"Anything. Everything."

"Well, story goes that our ancestors had the gift of foresight. The ability to sense the future."

"This again?" Brian said.

"Quiet, you." Her mom made no effort to capitulate to Brian's discomfort with the supernatural. And this part of the story was family lore, with enough time passed between then and now to be couched as a quaint tale.

"What about the past?" Simone asked.

"I never heard that. Why do you ask?"

Raina narrowed her eyes at Simone.

"No reason," Simone said. "Just a question."

"They also had healing abilities," her mom said.

"Couldn't that've been a knowledge of herbs?" Raina asked.

"Possibly."

"Maybe it was both," Simone said. "A skill and a magical ability."

"Not magical, mystical," Raina said.

Brian leaned against the far wall. "The mystical police detective."

"Don't start." Her mom hacked the tomatoes apart with her knife.

"How can you learn about these abilities?" Simone asked. "How can you control it? Make it work for you. Is there like, a manual or something?"

"Darned if I know." She turned back to the stove. "Like I told you the other day, I just get flashes here and there."

That wasn't entirely true. Raina's mom had a strong intuition, but it came from paying attention to her surroundings and working to understand people, not from any special ability. Still, it must've made her feel better to pretend, although Raina was never sure if she did so consciously.

Her mom's voice cooled. "Raina, though, why don't you ask her?"

"I don't know any more than you do." Raina dragged a chair away from the table and sat down.

Her mom dumped the chopped tomatoes into the pan. Their juice sputtered and spat.

"Why don't you consult your novels?" Brian muttered.

"What was that?" her mom asked.

"Nothing," he said.

Simone pressed on, ignoring the family dynamics. "Do you know anything about Celeste? Or Madeleine?" she asked.

"Celeste, no. Madeleine, a bit. There's an exhibit about her in the Acadian Museum in Miscouche. I visited it a few years ago. It focuses on the Acadian Expulsion of 1758. Horrible history, getting expelled from your home and sent to a strange country. All those children dying."

Images rose unbidden to Raina's mind. Flames and spectres swirled around her. She gagged on salty seawater mixed with the coppery taste of blood. Waves crashed over her head as something pulled her down into the depths. Her chest heaved as she struggled for air.

"Jesus, Raina." Brian's voice. "Are you okay?"

A spoon clattered on the floor and her mom was beside her. "Head between your knees," she said.

Raina flopped forward. Breathed in through her nose, out through her mouth. Stuck her hand behind her back to touch the journal.

"Is she all right?" Simone asked.

"I'm fine." Raina sat up. "Just a bit lightheaded."

"Too much whisky and not enough food, right?" Simone handed her a glass of water.

"Yeah," Raina answered. "Exactly."

"You were telling us about the museum, Aunt Kate," Simone said. "And I think your sauce needs to be stirred." She led Raina's mom back to the stove and got her chattering again.

Raina sent a silent thanks to Simone. She sipped her water and ignored Brian's stares. Her mom likewise kept an eye on her but, as far as they knew, she hadn't zoned out like that since before she'd moved to Wellington, so the incident passed without further comment.

The journal was helpful, yes, absolutely, but it could clearly only do so much to protect her, which was not enough.

Once Raina steadied herself, she steered the conversation away from the past by asking her mom if they'd had any more Airbnb requests.

After dinner, as her mom heaved herself out of her chair, leaning on the table for support, Simone volunteered to wash the dishes. "Go to bed, Aunt Kate. We'll take of this."

"Thanks, dear." Her mom and dad left the kitchen. Brian had departed a few minutes earlier with leftovers for Claire.

"We need to go to that museum," Simone said once they were alone. "Your mom said they have some Doiron family documents. How cool is that?"

"Why? She said it was just about the expulsion."

"As far as she knows. Ship manifests, lists of births, marriages, and deaths. But she doesn't know about Celeste. That she kept a journal. Or that Sébastienne wrote Madeleine's story. How could she look for something that she didn't realize existed?"

CHAPTER 15

Raina

Raina's head throbbed from the aftermath of too much whisky. Once she'd returned to the B&B, she had added two shots to her usual pour. She'd placed the journal on top of her pillow and handcuffed herself to the bedframe, and the combination had allowed her to get a modicum of sleep.

She itched to go for a morning run but had no time to waste before she was scheduled to report to the Coast Guard vessel. She checked with her department for progress on the smuggling cases and called a few informants about crystal meth or cocaine dealers. Nothing other than the usual unfortunate aftermaths. A few overdoses, one death. One human trafficking survivor had called the hotline from her cell phone in a bathroom stall and was now at a women's shelter. She likely had knowledge that would help others, but right now, the woman needed safety and security, not a police interview. So Raina returned to get Simone, keeping the journal close beside her.

Her cousin sat on the porch steps, chin in hands, contemplating the cloudy sky, which was thick with the promise of rain. When Raina pulled into the driveway, Simone popped up and ran to the Jeep.

"Road trip," Simone said. "Got snacks?"

"It's not even an hour." Along Highway 2, which thankfully cut through the middle of the Island.

"Still need junk food. Twizzlers are best."

Raina smirked. "Only if I have to stop for gas."

Simone looked at the full tank indicator on the dashboard. "You're no fun."

"I've been told." Raina turned onto the main road and increased speed.

Simone flipped the radio from station to station, stopping when The Doors started to play "The End." Raina reached to flick it off but, with Simone swaying to the music, she turned it down instead. Why did such depressing songs have to be so catchy?

"Did you check on if anyone's looking for the journal?" Simone asked. "Or me? Is this"— she sang the next words—"the end?"

"You don't seem too worried about stealing the journal anymore."

"I have you on my side."

"If you're caught, you need a lawyer, not a cop." Raina considered toying with Simone, just for fun, before letting her off the hook, but Raina didn't have the energy for it. "No reported theft from the archives."

"Good news all around," Simone said. "That means you and I get to hang out more."

"Right. Good news," Raina said.

"Why'd you move to Wellington?" Simone asked.

"Why do you think?"

"You moved to get away from the water, duh. But I meant, why not move to the Prairies or something?"

"The Island is my home. I wasn't going to let …" Raina searched for the right word to describe the phantom ship, but couldn't find one. "… anything drive me off it."

"I can respect that. What started the nightmares?"

"Not talking about them."

"Why do you think my premonitions are just about babies, and yours were, or are"—she shifted in her seat, peering at Raina for clarification she didn't get—"about finding stuff?"

"I've no idea."

"So, why'd you become a cop?" Simone tapped the portable warning light on the dash. "Can I turn this on?"

Raina slapped her arm away. "Can you go five minutes without asking a question?"

"It's how you learn. You're not against learning, are you?"

Raina pinched the bridge of her nose with the fingers on her left hand. Maybe if she squeezed hard enough, the pain would take her away from the conversation.

"C'mon, it's not like it's a secret, or personal or anything, right? I bet you get that question a lot."

She did. Far more than her partner, Liam. Raina gave her stock answer. "To protect people."

"Really, that's all you got? Isn't that written on the side of police cars? To serve and protect? You can't be more original than that?"

"No, it's not. And fine. I like the analysis of evidence. Clues that lead to a solution." Better than flubbing around with weird unreliable premonitions. Being a police officer hadn't been her original choice, but its logical underpinnings had called to her when her initial plans turned out to be completely unworkable.

"But you don't always solve cases, right?"

"No, unfortunately." The smugglers were like a leaky pipe, bursting out in one direction when another was welded shut. Taking advantage of people when they were at their most vulnerable, when they trusted the wrong person.

"Were your premonitions ever useful?" Simone asked.

"Had to block them out."

"Because of the nightmares?"

"How about trying a sentence without a question mark?"

"Do you miss the family business." Simone exaggerated a downward inflection on her last word.

"Not what I meant."

"But not a question mark."

"You're relentless."

"It's a skill. Your answer?"

"No, not anymore." Raina slowed as the traffic grew heavier.

"Will Brian take it over? Your mom was talking about retirement sometime soon."

"That's the plan." Brian wanted out of the business so he could focus on his realtor work and his own family, but her mom said she'd go to her grave early if they had to sell it. Brian, good son that he was, agreed to take it on eventually, with the help of a few cousins. He wasn't happy about it—that clearly hadn't changed based on their conversation the night before—but she didn't think he saw any other option.

They soon arrived at the museum's mostly empty parking lot. The museum was shaped like an L, the main door sitting at the point where two long red-roofed wooden buildings met. Instead of glass, the windows were filled with wood carvings of the Acadian Expulsion and framed with white shutters. Nine vertical banners whipped in the growing wind—three blue, three white, and three red—in a nod to the colours of the Acadian flag. The museum was surrounded by a school, a church, a post office, and a coffee shop. Everything a small town needed.

Simone hopped out of the Jeep, turned, and looked at Raina, still sitting in the driver's seat. "Aren't you coming?" she asked.

"Yes." But she needed a moment first. After so long resisting this…whatever it was…now that she was confronting it…

"Don't you want to figure this all out?"

Jesus, another question. "It's not like we're going to get inside and everything will magically fix itself."

"You never know. There's magic in these parts, after all." She winked, hummed the theme song to *Bewitched*, and grinned.

"Goofball."

"You adore me." Simone spun in a circle, arms wide, head back, tongue out to catch a drizzle of beginning rain.

Raina would never admit it out loud, but Simone was growing on her. Like mould on blue cheese, maybe, enhancing the flavour of life. "Let's do this," Raina said.

They entered the large lobby, with the requisite souvenir and book section in front, offices to the right, and exhibit entrance to the left.

A woman behind the ticket counter rose. Her sundress was patterned with purplish-blue lupins. "Good morning. Where are you two from?" she asked.

"Wellington."

"Yukon."

"That's quite a combo. But you're not originally from Wellington, are you? Your accent's not quite right."

"Rustico." Raina sighed.

"That sounds more like it. I've an ear for Island accents." She handed them a map of the exhibits. "Anything in particular bring you here?"

"Yes, actually," Raina said. "We're interested in the exhibit about the Acadian Expulsion. Madeleine Doiron in particular."

"We're Mad's relatives," Simone said.

"Mad, I like that," the woman said. "I'm sure she was plenty angry at how she was uprooted by the British."

Raina glared at Simone. Basic rule of detecting. Don't give out personal information.

"We're wondering if you have any documents from the Doirons?" Simone asked.

"Usually you need an appointment for that, to give us time to search, but for family, I'll make an exception."

Simone tilted her head at Raina as if to say, *See*?

"Why don't you take a look around? Madeleine's exhibit is around the corner of the first set of exhibits." The woman opened the map and drew a circle. "Right here. You can't miss it. I can answer any questions after. Make sure to try the step-dancing exhibit afterwards. There are video tutorials."

"Awesome," Simone said. "We could dance together."

"We'll see," Raina said. By which she meant *not likely*.

They thanked the woman and walked to the exhibit entry.

"Everyone's so friendly here," Simone said. Her voice soared in the empty hall. "In Montréal you're likely to get a grunt and a head-nod. If you speak English, not even that."

"Lower your voice," Raina said.

"Why? This is a museum, not a library. And there's no one here but us."

Raina strode past the first panels into the array of exhibits that snaked this way and that. Simone stopped in front of one describing the origins of L'Acadie. "Slow down."

"You can look if you want. I'm going straight to Madeleine, get this over with," she stage-whispered over her shoulder. Simone hurried to keep up.

Raina stopped in front of the exhibit about their ancestor. A statue, wearing a white dress and brown shawl, her head covered with a kerchief, sat in front of a spinning wheel. She was surrounded by cut-out figures and paintings of other historical figures, but Raina focused on Madeleine. Before this, Madeleine had only been a name. Someone lost to history. But now, Raina considered her as a real person—not a long-dead ancestor, but once a living breathing feeling human.

The centuries between them collapsed. Raina reached out as if to touch her, and the air around Madeleine seemed warmer than elsewhere. An invitation? Raina wasn't sure if she wanted to accept it. Would it help, the way holding Celeste's journal had? Or would it destroy the boundaries she'd erected between the explicable and the inexplicable? She stepped back from the velvet rope that divided Madeleine from the rest of the room.

"She was fifteen when she got married?" Simone gasped as she read the accompanying panel. "To a widower who was thirty? Gross. But common back then, I guess."

Raina scanned the words. Noted the important dates and places of Madeleine's life. Considered the connections, through the Doiron line. Madeleine, born in the eighteenth century in Rustico, followed generations later by Celeste in the nineteenth, then Raina in the twentieth, and Simone in the twenty-first.

"Not much about Madeleine herself here, is there?" Raina said. "Other than basic facts."

"Nope. She wasn't a queen, or a saint, or a scientist. If you're not famous, history doesn't care about you."

"But still, she's here. The centrepiece of a museum exhibit."

"Go Madeleine," Simone said. "And whoever's kept her story alive." She read an accompanying panel. "The Treaty of Utrecht between Britain and France in 1713 set the stage for the expulsion decades later. Imagine, kings in two different lands you've never even set foot in, forcing you out of your home and across the ocean."

"Not much has changed over the centuries. Rulers, politicians, refugees ..." Raina let her words trail off as she stared at the image of her ancestor.

"It feels warmer here than the rest of the museum, doesn't it?"

"Not sure why," Raina said. "There's nothing of hers here. Just representations."

"True, but it's still part of her story. I think she's encouraging us," Simone said.

"That's ridiculous," Raina said, only half meaning it.

"I'm going to check out the rest of the museum. See if I can find anything else about the Doirons." With a last glance at Madeleine, Simone walked away.

Raina pulled her cell phone out of her back pocket, snapped a few photos to document the exhibit, and focused on Madeleine. She reached out, slowly. The air temperature rose again. She snatched her hand back. This was absurd. Madeleine wasn't here. Raina tore her gaze from Madeleine, shook off the eerie feeling, and strode farther into the museum, past several exhibits, until she heard stomping and banging feet. She followed the sound.

"I wish I had clogs." Simone had earphones on and was staring at a video screen, her face intense with concentration. Her feet flew as she advanced from the beginner to intermediate step-dancing videos.

Raina's phone pinged with a message from her chief. He wanted her to check in at the detachment this afternoon. That'd eat up an hour or two she didn't have.

"I give up." Simone heaved a long breath which ended in a laugh. "The advanced steps are craaazy. Sure you don't want to try?"

"No more wasting time."

"You're no fun."

"We've established that fact." Raina turned towards the foyer. "We need to see those documents."

The woman from the front desk ushered them into a small room with a pile of documents and two sets of white cotton gloves. Simone thanked her and she left.

"No stealing anything," Raina said to Simone.

"No promises." Simone grinned.

Raina donned the gloves and turned over the only book. "Just a Bible." Her stomach clenched. Had she really expected Madeleine's story would be sitting here, ready to answer her questions, solve her problems? It was probably lost in a fire or forgotten on a shelf, never to be seen or read again.

"We'll keep searching," Simone said. "I've the rest of the summer off."

"I don't," Raina snapped.

"Yeesh. Sorry."

Raina shook her head and flipped through the documents. Just the expected ship manifests and birth records. An old newspaper was sandwiched in between them. Raina picked it up. Her fingers tingled, like the fizz when touching Celeste's journal. She stared at the front page, with an image of a thin woman seated primly on a bench, a ship in the harbour behind her. But that vessel wasn't what drew her attention. In the background was a flaming ship, blurry but recognizable. The phantom ship.

"What're you looking at?" Simone asked. "Is that the phantom ship, there in the corner? Let me see."

Simone's voice dimmed as if moving away from her. This time, Raina didn't see images or flashes. It was as if she were living it again, even though it had happened over a decade ago.

It had been one week before high school graduation. The plan was for her to spend the summer working on the tour boat. She'd considered starting at the University of Prince Edward Island that fall, but the tours were booked well into October, and her parents needed her help. Brian had just gotten his realtor's license so was dedicating time to building his client list. She was registered to start her business degree in the winter term, with holidays focused on adding more tours and finding opportunities for income in the off-season.

That morning, she woke just before dawn to light flashing outside her bedroom window. Usually, she'd ignore anything that woke her early and yank the covers over her head, but she was too excited. Her mom had promised she could lead the next tour, so instead of going back to sleep, she stood, once again practicing her spiel, trying out new material to make it her own as she parted the curtains and peered out.

Lightning ripped across the dark sky. One arc branched into another, as if an invisible creature sketched out dozens of trees, with long trunks and limbs intersecting one another. Everything was terrifyingly quiet. No thunder. No dogs barking. No rain pounding. The lightning forked and slashed, never touching the ground. She stared, mesmerized, until something else caught her attention. A translucent book danced before her eyes. Another vision. Moby Dick chomping on a whaling boat. She shivered as the temperature dropped. It was a warning about the tour. She blinked and let the curtain drop.

"You're awfully quiet," her mom said at breakfast.

"Just nerves." Raina poked at her cereal, the cornflakes now nothing more than mush.

"You never get nervous." Her mom put her palm on Raina's forehead. "You're a little warm. Maybe you're getting sick?"

"I'm fine."

"Do you want to stay home from school today? We could delay your inaugural voyage."

That's what they'd been calling it, her inaugural voyage, although Brian teased *maiden voyage* was more appropriate, though he'd never say so in front of their mom.

"No, I want it to be today. It's summer solstice. And there's going to be a full moon."

"I'm well aware, Raina. I can read a lunar calendar." She grabbed the milk off the table, which squished the carton and sent liquid squirting out the top. "Damn it." She swiped at the mess with a woven dishcloth.

"I didn't mean it that way, Mom. Just that I'll be fine." Raina swigged the coffee she'd only started drinking that year. She suffered through the bitter taste because she wanted to be sophisticated. Sugar would've made it more palatable, but sweet wasn't really her thing. "The storm this morning woke me up early, is all."

"What storm?"

"The electrical one."

"There was no storm."

"You must've slept through it."

"I was up at five trying to balance our bank account. Didn't sleep through anything."

"Right." There was no arguing with her mom. Especially about something like this. If Raina said anything more, that maybe she'd had a vision, her mom's jealousy of her abilities might make her revoke the invitation to lead the tour. "Must've been a dream."

At lunch, Raina talked through the vision with Hattie, huddled on the bottom stairs beside the library they'd been kicked out of one too many times for being loud. They always started out whispering but could never keep their volume low for long. Other students stepped around them, rattling on about graduation and summer plans. The chaos was great cover for their conversation. If anyone overheard a word, if they actually cared to pay attention, they'd assume Raina and Hattie were discussing books.

"Whaddya think?" Raina asked, after explaining everything.

"Creepy," Hattie said. "You've never had one like this, have you?" She offered Raina her open bag of ketchup-flavoured chips but Raina shook her head. Normally she'd have dug in for a handful, but her stomach couldn't handle it.

"No, which is why I'm not sure what it's telling me. Don't go on the tour, because something bad will happen. Or do go on it, so nothing bad will happen." Raina picked at the hole in the knee of her jeans.

"What do you want to do?"

"I want to go." Several lockers slammed in quick succession as the in-crowd rushed to the cafeteria. They always travelled in a pack.

"Because you think it'll be okay, or because you don't care as long as you get to lead the tour?"

Raina winced. "It's not that I don't care but, if I don't take this chance, Mom might never let me lead it again. I think she's afraid I'll summon up the ship, proving once and for all I have abilities and she doesn't. But she'll have to let me continue with the tours if I can do it. It'll be quite the tourist draw. Plus, it's the perfect intersection: first time..."

Hattie stifled a giggle, knowing Raina had tired of the joke.

"Summer solstice, full moon," Raina finished.

"Sounds like your mind's made up."

"Yeah, I guess so."

Their tour departed an hour before dusk, puttering away from the dock. Though early in the season, they were almost at capacity. Four families, with kids ranging from early to late teens, and one couple who seemed more interested in each other than the tour. They all wore bulky orange lifejackets with bright yellow straps and cheap plastic buckles. Brian sat at the back, his hands on the life preserver. Raina preened in her slim black life vest, which she'd put on her Christmas list last year, holding onto a stanchion and leaning out over the deepening water, her vision of that morning almost forgotten in her excitement. Once they cleared the harbour, her dad revved the engine. This was Raina's cue. Her mom nodded at her.

"Welcome, everybody, on board the *Spirit of Rustico*," Raina said into the microphone. "The finest tour on the Island. We'll spend the first half viewing the sights, best experienced from the water of course, and tell you the history of the area. Then, the second half, the one you're all really here for, I'm sure"— she winked to their chuckles, not bad so far—"we'll continue on our search for the phantom ship. We can't guarantee you'll see her, but the tale alone, out here in the open waters, will bring the best kind of scary shivers to each of you." One of the preteens covered her ears. "Don't worry," Raina said. "It's just a tale." Then, because the girl had turned away, Raina mouthed, "It's real." One of the older teen's eyes grew wide. The other rolled hers and crossed her arms. Not a fan. Can't please everyone.

Half an hour later, dusk fell, and the ocean darkened. As they crashed through the low waves, salty sea spray coated them. Her mom passed around blankets. Raina started the tale of the phantom ship.

"The Northumberland Strait is one of the most haunted places on earth, thanks to shipwrecks, drownings, and people lost at sea. The strait separates the Island from the mainland, on the south shore. Here on the north shore, we're not in the strait itself. But there are no real boundaries in water, so the legends are just as strong here. The phantom ship is the most famous tale. Sightings of it date back to the early or mid-1700s. People wonder why they started then, but I think it's linked to the Acadians. How many of you have heard of the Acadian Expulsion?"

A few hands went up. The teen who'd rolled her eyes complained to her mother that she'd already taken her history exam and didn't need another lesson.

Raina ignored her and continued. "Most know about the expulsion from the mainland, in 1755. How many of you have heard of the poem 'Evangeline,' by Longfellow?" Most of the hands shot up this time. "It's brought a lot of attention to the plight of the Acadians, but it's wildly historically inaccurate."

This was Raina's adlib. Her mom never brought up the expulsion on the tours. Said the story was too sad and at odds with the fun promised by the tour.

"Anyway, there was a later expulsion in 1758, from Île Saint-Jean, the former name of PEI. Hundreds died on the perilous journey across the Atlantic Ocean. Legend has it a few jumped over the side and drowned, rather than face deportation from their beloved island." This last bit was also historically inaccurate, but Raina was on a roll and it sounded good. "The phantom ship is a schooner, either three- or four-masted, with sails the colour of a cloudy sky, consumed in flames. It's seen most often in the Northumberland Strait in autumn, another reason I think it's linked to the deportation, which happened in November, but we might get lucky tonight. It is the summer solstice, after all, with a full moon to light our way." She gestured to the sky in a way that she immediately knew was too over-the-top. She'd adjust it next time. "In the early nineteen hundreds, a fishing crew saw the ship and tried to rescue the crew. They reported no living people, just wisps of ghosts and spectres. Then it disappeared."

"I read on Wikipedia that the ship is just a trick of the moon's reflection near sunset, paired with mist from a northeast wind," a man said. "And I don't buy that it's seen on the north shore."

Any mention of Wikipedia would set her mom to cursing just as much as the launch of Airbnb. But Raina had the microphone. "Some people need to rationalize everything. But certain things can't be explained." That was exactly the response her mom would give, plus a rant about the internet. "And the ship has increased its roaming range over the decades and centuries." Personally, she wondered if it had something to do with the Doiron family, though she wasn't sure how or why it would be connected to them. "Now, if you keep your eyes on the horizon …"

And there it was. Raina almost dropped the microphone. Not a mirage, or a reflection that could be interpreted as the ship if you squinted. She'd found the phantom ship. A three-masted schooner was awash in crinkling and crackling flames, sending sparks and ash into the sky. The smell of smoke drifted towards them. One of the tourists gasped. The others stared, as if not quite seeing something. The *Spirit of Rustico* headed straight towards the ship.

"Jesus Christ," her dad said from the wheelhouse. He jerked the wheel to port, towards the Island.

Raina flailed and fell over the side, splashing into the cold, deep, dark water.

Raina, Raina, spectral voices whispered.

"Raina." Simone's voice. "Raina."

Raina's eyes snapped open. She was in the museum.

"Are you okay? You zoned out. Do you need to sit down?"

Raina leaned against the wall and slid to the floor, breathing as if she'd run a marathon.

"Do you need a paper bag? What happened?"

"Just give me a minute."

"You look pale. Maybe you should eat something."

"Road trip snacks?" Raina's voice hitched and she forced it back to normal. "Just got a little dizzy."

"Nice try. You had a vision, didn't you?"

Raina considered lying, but was tiring of it. Maybe Simone being here was a sign to tell her whole story. "Not a vision. A memory." The newspaper was still in her hand. She focused on the byline. "Photograph by C. Haché."

"That's Celeste's photo. With the flaming ship." Simone's voice rose and her cadence increased. "Just like she wrote in her journal."

"You can see it?"

"Yeah. Creepy and cool."

"Cold, not cool," Raina said.

"What do you mean?"

Raina looked up. She wasn't quite ready to stand but she managed a steady voice. "I have to report in at my department. No time to take you back to Rustico. You can come with me. I'll drop you at a coffee shop."

"Sure," Simone said. "But just give me a sec." She plucked the paper out of Raina's hands, dashed out of the room, and darted back. "Will you be all right by yourself?"

Raina waved her away, face hot and chest tight. She managed to pull herself up before Simone returned. It wasn't just that the memory was so vivid, like living it over, but that it also had the hint of a foretelling. That it could happen again.

Simone returned a moment later. "I showed it to the woman at the front counter. Said something was out of focus in the corner. She explained it was probably from the process of making the photo into an etching and printing it. She couldn't tell it's the phantom ship."

Raina nodded. She and Simone were tied together not only by visions, but by the ship, though Simone had never seen it in real life. Hopefully she never would.

CHAPTER 16

Raina

After driving to Wellington and bringing Simone to the River Café, where she could get her fill of lemon cranberry scones and tea, Raina entered the police department. She was attached to one of four municipal police services on the Island, which worked in conjunction with the RCMP and had agreements with smaller towns such as Rustico. Some thought the patchwork of services was confusing, but it seemed to Raina as if they covered the Island like the dew, which also happened to be the motto for the province's newspaper, *The Guardian*.

The Wellington station was positioned like a guard between an inlet river and the town in an old brick mill with a dropped ceiling and rounded rectangular windows. It had a small but mighty force: one police chief, one inspector, one corporal, two detective constables—Liam and her—with three staff. A jail cell was tucked in the back corner of the main floor. Raina waved to the staff, knocked on the chief's door, and poked her head in.

He was seated behind his desk, pouring over documents, his bald head glistening in the fluorescent lights. He looked up. "Cormier. Good." He motioned her in with a meaty arm. "I need a break from this paperwork. You'd think computers would have decreased it, but it's a never-ending pileup. Everybody needs a fucking form filled out."

"Anything interesting?" She sat in the visitor's chair.

He clutched the empty ashtray he used as a paperweight, something he did whenever he had the urge for a smoke, which seemed to be constantly. "Got a Twitter complaint that the back seats in our cars are too small, with no leg room or offer of bottled water."

"You're kidding."

"Nope. Said the Charlottetown cars made for a better experience." He leaned back in his chair.

"Do you want a full sitrep on my cases?" She assumed a situation report was why he wanted her in his office. He was fine with short updates by text or phone, but he preferred in person for longer briefings.

"No, you can pass all that on to Liam. He'll take them over while you're with the Coast Guard. He'll fill me in as needed. I wanted to talk to you about the tasking. Your joining instructions should be in your email. I assume you've read them."

Raina nodded, even though she hadn't.

"The offshore patrol vessel has supported law enforcement before, but me and my fishing buddy, the captain of the Canadian Coast Guard Ship *Earl Grey* ..."

Raina knew not to laugh. The vessel wasn't named for the tea, but the British Prime Minister the tea was named for.

"... are considering proposing an ongoing collaboration. You're the most qualified to assist, and this will push you to the top of the promotion list. I'm going to wait until the last possible date to write your evaluation, so you get a chance to prove yourself in your week-long assignment. If all goes well, I'll recommend you for promotion. We'll consider a recurring position with a Coast Guard vessel."

"Recurring?" She wasn't sure she could survive a one-time week onboard, let alone anything longer or more frequent.

"You have an excellent record, and nothing ever takes you away from your duties," he said, which was code for *no husband + no kids = dedicated to the force*. "Perfect for sailing with the Coast Guard. Though I'm not sure about all the time your skills will be wasted, during water sample collection or transit time."

"But if I'm at the top of the list, then I get to pick my posting."

"Shit, Cormier," the chief said. "I thought you were a team player." He propped his elbows on his desk. "Don't turn into a fucking union stickler. This is for the public good." He looked at his ashtray as if he'd do anything to get a pack of cigarettes to appear there, then stared back at her. "Unless you've changed your mind about a promotion."

Raina forced a smirk onto her face. "Just messing with you, Chief. You know you can always count on me."

"Look at you, gaining a sense of humour." The chief jerked his thumb at the door. "Dismissed."

Raina nodded and strode away, forcing down her anger. Most of the time, her chief was a great boss. But as soon as anyone dared disagree with him, he turned into an asshole. Well, she wouldn't have to deal with him much longer. She'd board the Coast Guard ship, then get her promotion and a new posting. And while she was at it, she'd vanquish the phantom ship from her life. Her mom was right. Time to face her fears.

RAINA MET SIMONE AT THE JEEP AS A MASSIVE RAINSTORM DESCENDED ON them. Thunder snapped and lightning ripped across the sky, mirroring the day she'd first seen the phantom ship.

"You looked pissed," Simone said, as they got in. "Please don't tell me you got in trouble because of me. Did the journal get reported? Did they think you're involved?"

Raina started to snap at Simone, but she looked so earnest Raina checked herself, and her temper. None of this was Simone's fault. Raina tapped her fingers on the steering wheel. Tap-tap-tappity-tap.

Simone repeated the rhythm on the dashboard. "You do that, too?" she asked. "Weird."

Raina stopped tapping, wiped her wet hair from her face, dialled the phone, and put it on speaker. Her mom picked up on the first ring.

"You're up," Raina said.

"It's almost noon, sarcastic Sally."

"Sorry." This wasn't a great way to start out.

"Is Simone with you?"

"Yes, you're on speaker."

"Hey, Aunt Kate," Simone said.

"Hey yourself."

"Did you get my note?" Simone asked.

"Yes, though 'off with Raina' isn't very specific."

Raina turned on the ignition, selected the fastest speed for the wipers, and indicated a left turn. Swishes and beeps competed with the rain for noise supremacy.

"Are you driving?" her mom asked. "You should be keeping your attention on the road, not talking to me.

"I'm a perfectly safe driver," Raina said. "I have advanced driving courses."

"For chasing felons. Not talking to your mom."

Her mom had her there, though that was a course that might be useful. Her mom said something inaudible. "Can you turn her up?" Raina asked Simone, something she never thought she'd say. "I need a favour." Something else that was new to her lips.

"Well, I never. You need help from your mom."

"Yes." Her mom was going to make this painful. "We went to the Acadian Museum. We're doing some research on the Doirons for Simone."

"Just for Simone?"

"I tried a super cool step-dancing exhibit. You'd love it," Simone said.

"I suppose I'm learning some things as well," Raina said.

"Just tell her everything already," Simone said.

"Tell me what?" Mom asked.

"We're leaving Wellington and are headed to the old Union Bank in Charlottetown," Raina said, in partial answer.

"We are?" Simone asked.

"Why?" her mom asked.

"Turns out some relatives used to live in its attic."

"Really? Who? I bet it was your first cousin twice removed's son. An attic seems about right for him."

"Ooh, who's that?" Simone asked. "Fred, Darryl, or maybe Nigel? Tell me the gossip."

"We don't have a Nigel," Raina's mom said. "But there is a Nathan."

Raina jumped in to avert a who's-related-to-whom lesson. "No, Mom, in the 1860s."

"Celeste," Simone said. "The one we talked about yesterday. Madeleine's great-great-granddaughter."

"You found something at the museum."

"Sort of." Raina braked at a stoplight and peered at the rain.

"We found a photograph of the phantom ship and Raina had a vision or something," Simone blurted.

"Raina, what's going on?"

Raina sighed. Screwed up her courage. "I want to get into the Union Bank to see if Celeste left anything there that would help me—us—understand ... something difficult to explain." The light turned green and she accelerated.

"What do you mean by 'us?'"

"Simone has premonitions too."

Her mom was silent. Finally, she said, "Well, I'll be. You're admitting it now. So you *and* Simone, but neither of your mothers. Sometimes it does skip a generation or two, like your grandma said. It was never my fault I couldn't harness it."

"What do you mean, 'your fault'?" Raina asked.

"Nothing. How can I help?"

"I saw a police report a few weeks ago about a protest against the renovation of the building the Union Bank used to be housed in. It's a heritage property that's being turned into condos. The protestors wanted assurances the developer would not only abide by restoration rules, but go beyond it to preserve as much as possible. Apparently, much of the original construction remains, and they don't want that to change."

"Brilliant," Simone said. "Madeleine's book might be there."

"Something's there, that's for sure," Raina said. "I can feel it."

"Where do I fit in?" her mom said.

"We need your help getting access to the building."

"You're a cop," Simone said. "Wave your badge. Tell them you have a case."

"It doesn't work like that. I can't just barge on in anywhere." Maybe she wished she could, but that didn't mean she would. "I can ask questions, but I can't gain access without probable cause."

"Then what's the good in being a cop?" Simone asked.

"What can I do?" her mom asked.

"The developer is Deidre Green."

"Ugh. That's a name I haven't heard for a while," her mom said.

"Do you know her?" Simone asked. "Has she done something wrong you can hold over her? Is there a classified database filled with her misdeeds?"

"You watch way too much TV," Raina said. "They played high school field hockey together."

"So, Aunt Kate, you can just ask for a favour. Friends always help out."

"I'm not sure you'd call us friends."

"Frenemies," Simone said. "That's the best kind. Do you have gossip on her, Aunt Kate?" Simone's eyes gleamed.

Raina reminded herself Simone was only nineteen and probably had a fair number of frenemies herself. "I thought you were a philosopher, not a would-be blackmailer."

"Philosophy has multiple real-world applications," Simone said.

"Mom, could you see if she can get us in?" Raina asked. "Surely you've put high school behind you by now."

"We did. Until we tried to pair our tours with a few of her short-term rentals. Let's just say it didn't end well."

"Tell us more," Simone said. "What happened? More drama? It's like a soap opera around here."

"You watch soaps?" her mom asked.

"I've been streaming *Another World*."

"That was one of my favourites. Especially the matriarch. What was her name?"

"Rachel Cory," Simone said.

"That's the one."

Raina interrupted what was sure to become a long, irrelevant conversation. "I didn't know you were trying to expand the business."

"That's hardly surprising, now is it, Raina?" Her mom's voice lost its friendly tone. "You're not exactly involved."

"I know, Mom. Just, can you ask her to let us into the building? Today?" She paused. "This is important to me."

"Are you okay?"

Raina rubbed the back of her neck. Decided to answer honestly. "Actually, no."

Simone punched the air with her fist. *Progress*, she mouthed, doing a victory dance in her seat.

"I'll make the call now, but on one condition."

"What's that?"

"I'm coming with you."

Raina's stomach dropped. "Mom, that's not necessary."

"That's my price, if you want me to suck up to Deidre."

"You never suck up to anyone."

"Exactly."

"What about your tour tonight? You can't miss that."

"So thoughtful. Look up, Raina. This storm's not going anywhere soon. We were just about to cancel the pre-bookings anyway."

"Fine. I'll meet you—"

"In Hunter River."

"I was going to say Charlottetown."

"Nonsense. No sense in taking two cars into the city. Besides, your father is headed to his cribbage tournament in Summerside. He'll drop me off in Hunter River on the way. We should get there at about the same time you do, if you're just leaving Wellington now. I'll meet you at that diner by the furniture place. The one that used to be a grocery store."

Arguing with her was useless, so Raina agreed and ended the call.

AS RAINA WALKED TOWARDS THE DINER, HER MOM'S VOICE FILTERED OUT THE open door. The rain had tapered off for a moment and the owner was a proponent of fresh air, to the great chagrin of tourists looking for air-conditioning. Her mom's charm bracelets rattled as she complained that no Islander should serve anything other than Red Rose tea. The server said she was from Nova Scotia, and her mom chuckled. "Touché," she said. "I'll take a coffee instead. To go. Lots of cream and sugar."

Raina poked her head in. Her mom sat on a red counter stool, looking slightly slumped over. When Raina said hi, her mom straightened.

"Ready, Mom?"

"Always in such a hurry, dear." She turned to the server, who had on a red checkered apron. "This is my daughter," her mom said. "She's a police officer. About to be promoted."

"Not necessary, Mom."

"Then congratulations are in order," the server said, pouring the coffee. "Why not stay for Happy Hour? We make a mean Long Island Iced Tea." She gestured at the mostly empty diner. "It's quiet now, but we fill up fast for dinner. You can pick any table."

"That sounds fun, but my daughter needs me. I'm helping her on a case."

"It's not a case," Raina said.

"Another day, then." The server placed the coffee on the Formica countertop.

"Much obliged." Her mom's hand trembled as she reached for the take-out cup, almost knocked it over. "Didn't expect it to be so hot," she said.

Raina peered at her. "Do you need it double-cupped?"

"It's fine," her mom said as they exited the diner. "Where'd you park?"

Raina pointed across the street to where Simone leaned out the Jeep's window. "Hi, Aunt Kate."

"Why didn't she come in with you?" her mom asked.

"Because you two would've decided to stay to chat. Enjoy Happy Hour. Order the daily special. Talk some more."

"Can we?" Simone asked, getting out to give Raina's mom the front seat.

"No time," Raina said as they climbed into the Jeep. "Didn't you get snacks at the corner store?"

"I did." Simone belted herself in the back. "Anyone want a Twizzler?"

"Do you have anything chocolate?" her mom asked.

"Pretzel M&Ms."

"Perfect."

"Raina, do you want anything?"

"No. No coffee, no iced tea, no Twizzlers, no candy."

"Enough, Raina," her mom said. "What's going on?"

Raina had thought she'd come to terms with telling her mom everything, but switching from *keep everything buried deep down inside* to *spill your guts* was not like flicking a switch. "Did Deidre give us permission to enter? And the security codes?"

"She did, after I promised we wouldn't touch anything and I'd give her five free family tour passes for her off-Island clients. No more stalling."

"I'll tell her," Simone said. "What I know of it, at least."

"You will not. This is something Raina needs to do."

Maybe it was her intuition, or simply because she was her mother, but she was right. Raina's chief had once told her that every cop gets scared at some point or another. They rarely admit it but, sometimes, confiding in a partner can make the fear manageable. "But you didn't hear that from me," he'd added, not wanting to admit to any fear himself. Liam knew a sliver of her story, Hattie a fair bit more. No one knew the whole of it.

As they drove down Highway 2, towards Charlottetown, Raina took a breath and forced away the old habit of retreating into herself. She told her mom she'd been having nightmares since the summer she'd graduated from high school, that she'd lied when she said they stopped, and that was partly why she avoided Rustico, especially their tour boat. How Celeste had written a journal, though Raina skipped over the part about Simone's theft of it. That they wanted to find Madeleine's book to get more information about how to control and deal with their abilities.

Her mom listened with a stoic look on her face. Raina figured she'd guessed at some of this before, especially the fact that her nightmares continued. Her mom had clearly known something was up with her and Simone. Not exactly in Raina's character to spend time with a nineteen-year-old, especially one she barely knew. Raina suspected the bit about how the Doiron abilities were capricious, skipping generations at seeming random, was equally comforting and frustrating. Nothing would've enabled her mom to harness them, but she had to watch her daughter inherit and then reject what she herself craved. For Raina, it meant she'd been left dangling, like a leaf on a dying tree, at the mercy of a wind stronger than itself.

"Celeste wrote her journal in jail," Raina continued. "At some point after that, it found its way into the archives. In it, Celeste mentions Madeleine's book. Although Celeste included some information about Madeleine in her own journal, she said the book itself was important. Regretted losing it. We want to find it. It has vital information for Doiron women."

"The journal." Mom's fingers twitched. "Give it to me."

Raina hesitated, then leaned forward and pulled it out from behind her back.

"Why do you have it there?" her mom asked as she took it.

"I'll get to that." Raina forced away the chanting of the ghosts that'd started as soon as the journal left her hands. It was worse than ever, even now, in the daytime.

"You said you felt something when you first touched it?"

"It hummed and sizzled. And then it was like a rock that'd been warmed next to a fire," Raina said, although that wasn't quite right. Rocks weren't living things, and the journal almost seemed to breathe with Celeste's words.

"It gets hotter the more pages you turn, the more you read," Simone said.

Her mom skimmed a few paragraphs, flipped to the back, closed it. They were almost at the turnoff for Charlottetown.

"Anything?" Simone asked, leaning as far forward as her seatbelt would allow.

"No," her mom said, "other than the fact it's a precious family heirloom. There's no way we can return it when it's due back."

"Exactly," Simone said.

If her mom thought it was like a checked-out library book, that was fine for now. What to do with it was a problem for another day.

Her mom pressed her lips together. "Tell me more about how your nightmares started, Raina. It wasn't just that brief sighting of the phantom ship and falling overboard, was it? Something else happened."

Raina's hands trembled as she steered onto a side road to find a place to park. Any attempt to think about what happened, let alone talk about it, flashed her back to that night, and she didn't want to cause an accident. The Jeep's tires crunched on the gravel as they rounded a curve. Ahead was an unobstructed view of the ocean. There was no getting away from it. She could hear waves crashing against the shore even though they were still too far away for that to be possible. She stopped.

"What're you doing?" her mom asked. "We're in the middle of the road."

Raina pressed her lips together. If she was going to tell her story, then here, by the ocean, was the most fitting place. She eased her foot onto the gas and continued until the gravel ended. She thrust the gear into park and fixed her gaze on the water. Rain sputtered onto the windshield. Seaweed dotted the shore, pushed inland by the rising tide. She held her hands out for the journal and her mom handed it back. Raina let its warmth soothe her.

"After I fell in," she began, the words rushing out after being trapped in her memory for years, "the water grabbed at me, and I struggled to catch my breath. I thrashed to the surface. The waves grew, whipping over my head. I kicked, forced myself to calm. I had a lifejacket on. I was a strong swimmer. We'd practiced for this. Dad would turn the boat, Mom would spot me, Brian would throw the life preserver, and they'd haul me in.

"But the sea state rose. A wave crashed into me, dunked me under, forcing water down my throat. I spat it out. Spun in a circle. No sign of our boat. Mom, you called my name, but you were searching in the wrong direction. I yelled for you, but no one answered. My leg muscles cramped as I treaded water, fought to keep myself upright. As the waves rose and fell, the phantom ship emerged between the swells. Fire spread across its deck as it approached. Wood splintered. A sail disappeared in a whoosh of flame, then appeared again. I swam towards it.

"The phantom ship drew closer. A ghostly captain tipped his hat at me. Spectres of sailors worked the rigging. A small, shadowy figure waved from the crow's nest. The crew sang a low chant that pulled at me.

"Raina, Raina.

"Come aboard, Raina.

"Swim to us, Raina.

"Come aboard, come aboard ...

"Waves closed over me. Something pushed against my feet, nudged me to the surface. I glimpsed a horse's head and a serpentine body. I reached out and nestled my fingers in its oily fur but it slipped from my grasp and disappeared.

"Smoke filled my nose. The ship sailed in a spiral around me, coming ever closer but so slowly, I wondered if it would ever arrive. I tried to intercept its course. My limbs grew heavy. I drifted underwater, my arms floating above me, my body weighed down despite my life jacket. Specks of light dotted my vision.

A charred hull materialized beside me. I kicked up, spurting out water, its brininess searing my mouth. The spectres cheered and I grinned. They threw out a rope ladder. I grasped onto it, firmed my grip when the rising seas threatened to toss me off. I pulled myself up, found myself humming their song. My energy returned as I climbed. What a beautiful madness, becoming one with them, as if the secrets of the universe were opening up to me. I reached the top and the captain himself took my hand to help me onto their deck. Flames licked over my wrist, but they were glacial instead of hot.

"Something snagged my other arm. Tugged. I turned. Through a wall of ash, I could see our boat, though the faces of those on board were obscured. I turned back to the phantom ship. Put one leg over the railing. The spectres danced from bow to stern. I would've clapped for them, but one hand was encased in the captain's, and the other...something held on to it. Dad. I heard his voice saying, 'Grab on to me.' I told him to leave me alone, but he wouldn't let go.

"The captain opened his mouth and roared, 'She's choosing us.' His black tongue flickered with the words. 'Aren't you, dearie? Just one more step. You have to do it yourself. Them's the rules.'

"I lifted my other foot off the ladder.

"A chorus, which seemed to come from the water, grew louder and louder, but I couldn't make out what they were saying. Why wouldn't they go away? I'd found a new home and wanted it. This crew understood me. Needed me. A wave somehow crashed over my head, though the sea seemed now far below. I licked the salt off my lips. Shivered. My foot hovered over the flaming deck. One of the spectres, long, fiery hair flying, raced towards me. I thought she meant to welcome me, but she peeled my hand out of the captain's as a spark danced around her head. 'No,' the spectre said. 'Let go.'

"So I did," Raina told her mom and Simone. "The captain roared in frustration, the phantom ship disappeared, and Dad pulled me onto our boat."

"Wow," Simone breathed. She'd taken off her seat belt and was practically perched between the two front seats.

"I almost died that night," Raina said, the first time she'd ever vocalized it. "I wanted to join their crew. Thirsted for it."

"That is so wild. Amazing," Simone said.

"It most surely was not," her mom said. "Seeing Raina go overboard. Searching for her . . . ." She trailed off. "When we did find her, she was flailing, waves crashing over her head."

"But what about the phantom ship?" Simone asked. "Was the captain holding Raina's hand?"

Her mom's breath came out in a rush. "There was something strange about it all, but when we found her, all I could see was Raina alone in the water. No phantom ship, no captain."

"Did Uncle Warren see anything?" Simone asked.

This was something Raina had wondered, but never asked.

"He wouldn't talk about what happened at all," her mom said. "But I know he thought it was his fault Raina fell in, because he'd jerked the wheel too hard."

"He saved my life," Raina said. "Twice. Once for getting through to me, coaxing me to let go of the captain's hand." Though one of the spectres had helped him for some reason. "Second for pulling me out of the water."

"You were delirious," her mom said in a hoarse voice.

"After that my premonitions grew stronger," Raina said, eyes on her mom, who clenched her teeth but didn't respond. "Every night I dreamed of that ship, wished I hadn't let go of the captain. I woke each morning to sadness, with the memory of my hand slipping out of his grasp."

Her mom stared at her. "Once you were safe, you still wanted to join them?"

Raina turned the words over in her head, trying to find a way to explain. "I was entranced with the idea of becoming one of their crew. Craved it like I'd craved air when I'd slipped under the waves. To see what they saw …" She rubbed her wrist where the fire had caressed it, stopped when she noticed Simone watching her. "Whenever I got too close to the ocean, it pulled at me in a familiar way. They were waiting for me. If I went back on our boat, I was afraid I'd jump overboard first chance I got."

"Do you think," Simone said, with a glance at Raina's mom, "that you could, I dunno, visit them for while?"

"One-way ticket," Raina said. "That much was clear."

Her mom leaned her head against her window.

"I managed to handle it for years. I knew it was too dangerous. So I treated it like an addiction. Quit cold turkey."

"Moved inland, away from the water, away from us," her mom said.

"Yes," Raina whispered. "Poured everything into my job. But now that's at risk."

"What happened?"

"Long story. Suffice it to say, we need Madeleine's book." Not just for Raina's job, but for her life.

"Why didn't you tell me all this before?" her mom asked.

Raina shrugged. "Got used to keeping it to myself."

"But I could've helped you," her mom said. "Saved you all this time. And difficulty."

"How? You know nothing about any of this. If it weren't for Simone and the journal, I'd still be where I've always been, avoiding the ocean, warding off the ship."

"I could have tried."

Raina shook her head and clenched her jaw, so she wouldn't say anything she might regret.

"What? Why not?" her mom asked. "At the very least, you could've had someone to talk to, share your difficulties with."

Raina turned to her mother. "Seriously? You didn't want to hear that my visions were strong. That I was able to interact with the supernatural. You couldn't—wouldn't—help me."

Her mom leaned back against the seat, staring at the ocean. Raina tapped her fingers on the steering wheel, stopping when she realized Simone was doing the same on her window. Their eyes met in the rear-view mirror. Simone flicked her gaze to Raina's mom. *Apologize*, she mouthed. But Raina would not. Her words were more than fair to her mother. Raina was a scared teenager back then, and the one person who should've understood her, a Doiron woman, had refused to try.

"What a mess," her mom said. "I always felt ... less than. Like I wasn't good enough for our family's abilities. For the Doiron women. Even though your grandma kept insisting it was something you couldn't choose to have or not. Like hair or eye colour. Something you get at birth. I thought if I just tried hard enough, wanted it enough. It seemed so easy for you. When you threw it all away and left, I was angry. It's a tough habit to break." She reached over and held Raina's hands. "We've wasted so much time. Both of us."

Raina forced herself to accept the explanation. "Thanks, Mom."

"Aunt Kate, you may not have the abilities, but you have Raina. If you think about it, you were crucial in continuing the line. That's just as important as having the abilities yourself."

"Aw, that's so sweet, Simone. Thank you."

"Sweet as pie, my mom says."

"Sure, maybe key lime," Raina added. "Mostly sour. Or mincemeat. No one likes that."

"Raina," her mom said.

"I'm kidding," Raina said. "Simone knows that."

"I do." Simone reached into the front seat and hugged her. "I'm her favourite third cousin once removed."

"That is likely accurate."

"I've been thinking," Simone said. "Maybe you didn't need to quit. I mean, you seem calm now, with the journal and everything, but your go-to state is all suppression and repression. No wonder you're so uptight. Keeping things in just means the volcano's gonna blow, and it's gonna blow big." She raised her hands to her ears in loose fists and mimed an explosion. "Kablam. Least that's what my Intro to Psych prof said. Not that you need a degree to figure that out."

Great, now Raina had a nineteen-year-old as a therapist.

"Maybe you shoulda done the opposite. Embraced the spookiness," Simone said.

"Be more like you, in other words."

"Wouldn't hurt. It's not like I've had the urge to swim out to a ghost ship."

"But you've experienced the pull, haven't you?"

Simone tilted her head, considering. "More like a buzz of excitement swirling around me. My premonitions seem steady on the Island, but the buzz, it's strongest in Rustico. Do you think we're different that way? Will I feel the pull if I go out on the tour?"

"No frigging way you're getting on that tour boat until we figure this out," Raina said.

"Wait a minute," Simone said. "Do you still feel it?"

Raina watched the whitecaps as they crested in the wind. "I do."

The spectres' shanty floated towards her.

Raina, Raina.

Come aboard, Raina.

Swim to us, Raina.

Come aboard, come aboard ...

She resisted the urge to hum along. Tore her gaze from the ocean. "Now that I've opened myself to it, it's taking everything I have not to race out there. It'll get worse at sunset. Celeste's journal helps, but I'm not sure for how long."

Her mom lifted her head, straightened her back. "I didn't help you then, but I can sure as hell help you now. Let's find that book."

CHAPTER 17

Raina

When they reached Charlottetown, Raina searched for somewhere to park. The downtown traffic was snarled with people descending on the shops and restaurants, having been chased away from the beaches and parks by the nasty weather.

Her mom was occupied with Celeste's journal, which Raina had reluctantly given back to her, but she glanced up when Raina cursed at the lack of spaces. "If you can't find anywhere, just go to your uncle's apartment lot. He's in Spain, hiking the Camino de Santiago. Took his car to the airport."

Raina turned onto a side street. "Which spot is his?"

"Back corner under the oak," she said, without looking up.

Raina pulled in and turned the engine off. The Jeep was cocooned under the leafy tree, as if they were the only three people in the world.

"Do you think maybe it wasn't an accident?" Simone asked. "That something—or someone—was, I dunno, directing you, so you'd go overboard, interact with the ship like that?"

"You mean fate?" her mom asked.

"Not quite. More like a teachable moment. I had a prof who loved that term. We joked about starting a drinking game off it, but no one had enough guts to sneak alcohol into class."

"Sounds like you need a teachable moment," Raina said.

"We never did it. Although we did keep count for later. Anyway, if no one was alive to teach you about your powers, and you were just messing around with them, maybe this was a push so you'd take them seriously. You said your abilities increased afterwards."

A test. That made a weird sort of sense. Showing she couldn't be trusted to have a relationship with the supernatural. Maybe that encounter with the phantom ship had happened on purpose. The premonitions warning her were intended to prepare her, not scare her away.

After it happened, that night near the end of high school, Raina had checked out dozens of library books and immersed herself in research, in the late hours when she didn't want to close her eyes. She searched for information about her peculiar abilities, trying to get a handle on them, to tame her nightmares—similar to Simone's more recent exploration of baby fortune-telling, though not quite so specific. Raina couldn't figure out an index term that covered premonitions, phantom ships, a sea of spectres, and an oceanic pull. Information about supernatural powers, psychics, and fortune-tellers was easy to find, but not overly helpful. She stepped up her research on the phantom ship itself, scouring the internet for any new theories, but found nothing she wasn't already familiar with. In her tour, she'd decided to focus on the Acadians, but other theories existed: American privateers, Scottish immigrants, an unlucky fishing crew. None of which explained the ship's interest in her. Tourists loved a good mystery, but not Raina. She needed answers, not more questions.

Now, after reading Celeste's journal and learning a bit about Madeleine, she didn't know much more about the phantom ship, but at least she'd learned that each woman's premonitions and abilities were slightly different from another's, were passed down through the Doiron line, and were stronger in some generations and weaker in others, bringing hope and despair, the latter more likely if one didn't know how to interpret them. Celeste hadn't known how until it was almost too late, and wrote that Madeleine's story had helped her understand them.

Her mom flipped another page.

"We need to get going," Raina said. "I think there's an umbrella in the back."

"Yeah, sorry. Deidre said there's no power in the building—they're upgrading something—so we should get in and out before full dark." She handed the journal to Raina, who tucked it back against her skin.

A few moments later, they emerged onto Great George Street, her mom huddled under the umbrella, Simone and Raina with their hoods tightened over their heads. The harbour was a few blocks behind, far enough to dampen the phantom ship's ghostly chant. It seemed to be following her now, getting closer with every story they shared, everything they learned about their ancestors. She unzipped her jacket and threw off her hood, letting the cool rain invigorate her, glad she was at least away from Rustico.

The streets were full of tourists, easy to pick out with their fanny packs, souvenir-filled shopping bags, and backpacks carried on their chests, snapping photo after photo they'd likely never look at. Locals relaxed in outdoor cafés under large canopies, happy to leave the scurrying about to others. The Union Bank soared in front of them, a tall brick and stone three-storey building with a dormer roof and arched windows, covered in metal scaffolding, reminding Raina of the wooden scaffolding Celeste had written about around the Pownal Street Jail. The jail had since been replaced by the Queen's County Jailhouse and was now a Pizza Delight, Maeve's favourite place to eat.

"The Union Bank was built in 1860 as a flagship bank," Simone said, reading from her phone and almost smashing into a family walking towards them, with the parents trying rather unsuccessfully to corral three boisterous children who looked to be under the age of five. Simone glanced up. "Eek. That poor woman is pregnant with twins." Her voice was too loud and the woman stared at her in horror. Simone shrugged and said, "Sorry," as the woman passed them, her hand flying to her stomach.

"Simone," Raina said. "You can't do that to people."

"I couldn't help it—it just slipped out. Besides, better she knows about it now." She returned to her screen. "The bank used a mishmash of pence, shilling, and dollar paper notes, had liquidation problems due to involvement in the railway, with some sort of scandal, and by 1883 was taken over by the Bank of Nova Scotia." She put the phone in her pocket. "The bigwigs got taken down in the end."

Raina would've loved to have been there to see that. Not that she condoned what Celeste had done, but Noelle had been unjustly accused. Unless...unless Celeste's journal wasn't accurate. She could have rewritten her history so, in case it was found, Noelle wouldn't be penalized. Not that it mattered now. What Raina needed to be true was that learning about family would connect her to her abilities in a way that wouldn't destroy her. Or would allow her to get rid of them entirely. That was a distinct possibility, now that she thought about it. Her mom had always wanted abilities, but that's because she never had them.

"Here we are." Her mom opened the flap on the keypad door lock and punched in four numbers. The access light stayed red. "Dang it," she said. "2-5-6-3," she read from a piece of scrap paper as she tried again, to no avail.

"Lemme see that, Mom. It's 3-6-5-2. You had the numbers backwards. I'll do it."

"Must need new glasses," she muttered, surprising Raina as she stepped away and let her input the code. The light turned green, Raina pushed the door open, and the interior gaped before them, almost entirely encased in shadows. A few tools were scattered about, with hardhats on a nearby shelf.

Simone grabbed one and took out her cell for a selfie. "I'm way behind on my posts."

"Don't you dare. Deirdre read me the riot act. We're not technically allowed to be in here."

Simone put the hat on her head but pocketed her phone.

"This used to be government offices," her mom continued. "Cubicle torture, I bet. Condos will fetch a fortune. Deidre said only the exterior is designated historical, so she can do whatever she wants inside, which led to the protests. Good thing we're in here now. Who knows what they'll tear up in the next few months."

"Do you think there are ghosts here?" Simone peered into the corners.

"Of government workers sweating it out in purgatory?" Raina asked.

"There's ghosts everywhere," her mom said. "We just can't always see them."

"I'm not sure if that's comforting or not," Simone said.

"How so?" Raina asked. Ghosts were never comforting to her.

"Well, ghosts mean maybe we get to hang around when we die," Simone said. "Not phantom ship kind of ghosts, just the everyday people kind. But, seeing them all would be too creepy even for me."

"That's an understatement," Raina said as she stepped into the centre of the room. Her words echoed back.

Simone raised her voice. "Hello…" The word bounced off the walls, becoming one, then two, then three, getting softer with each repetition.

"Don't do that," Raina said.

"Why?"

She didn't say that it sounded like Simone was waking up ghosts. The phantom ship was enough to deal with. Adding more spirits would not improve their situation.

Her mom propped her umbrella against a wall. "The stairs are back here," she said.

Raina and Simone followed her up the winding staircase, but her mom's steps slowed as they neared the top. She stopped on the last landing, leaned against the handrail, and looked out the window.

"You okay, Mom?"

"Just taking in the view. Never seen Province House from this perspective." She pointed at the sandstone building fronted by four pillars.

Province House. Celeste could've watched Sir John A. Macdonald, Canada's so-called Father of Confederation, pose for a photograph before he entered the building. She could've taken one of him herself, had things been different.

Raina made herself wait until her mom seemed to have caught her breath, then stooped to enter the attic, a large, undivided space with a low ceiling and several dormer windows, all encased in dust and grime. Cobwebs covered the walls. Raina shivered, even though the attic wasn't cold. She clicked her phone's flashlight on and started to search, tapping and pulling on bricks, moving from left to right, bottom to top. Her mom scoured the floorboards. Simone stood in the middle of the room.

"Aren't you going to help?" Raina asked.

"Celeste wrote that she hid it under her bed," Simone said.

"Yes, but there's no bed here, my dear Watson."

"No duh. But think about it. They didn't have the whole attic, only a room in it. The rest was used for storage. Their section was near the stairs, and she had a view of the harbour, so..."

Why hadn't Raina thought of that? She was too distracted by the phantom ship. Now that she had the journal to anchor her, maybe, instead of trying to repel the lure, she could use it. She leaned into its power.

Raina, Raina, it whispered.

She pulled the journal out from her waistband and held it loosely in her hands. She let the voices wash over her, around her. She focused on the room, using Celeste's journal to control the call and use it for her own purposes. She doubted her ability to restrain it for more than a few moments, so imagined Celeste living in this attic, worried about a lack of money and a lack of independence, making bad decision after bad decision. Shadowy furniture appeared. Prickles raced across Raina's arms, as if she'd travelled over a century and a half into the past, to visit her ancestor.

"I can see it," Raina whispered. "Celeste and Noelle's room. Their door was here," she pointed, "table there, stove there," her voice rose, "and bed there."

Simone's eyes darted from wall-to-wall. "I can't see anything."

"It's the journal," Raina said. "It's warming. Sizzling." She held it towards Simone and her mother. Simone touched it and gasped, eyes wide.

Her mom placed her palm on the journal and shook her head. "I can't sense anything," she said.

"Celeste is here," Simone said. "Her presence has given the journal more power. I can feel her emotions. She's afraid."

With those words, Celeste herself appeared across the room, a book in her hand. Raina almost dropped the journal. "I can even see the knitting needle in her hair," Raina said.

"Is it a ghost?" her mom asked.

"A memory," Raina said.

"She's all blurry to me." Simone reached towards where Celeste stood with one hand, the other still on the journal.

Raina pulled her back. "Don't disturb her. Just watch."

Celeste crawled underneath the bed and scrabbled at the wall.

"She's hiding Madeleine's book," Raina said.

Celeste backed out and turned. Lightning flashed. She looked directly at Raina. Their eyes met, then Celeste disappeared.

"Thank you." Raina's words weren't likely to reach Celeste, but maybe her sentiment would. Somehow.

"What's she doing now?" her mom asked.

"She's gone," Raina said. "Showed us what we needed to know."

"I told you we needed the journal itself," Simone said. "The thing has frickin' power itself. Amazing." She walked to the wall, tracing her fingers over the brick.

Raina's hands shook as she put the journal into her waistband. She scanned the room and grabbed a screwdriver sitting on a windowsill. She crouched, gave Simone a none-too gentle shove out of the way, and chipped at the mortar.

"Need me to help?" Simone asked. "Maybe I can find an axe or something."

"We can't risk damaging the book." Raina scraped until the brick came loose, dropped the screwdriver, grabbed the brick with her hands, and jiggled at it. Her fingertips chafed as her nails dug into the wall, drawing blood, but she didn't stop until it finally yanked free. She peered into the opening. Inside, settled into the darkness, was a leather-bound book.

"Is there anything there?" Simone asked, standing over Raina's shoulder.

"It's Madeleine's book, I'm sure of it."

"Well, take it out already," Simone said.

Raina reached in, her hand hovering over the book. She steeled herself for what might happen when she touched Madeleine's story. She grasped the book's bindings and the phantom ship roared at her.

Raina, join us, now Raina, now, join us, join us.

She gasped and fell back, releasing her grip, and the voices hushed.

"What happened?" her mom asked. "Did something bite you?"

"Did it talk to you?" Simone asked.

"Maybe a bit of both," Raina said. The journal dimmed the call, but the book increased it? Or was it because she was combining the two or had seen Celeste? She focused on Madeleine and her life, what she knew of it from Celeste's journal, and touched the book again. The phantom ship was only a murmur now, the fading voices replaced by an image. A wooden cross and crescent moon threaded onto a thin rope.

Madeleine's necklace.

The key to everything.

Raina shone her phone into the hole. Rubbed her hands along its inside. Nothing. If anything else had once been there, it was gone now.

OUTSIDE, RAINA SHIVERED AS RAIN FELL. SHE'D WRAPPED MADELEINE'S STORY—with Celeste's journal—in her jacket to keep them safe and hugged them both tight. She wound through the tourists, headed for her Jeep. Her mom and Simone trailed behind.

"Raina, slow down already," Simone said.

Raina turned. Simone held onto her mom's arm, keeping her steady. Her mom was using the closed umbrella like a cane. Raina rushed back. "Are you okay?"

Her mom shook Simone off. "I'm fine. Just can't run like a racehorse. Your uncle was the sulky driver, not me."

"What's a sulky driver?" Simone asked.

"Someone who rides in a two-wheeled cart that the horse pulls, instead of in a saddle." She seemed to get her wind back. Only her mother could manage to do that while talking. "You should catch a race before you leave. The best time is during Old Home Week, which ends with the Gold Cup parade. We don't usually go, we're too busy with our tours. But Raina can take you. Traffic will be a nightmare, but it's fun."

The ghostly chant started again. *Raina …*

"Mom, I don't give a shit about jockeys, races, Old Home Week, or the parade," Raina blurted.

Her mom's eyes widened.

"Raina, what the hell?" Simone said.

Raina slipped her fingers under her jacket, touched Madeleine's book and Celeste's journal, focused on her ancestors. The chant faded. When she felt she had control again, she said, "I'm sorry."

Her mom stepped closer to her. "What happened in there? Why are you in such a hurry?"

"The book conjured an image," Raina said. "Madeleine's necklace. It's powerful. Grown even stronger with time. It's searching for a Doiron woman."

"May I?" Her mom held out her hands, palm up, for the book.

Raina stepped under the awning of a bakery shop and unwrapped the book. "Are your hands dry?"

Her mom wiped her hands on the inside of her sweater. Raina gave the book to her. "Anything?"

"No. It's just a book." She sighed. "Simone?"

Simone picked it up. People passed them by, their flow dividing on one side of them and joining on the other. "Nothing," she said. "Maybe it only works for you?"

"But why?" Raina asked. "If we both feel something from the journal."

"Maybe it was something to do with Madeleine," her mom said. "Something about her connection to the necklace. Maybe the necklace is lonely."

"That's impossible," Raina said. She wrapped the books back up and they continued walking.

"Seriously?" Simone said. "You believe in premonitions, ghosts, phantom ships, and magical—mystical—books, but not a lonely necklace?"

Raina shrugged. She had a point. The necklace belonged with a Doiron woman, after all.

"What does it do?" her mom asked.

"I think it gives more control to the wearer. Protection and strength. Like a talisman." Like Celeste's journal and, maybe, Madeleine's book. "Which means I should be able to repel the ship's call if I have it." Or maybe it'd let her interact with the phantom ship without being overtaken, without losing herself. The possibility of that sort of resolution was enticing.

"What does the necklace look like?" her mom asked.

"Rope thread, wooden crescent moon, and cross." An image of it zoomed into Raina's mind's eye. It hung there, lit from within.

"Would it still survive?" Her mom's words dispelled the vision.

"Of course," Raina snapped. "What was all this for, otherwise?"

Her mom softened her voice. "Just because you want something, doesn't mean you'll get it."

Didn't Raina know that. She'd wanted to rid herself of this wrenching influence that lingered over her, almost her entire life.

"Where do you think it is?" her mom asked.

"Celeste hid her journal in the jail. It ended up in the archives. Maybe the necklace is there?" Raina said.

"Nope," Simone said. "The archives only keep documents, not artifacts. What about a museum?"

They'd reached the Jeep and climbed in. Raina passed her mom a water bottle and Simone handed her a bag of pretzels.

Her mom took a few sips and bites. "That's better," she said, after a moment. "So how will we find it?"

"We play hot-and-cold." Simone grinned. "Walk Raina around the Island and see if she can feel it."

"Don't be absurd," Raina said.

"It makes some sort of sense," her mom said. "Games have their own history rooted in fact. Ring-a-Ring o' Roses is about plague deaths. Hide-and-Seek is based on predator-prey relationships. Capture the Flag derives from warfare ..."

"Okay, I get it. Kids are ghouls," Raina said.

"It's not like they know the games' origins," her mom said. "You used to love them."

"So hot-and-cold is like hunting," Simone said. "Or, put another way, detecting. A cinch for you, right Raina?"

If there was one thing Raina knew, it was that nothing was ever a cinch.

"We can start with Rustico," her mom said. "Where the Doirons settled when they returned to the Island. Historical places. Farmer's Bank. St. Augustine Church and its cemetery. Doucet House." Touristy stuff was her bread and butter.

"Hot-and-cold is not at all like detecting," Raina said. "It's ridiculous. We need something more systematic. What about our family members? Might anyone have it in a drawer somewhere? Or in a trunk, where Celeste found it?"

"Maybe, but I've never seen it. Never heard anyone talk about it," her mom said.

"There could be a clue in Madeleine's book," Simone said.

"Doubtful. She wouldn't know what happened to it after it was passed down. Celeste is our most recent clue. But skim through anyway." Raina passed the book back. "There must be something we can learn from Madeleine's story. Especially about the phantom ship." A mystery she could finally solve. The ship seemed tied to Madeleine, somehow, with the way the voices of its spectral crew increased as soon as Raina touched her book. She considered asking Simone to drive so she could read it herself. The book contained not only potentially crucial knowledge, but also a source of connection to a woman who, centuries ago, faced some of the same struggles Raina did. In some ways so different. In others so similar. But the roads were treacherous from the rain and Raina didn't quite trust Simone at the wheel. If she'd been alone, she might've found a place to park under a streetlight to read the book through, but she had less than twenty-four hours now before she had to report to the Coast Guard. With Simone reading, they could multitask.

"How are you doing, Aunt Kate? Should we stop for dinner?"

"We can eat back at Mom's place," Raina said. "It's only a half hour." Maybe a bit longer depending on the strength of the rain. The quicker they got back, the quicker she could search her mom's attic, where some old family stuff was stored.

"Raina, stop being so selfish," Simone said.

"What? Mom's fine."

"She needs an actual meal."

"Jesus, would you two stop talking about me as if I'm not here?" her mom said. "Let's just get takeout. Gahan House is only a few blocks away. I'd kill for their lobster burger."

"Yes, of course." Raina was being selfish, putting her needs before her mom's, but her body twitched and hummed with the possibility of finding some sort of peace. She could afford to stop for a few moments, though. With some additional concurrent activity. "Simone, can you do a Google image search for the necklace?"

"On it." Simone put the book down and pulled out her phone.

"Why the rush, Raina?" her mom asked. "You want to escape the lure of the phantom ship. I get it."

"Mom ..." Raina shook her head as she pulled the Jeep into traffic.

Her mom held up her hand. "I know I can't truly understand what you're going through, what you've gone through, but I do understand *you*. So, what does an hour or two matter, even a few days, after all this time?"

"I have a deadline," Raina said. "My chief assigned me to the Coast Guard. I'm supposed to report to an offshore patrol vessel tomorrow afternoon."

"You agreed to go back on the water?"

"I didn't so much agree, as it's a precondition for my promotion."

"Your promotion? That's what all this is about?" Her mom sat back and stared out the window. "You've always cared about that job more than anything else."

Raina might have been insulted, except it was partly true. "It's been my way to cope. To live my life."

"Life is only worth living if you live it."

"I've been living it the only way I know how." But now, maybe there was another way. She tapped the wheel to calm herself. Tap-tap-tappity-tap.

"Hey, we get that from Madeleine," Simone said. "The tapping. It was a game she played with her kids. It was right at the beginning of the book."

Raina stopped tapping. It was helpful, but insufficient. "Did your search turn up anything about the necklace?"

"Not really. There's like, millions of hits with a wide search and next to nothing with a narrow one."

"What do you mean?" her mom asked.

"When I use terms like wooden, cross, moon, necklace, there are massive results. When I add in Acadian or PEI, all I get are a list of pages without those terms."

"If we don't find the necklace tonight, in Mom's attic, we need to contact the archives first thing in the morning," Raina said.

"It won't be there," Simone said.

"I know that, smartass. But we can follow the evidence. Find out who donated the journal. Maybe that person has the necklace. It could be linked to the guard Celeste gave the necklace to. He might've picked up the journal. Kept it for posterity or something. Their case was infamous at the time."

"Great idea," her mom said.

"Horrible idea," Simone said.

"Why?"

"Simone, time for you to explain yourself," Raina said.

"But Aunt Kate has such a high opinion of me. I'd hate to ruin that."

"Simone, what did you do?"

Raina caught Simone's gaze in the rearview mirror and smiled. Watching her squirm was enjoyable.

"Fine, Aunt Kate, but just remember you yourself said we shouldn't give it back," Simone said.

While Simone detailed her theft, Raina pondered that very issue. How to find out more about the journal, and the necklace, without the archives discovering the theft and linking it to them? She didn't relish being an accessory after the fact, but it seemed as if the journal and necklace had been taken from their family centuries ago. Through desperation and circumstance. Raina was just restoring them to their rightful place. With the Doiron women.

Shit. That sounded like something Celeste would think.

BY THE TIME THEY ARRIVED BACK IN RUSTICO, THE STORM HAD REENERGIZED itself, lashing out with wild thunder and lightning. Her mom went straight to bed, but told Raina to wake her if they found anything. Raina and Simone spent a few hours ensconced in the attic, rummaging through box after box, but found nothing other than old clothes, gaudy Christmas ornaments, lopsided pottery from elementary school projects, and a mass of trinkets. When they finally gave up, Simone claimed a vintage pair of jeans, declaring that the evening hadn't been a total waste, and said goodnight.

Raina texted the B&B she wouldn't be back that night and followed Simone into the basement, wondering why Simone got to keep the spare room and she was relegated to the cot. Raina flipped through Madeleine's book, but she couldn't concentrate on the words. Her brain was occupied with finding the necklace. Its image grew larger in her imagination. The book and journal opened a connection between present and past, giving her crucial information about her ancestors and, as long as Raina concentrated, helping to stem the call of the phantom ship. Which wasn't exactly practical. She couldn't ask someone wanted by the police to please not run away because she couldn't chase them with a book in one hand and journal in the other.

When sleep finally found her, she dreamed of flaming ships, spectres, feux follets, and Madeleine's necklace. She roused occasionally, pushing away one dream as another took hold. But then the woman in white appeared. She flitted just outside of Raina's sightlines, but, in the manner of dreams, Raina knew who it was all the same. She tried to turn to see the woman, to run from her, but Raina's limbs were leaden, refusing to obey her commands. The woman's grey hair tickled Raina's face. She screamed. Woke up.

She sat upright, calmed her breathing. She was used to nightmares. She could manage this one. It wasn't a premonition. Couldn't be. Simply her mind sorting through what she'd learned from Celeste and Madeleine. It was just after dawn, so she tossed the blankets aside, giving up on sleep. She sat there for a few moments until the last vestiges of the dream fell away, then went to the kitchen in search of tea. The rain had let up but fog encased the house, obscuring the ocean.

While the tea brewed, she programmed the phone number for the archives into her cell. She'd call as soon as it opened, gauge any reaction to a question about the journal, see if they'd give her any information over the phone. Then she plunged back into Madeleine's story. A short while later, Simone's footsteps trod up from the basement, her mom's down the stairs from the second floor.

Raina poured them both a mug of tea and sat at the table. Her mom turned to take hers to the back porch, already staring into the fog at the hidden ocean beyond.

"Isn't it too damp out there?" Raina asked.

"I'm a grown adult. Think I can decide where to sit." She closed the door behind her.

"So, what's the plan?" Simone asked. "I know you've got one. Heard you tossing and turning all night. Your mind working overtime?"

Raina opened her mouth to explain, but her mom's mug crashed onto the deck and shattered. She slumped over the left side of her chair. The woman in white leaned over her, her grey hair brushing over her mother's.

Simone dropped her own mug.

"No!" Raina shouted. She lurched to her feet, forced her knees to lock so her legs would hold her weight. Adrenaline coursed through her and every part of her body shook. She gaped as the woman in white turned her cavernous eyes to Raina's, tilted her head, and gestured towards the phantom ship that had appeared in the water, close to the shore. Too close. Raina froze.

The spectral sailors called to her, waved her forward. *Raina, Raina.*

Raina took a step, held out her hand to them. Forced it down. The pull was stronger than ever, as if her very veins coursed with their energy. Her mind filled with visions of life on board, the secrets that would be unlocked to her, the seas they would explore. She would be part of a crew that understood her, as they balanced between the worlds of life and death, seeing all.

Raina hummed their chant, whispered her own name. *Raina. Raina.* The captain saluted as the ship sailed ever closer, then held out his hand to her. If Raina stepped outside, she'd be unable to resist the invitation.

She should run. She could reach her Jeep in seconds, be miles away in moments.

The woman in white grinned. Her mom struggled as if trying to stand. The woman put one wispy finger over her mom's chest and her mom fell back. Raina squinted to block out the ship, focused only on the woman, and ran outside to stop her, but the woman waved her arm at Raina, unleashing an invisible force that threw Raina against the edge of the deck. Her head bounced on the wooden rail. Pain shot through her, blurred her vision.

When it cleared, a spectre was just in front of her. The captain who'd reached out to her almost two decades ago had crossed the distance from the ship to Raina. "Raina," he beckoned. She brushed her fingers with his. "Join us, our Raina. Come aboard."

Her mother murmured something, her words a jumbled mix of nonsense, but they were loud enough to reach Raina. She shook her head at the spectre.

Raina turned to the woman in white, who raised her hand, clenched her fist, and stretched out to the side of the house. She rapped once. Raised her fist again.

"No!" Raina jumped through her translucent body. The woman lunged at Raina with icy tendrils but Raina dodged her.

The woman in white hissed, twisted, retreated. Rapped again. Raina grasped at her wispy body, her hands uselessly passing through. She couldn't vanquish her. Raina turned to the phantom ship. Opened herself to them, told them what she needed. She'd fought their lure for long enough.

If they took her now, so be it. It was a worthwhile trade to save her mother.

A spectre with long, fiery hair leapt off the ship, followed by a smaller one. The taller one tackled the woman in white while the smaller one nudged Raina's shoulder. Its coldness helped Raina focus her energy. As the woman in white flailed in the spectre's arms, Raina reached out, managed to latch onto the woman's shoulder, and heaved her towards the ocean. The woman in white screeched as she lurched off the porch, rolling away into the mist in the blazing arms of the spectres.

CHAPTER 18

Celeste

As time wore on with no sign of Mr. Campbell, even though Mr. Murphy had sworn he'd delivered her message, Celeste's doubts about her plan grew until they seemed to fill their cell. Her dreams were filled with flashes of the phantom ship and the woman in white.

She should have asked for someone else. Mr. Morrison, maybe. But he was too important a man, as a newspaper editor, with no need to chase a story. Surely Mr. Campbell had seen her name on the bylines that would have been his if he hadn't been quarantined. She counted on his curiosity, even a bit of vengeance. Might he not want to see her in jail, gloat a bit, after she had stolen his job, at least for a time, without so much as a how-do-you-do? Although, he could do that with just the knowledge she was a prisoner. Leaving her to rot might be better satisfaction. She didn't know anything about him, hadn't been able to meet him, observe him, eavesdrop on him, as she had done with Mr. Murphy. As she had done with the bank's executives. Each thought chased the other as she paced the length of their cell, along the cracks and bumps of the cold, uneven floor.

Noelle drew further and further into herself. Celeste continued to write in her journal, scratching out her story and the lessons she had learned, hiding it under the corner of the mattress whenever a guard approached. She didn't think Mr. Murphy would confiscate the journal, but didn't want to take the risk, and she had much less of a measure of the other guards.

When the fountain pen ran dry, she sighed. She hadn't been able to include much about Madeleine, hadn't even noted where she had hidden Madeleine's story. Maybe it was better that way. If the book couldn't find its way to a descendant, then she'd rather it and her journal stayed hidden. What if children were not in her or Noelle's future, only jail or life as convicted felons? Had she risked their familial line for a chance at independence? She didn't voice these concerns to Noelle, but kept them locked inside of her, as tightly as she and Noelle were locked behind bars.

Celeste passed her time listening to the conversations of the other prisoners and the guards. Seems there was a backlog of cases, which was why their trial date had not yet been set, but it was slowly clearing. Though Celeste did not want to prolong their stay, she needed the trial to be delayed until she heard from Mr. Campbell. If she heard from him.

Every time a guard walked down the corridor towards them, she held her breath, waiting for him to inform her she had a visitor, then let it out when no such announcement was forthcoming.

The pity on Mr. Murphy's face grew every time she saw him until, early one morning, he came back on shift whistling a cheerful tune. Celeste stood at his approach. Noelle turned to the wall.

"Ye women decent?" he asked.

"Yes, Mr. Murphy," Celeste said.

Mr. Murphy passed by the curtain and into sight. "Good morning to you both." He fixed his eyes on Celeste. "You've a visitor," he said, with a raise of his eyebrows.

Celeste pressed her palm to her forehead. "Thank you, Mr. Murphy," she said. "Thank you. Thank you. I was beginning to give up on him."

"Can't have that now, can we?" Mr. Murphy said. "But it's you I should thank." He seemed bursting with news.

"The necklace," Celeste said. "It worked, didn't it?"

"Quite possibly," he grinned.

"Congratulations."

"I'm grateful to you." He placed his hand over his heart. "Truly. That's why I went to see Campbell again. Yesterday. Waited 'til he left the newspaper offices and followed him, just like the first time. But this time, seems I persuaded him to give you a chance, that whatever was in that letter would be true, and likely a benefit to him."

Celeste bounced on her toes. "Mr. Murphy, I could kiss you," she said.

Mr. Murphy blushed, emphasizing his freckles. His keys jangled as he unlocked the cell door.

Noelle jumped up. "Are we being released? What's happening?"

"I have a visitor," Celeste said.

"What? Who? I'm coming with you," Noelle said. "Anything to get out of here, even for a moment."

"I'm sorry," Mr. Murphy said to Noelle. "Only your sister has been cleared for a visit."

Celeste was glad to hear it. Having Noelle with her would complicate things, interfering with her ability to frame events to their benefit. "I won't be long." Celeste bent to hug Noelle but she leaned away. "See you soon, little goose." Celeste turned to Mr. Murphy and held her wrists out to be cuffed.

"Sorry," he said. "Procedure."

"I understand," Celeste said. Though she resented every second the cuffs encircled her wrists, it wasn't Mr. Murphy's fault. She walked down the corridor, careful to remain in the centre, with her head held high as the other prisoners jeered at her. If she could handle being in jail, handle being surrounded by all these angry men, she could handle Mr. Campbell. She would have to go slow, give him just what he wanted, so she could get what she needed.

Once into the main area of the station, she breathed in comparatively clean air. Police constables darted about. Witnesses and suspects sat slumped in chairs. A few journalists yelled out questions that went mostly unanswered.

"Nice day, isn't it?" Mr. Murphy said. "Got the doors propped open."

Celeste glanced towards the main door. It might be opened for others, but not her or her sister. She aimed to change that.

She followed Mr. Murphy towards a series of rooms on the station's left-hand side. He opened the first door and ushered her in. "Here you go. Ye got thirty minutes."

"I appreciate your help, Mr. Murphy."

"We're helping each other," he said.

She stepped in and the door closed behind her. The room was not much bigger than her cell, but a tiny window sat midway up one of the walls. Not big enough to crawl through, more like a porthole than anything, but large enough to see the sparkling blue sky and bright yellow sun. Celeste pressed her face against the glass. How long would it be before she could step foot outside? How had Madeleine managed all those weeks in the hold? Would Celeste's fate be any better than her great-great-grandmother's?

"Thought you came to see me, not stare out a window," a voice from behind her said. She turned her attention to a man in an ill-fitting suit, with scrapes on his chin from a bad shave, sitting at a rickety table.

"Mr. Campbell, nice to meet you," she said to the photographer.

He nodded. "Miss Haché." He leaned back in his chair so that only the rear legs touched the floor. With only a slight push he would surely topple over. His leather satchel sagged on the wooden table. Relatively empty then. Good. In her letter, she had warned him not to bring his camera. No one must know he worked for the newspaper, for her own sake and for Mr. Murphy's. Noelle would be even angrier with Celeste if the guard was sacked, and Celeste would have to cultivate another relationship, which wouldn't be easy, based on the stand-off interactions she had with the other guards.

"Thank you for coming." She perched in the chair opposite Mr. Campbell.

"You got my attention, sure enough. Sending that guard after me." He peered at her as if framing her for a photograph. "Twice."

"He was simply passing on a message. One I was beginning to doubt had interested you. I assumed if you wanted the story, you would have shown up immediately."

He laughed. "There's more going on in this city than you. Delegates from the Maritimes and Canada, don'tcha know, accompanied by the premier himself. Managed to get a photograph of them on the steps of Government House, though it was quite the gaggle. Why they want a union when the representatives can't even agree on where to stand for a photograph, I'll never know. But it made the front page, so what do I care?" He leaned forward, slamming the front legs of his chair back onto the ground. "You know all about front pages, don'tcha?"

Celeste rested her hands in her lap. "I'm sorry you were stuck on the quarantined ship."

"Are you, now?" He reached into the front pocket of his suit jacket, rummaged around, pulled out a toothpick, and jammed it into his mouth. "Darn suit. Can never find anything in these pockets. But figured it might help me get in the door. Gotta look respectable."

She patted the knitting needle that held her hair demurely up. "Indeed. I trust your health is fine."

He scoffed. "Did my best to stay as far as possible from the passengers and crew. Once I'd taken enough photographs of them, I had more film delivered with the next food supply. Got some lovely shots of the city. Mr. Biset bought them off me. Says he thinks he might be able to sell them as souvenirs to some of the delegates. Only reminder they'll have. PEI will never join the union with Canada."

"I'm sure your photographs are wonderful and will be well-received."

"Aren't you the polite one." He pointed his toothpick at her. "Not quite what I expected from a woman chasing stories across the city, filching bylines."

"I did no such thing. They were bylines you couldn't have gotten on your own. I was doing a service to the newspaper."

"Quite the rationalization. Mr. Biset's rather furious with you."

"I regret that," she said. Her chin quivered so she clenched her teeth to keep steady.

"So you did steal the notes?"

"Absolutely not." Her aggrieved tone was more than passable.

"Then how'd they come into your possession?"

"Are you here to interview me about the charge or follow up on my tip?"

"Both, maybe. And it's charges." He emphasized the plural. "Assisting with a jailbreak. My oh my." He chewed on his toothpick.

"That's even more ridiculous than the first charge. And I don't agree to be interviewed for both. Unless, of course"—she inclined her body towards him—"you plan to portray me in the best possible light. It could be a good story for you. Sell lots of newspapers. Mr. Morrison would be pleased with that."

"And the jurors might be predisposed to find you innocent? That's rather …" He paused. "Clever," he said, drawing each syllable out.

She drew back. "You say that as if it's an insult."

"I'm not rightly sure at the moment. You're a quick learner. Your photographs were impressive. For an amateur."

Celeste bristled. "They were good enough for the front page. More than good enough."

He shrugged. "They never could've vied with mine but, as I was indisposed, they fared well enough."

All those people suffering with smallpox. She regretted wishing the quarantine would last longer once she'd made her first front page. "Did anyone die on the *St. Cecilia*?"

"Yes, several. Sad, but hardly a tragedy. It happens all the time. Surely you know that."

She swallowed her guilt. She had to focus. "I do. Please, go on."

"Do you have the goods to back the accusations you included in the letter or don'tcha? I figured a bunch of vague claims weren't worth my time to follow up. But Mr. Murphy convinced me different. So don't disappoint me. I need more details."

"My apologies. I couldn't include too much, in case Mr. Murphy read our correspondence." Plus she'd worried that, if she'd put too much information in the letter, Mr. Campbell might've chased the story on his own, without visiting her. She wanted him in front of her, so she could get as much as possible from their interaction. Information, promises, curiosity. All three would assist her.

"How did you manage that, anyway?" he asked. "Getting a guard to pass on a message?"

"That's my business. So, will you help me?"

"Seems like you help yourself. My only job is to get a newsworthy story that I can tell in a photograph. Helping anyone else is not part of it. Why're you so eager to give me this information?"

"Because it'll assist my case." Discredit the bank's executives. Cast doubt on any testimony against her.

"Should've known it. How can I trust you're not just inventing all this?" He threw his hands up. Stared at her.

She met his gaze. "Please, Mr. Campbell. I'm accused of being a thief, not a liar."

"In my experience, those two things go together quite well. Like island potatoes oozing with melted butter. Can't have one without the other. Besides, you're also accused of assisting a jailbreak. Rather like you're trying to do now, I suppose."

"I'm not trying to break out of jail." Though she would if the chance presented itself. "Simply to bolster my defence."

"Got a lawyer?"

"Unfortunately, we don't have the funds for that."

"Should've counterfeited more notes, eh?" He chuckled at her frown. "Don't suppose you think that's funny, do you?"

"Not particularly."

"Tell you what. If your information is newsworthy and accurate. And if you can corroborate it. That means that you have something that can prove—"

"I know what corroborate means, Mr. Campbell."

"Don't get testy. If there's corroboration, then I might ask the newspaper if it might consider lending you their solicitor."

That was a lot of *mights* and *ifs*, but it was more than she had at the moment. "That would be much appreciated."

"So formal. Not a lady in disguise, I suppose?"

"I had an excellent English teacher." The travelling teacher who loved baseball. She smiled at the memory of her brother Yvon playing catch with him.

"Was he the King of England?" Mr. Campbell asked.

"I can get you documents to corroborate"—she said the word slowly, as if he was the one who might not understand it—"my story."

"How?"

"Once I'm set free." She could sneak into the bank, ensuring no one saw her, as familiar as she was with the layout and with employee movements. Any documents that would help her would either be in the file cabinet in the bank executives' salon or on Mr. Forbes's desk. As long as he hadn't gotten more security conscious of late. Or, she could disappear, and Mr. Campbell could chase the story on his own.

"Let's go over the facts of your case, shall we?" He counted each off on his fingers. "One—you had access to the office the notes were stolen from. Two—you were caught trying to pass off one of them. Three—you had an expensive camera in your rooms which you never could've afforded on your own."

Three strikes, you're out.

"What if you don't get released? Then where would I be?" He shrugged.

"I can tell you where the documents are. You can get them yourself."

"At the bank?" he asked.

She nodded. Was he the type to do anything for a story? Take risks?

"What, you'd have me break in? To a bank? I'd be sitting in a cell beside you soon as anything. We're finished here." He stood to go, his chair rasping on the floor.

"No, wait," she said. Apparently he wanted an easier way. She could give it, although she feared it might take longer. "I can give you names. Of people to speak to. Do whatever you need to get them to trust you. They'll tell you what's going on at the railway."

"The railway?" He tilted his head.

"Yes. It's all connected." She lowered her voice, pulling him in. "The offer of confederation, the railway, the bank's dealings."

"Now you're talking." He sat and pulled out his notebook. "Tell me everything."

"You'll use this information to help me? Get a lawyer and assist with my case?"

"I'll use it to sell papers. If it helps you, then that's fine by me."

He had dodged the lawyer question, but keeping the information to herself wouldn't do her any good. So, she told him about the events leading to their arrest and her knowledge of the bank's executives. Everything she'd heard while listening at the salon's door, about bribes and loans, who'd given them, who'd taken them, and how it related to the railway. He filled page after page.

"The last charge," she said as she finished her story. "Assisting the jailbreak. It really is ridiculous. I think the bank had that added on."

He ruminated on the idea. "It's possible. The executives are powerful enough. Got a lot at stake with this railway deal. If half of what you've said is true, there might even be more to find."

"So, the lawyer you promised?" she prompted.

"Ah, Miss Haché, you know full well I didn't promise anything. I'll check all this out." He rapped on the door. "We're done here," he called. He plastered a bowler hat on his head and tipped its brim at her. "Pleasant day."

Mr. Murphy, whistling once again, escorted Celeste back to her prison cell. Now that the necklace had done its job, maybe she could ask for it back. But what if his wife needed to wear it for her entire pregnancy and the babe's birth? What if she needed it to conceive again? Her deal with Mr. Murphy wasn't time dependent. It was a one-for-one, which she had to honour. The necklace was well and truly gone.

"SO? WAS IT MR. CAMPBELL?" NOELLE ASKED WHEN CELESTE ENTERED THE CELL and the door clanked shut behind her.

As Mr. Murphy secured the lock and sauntered away, Celeste sagged against the wall and onto the floor. She had originally taken care not to touch the grimy floor with anything other than the soles of her boots, but she had grown used to these living conditions. One could get used to anything, she supposed. That should have been a hopeful thought, but it seemed grim instead. She nodded in answer. Now that she had spoken with Mr. Campbell, she was sapped of energy. Her and her sister's futures were in the hands of a photographer who cared for nothing more than a byline on a front page. She had yearned for more. That he might want to help them, like Mr. Murphy. But he was a different sort of man entirely.

"When are we getting out of here?"

Celeste closed her eyes to block out Noelle's pleading face. Did her sister not appreciate everything she was doing for them? All Noelle had done for the last several days was accost her with accusing eyes, give her the silent treatment, sit on the mattress, and mope. "I'm not sure."

"I can't stay here any longer. You must get us out now."

Celeste opened her eyes. It took such energy to just focus on her sister. "It's going to take a little longer than I'd expected. Mr. Campbell has to do some investigating."

"How long?"

Celeste had no idea. "Maybe a few days," she said.

"Days? Days? I can't handle another hour. Do you know what the other prisoners called us, after you left? The twisted sisters. I'm not twisted, you're twisted.

And enough with your not-guilty plea. Your *protection*." She spat out the word. "I'm going to tell the truth about what happened."

Celeste's eyes flew open. She lurched towards her sister. "Just be patient," she cooed. "As soon as Mr. Campbell corroborates my information"—if the railwaymen would actually speak with him—"then I'll be considered an informant. We can say the bank planted those notes on me to discredit me, if I said anything about what I'd overheard."

"But that's not true." Noelle pushed Celeste away.

Celeste could see her sister would not be appeased. Noelle seemed to have spent the last several days whipping herself into righteous indignation. Celeste had to cut through it, dissipate its danger. She jerked herself upright. "True? True? You care so much about the truth but nothing about surviving. See how much the truth will get you." Noelle shrank back at her words. "Go on. I'll call the guard myself. All it'll do is get both of us a long sentence. But, if that's what you want. If you value misbegotten honesty over your sister? If you want to betray me, so be it." Celeste gripped at the cell bars and raised her now trembling voice. "Mr. Murphy. My sister has something to tell you. Mr. Murphy!"

The other prisoners added to her call.

"Hey, Mr. Murphy."

"The twisted sisters want to speak to ya."

"Better get in here, Murphy."

They banged their tin cups on the bars, adding to the din.

"No!" Noelle thrust her hands over her ears. "No, that's not what I want. I'm sorry."

"Isn't it?" Celeste yelled. "Isn't it?"

Mr. Murphy banged the main door open. "What the hell is going on? Anyone who says one more goddamn word is getting thrown in the stocks."

The prisoners' shouting fell to a few mutters.

Celeste gestured towards the cell door. "Well," she whispered. "Here's your chance." She put her hand on the grubby curtain, pulled it back a bit. "I can get his attention."

Noelle shook her head and collapsed in the corner. Celeste dropped the curtain back in place. Her sister was sweet and honest, positive characteristics in certain situations. But she was also quick to back down when confronted. Celeste hated herself for manipulating her, but she'd had no other choice.

Footsteps approached. Celeste pasted a calm smile on her face.

"Sorry about that, ladies," Mr. Murphy said. "Don't know what got into them. I've news for you, anyway."

Had it happened that quickly? Mr. Campbell found something and scared off the bank? Or did he actually get them a lawyer? Celeste clutched her hands together to keep them steady.

"Your trial's in three days."

Noelle burst into tears. Celeste wanted to do the same. The chances of Mr. Campbell coming through for them in time were dim indeed.

THE SUPREME COURT JUSTICE SAT ON HIS BENCH, SWATHED IN A RED ROBE WITH a white wig propped on his head. He called the room to order. Their trial was in the same place as when they had gone before the magistrate, but this time, instead of a bustling crowd intent on their own business, all eyes were on Celeste and Noelle, two sisters with no representation and little hope. They'd been uncuffed and allowed to sit, as the trial might take an hour or two. Celeste forced her back straight, placed her hands in her lap, and projected an outward calm, despite the dirt on her face and her bedraggled clothes. Her mind whirred like clockwork as she struggled to figure out what she would say and how she'd say it, if she was given a chance to speak. She didn't know the rules or the process, so could only guess at the best approach. How could she get them both free?

Her head pounded from lack of sleep the night before. Whenever she had closed her eyes and begun to drift off, a vision of the woman in white had flashed in her mind. She had shaken herself awake, telling herself that if the vision didn't fully form, if the woman didn't knock three times on the bars of their cell, then she wasn't a true premonition but simply a dream, an indication of her distress. But exhaustion soon overtook her and the woman pounced. Celeste fought with the woman, trying to claw out of her grasp, when flashes of light illuminated the cell and shadowy flickers skipped over the walls. Not a storm, not lightning, but a reflection of the phantom ship. The woman in white faded.

Celeste reached towards the fiery silhouettes. Her fingers found purchase on a spectre with long hair blazing in the night. The spectre beckoned her up and out of the jail. Through a flash of flame, Celeste was now at sea, floating over the deck of the phantom ship. Ghostly beings danced in the fire below as they chanted and cavorted about.

The spectre tilted its head at her. Celeste had never feared the phantom ship—though she hated it—but the judgement of this spectre terrified her. It led her towards the starboard railing. When she grazed the blazing wood a fierce iciness shot through her body. Visions of war, death, and isolation flashed into her mind. Pain and sacrifice. But more than that, threaded throughout it all, was a shame that marked Celeste alone. She had made mistake after mistake by putting herself first, by ignoring premonitory warnings in favour of her own gain. She had warped the abilities that had passed through the generations to her. Celeste shivered. She had risked her sister's life by intertwining their fates.

But then the spectre wrapped its arms around Celeste and hugged her, tapping her fingers on her back. Celeste had a vision of Yvon, rowing out to the phantom ship, and she suffered the spectre's grief. It had been an accident. The ship wasn't calling Yvon the way it called to others. It hadn't even understood what Yvon was doing until it was too late.

The ship and the spectre disappeared. A keen and unexpected loss came over Celeste, paired with an uneasy peace as she came to a decision. She must separate her own future from Noelle's. To save her sister. The air warmed. Celeste had closed her eyes, with this resolution repeating itself in her mind, searching for a way to open a door for Noelle's freedom in the morning.

Now, a bailiff led twelve jurors, all men in suits, towards two long rows of benches. As they sat, a few fixed her with irate stares. They looked familiar, but she couldn't quite place anyone.

The justice drew Celeste's attention away from them as he read out the charges. "You are accused of larceny and forgery. Although there are no allegations of violence, due to the significant amount of the theft, paired with the trusted position the defendants were in at the bank, the charge has been advanced to grand larceny."

Celeste groaned as Noelle gasped. A buzz of conversation erupted from the observers behind them. Mr. Murphy, standing near the bailiff, grimaced and shook his head.

The justice continued. "For which the maximum penalty is death by hanging."

The full force of what Celeste had done, of the situation she had put her sister in, piled on her as if a thing alive. She slumped in her chair, her thoughts racing. She hadn't considered this possibility, that they would upgrade the charges. She had been careless. Stupid. She turned to her sister to apologize. "Little goose," she said. But Noelle had a glazed look on her face, just shook her head in a barely noticeable way. Celeste squeezed her sister's arm, opened her mouth to assure her she would think of something, but she had no assurances, no words.

The woman in white appeared behind Noelle. Celeste cringed, yanking her sister's chair closer to herself.

"The other charge of assisting an escapee will be dealt with separately this afternoon," the justice continued.

The ghostly apparition wagged her finger at Celeste. Then she disappeared.

Celeste pinched her knee to push away a growing hysteria. Clapped her mouth shut to stop a long, low moan from escaping her lips. If she let it start, she didn't think she could ever stop.

The voice of the prosecutor dragged her attention back to the trial, which had started. Mr. Forbes was on the witness stand, his eyes on Celeste as if he were standing over her grave, shovelling dirt over her mouth, her nose, her … She blinked and pinched herself again.

"You are an executive of the Union Bank?" the prosecutor asked. "The director, I believe."

"That is correct." Mr. Forbes turned to the prosecutor, adjusted his cravat, and squared his shoulders.

"How do you know the defendants?"

"They cleaned my office every day."

"Were they ever unsupervised?"

"Yes, indeed," Mr. Forbes said. "Our head housekeeper, dear Mrs. Pierce, had much else to deal with. So we took special care in their hiring, advertising for women of moral means and interviewing them carefully."

"What about the bank notes? Where were they stored?"

Mr. Forbes looked away from the prosecutor, towards the spectators. "I am extremely careful about securing all notes, signed and unsigned, in our state-of-the-art Palmer safe."

Celeste clenched her hands into fists, her nails cutting into her palms. He lied so easily. She recognized it as a skill she herself had.

"I keep the key to the safe in a locked drawer, and the key to that locked drawer in my own pocket"—he tapped his chest to indicate its position—"all day. That second key is hidden in another drawer at night, in accordance with procedure, so it can be accessed if needed by another executive during an emergency, or if something should happen to me. The need for two signatures—the cashier's and the president's—was another layer of security which the sisters breached.

"They must have been paying careful attention, snooping and prying, in order to ascertain both hiding places and to learn to forge the signatures. Indeed, Miss Celeste Haché was caught lurking outside our salon, where we held our executive meetings, by Mrs. Pierce just a few weeks before. We gave her a warning. Miss Haché assured us she was simply cleaning a stain and would never linger again. Clearly, that was an untruth." He cleared his throat. "It is my opinion that she and her sister took their jobs merely to get access to the safe. I keep careful books, but who knows how many notes they have stolen? They could have changed my records as well. It is unconscionable." His voice rose. "We generously allowed them to room in the bank's attic. Fed them thrice daily. They repaid our kindnesses by stealing. I'm sure it was only a matter of time before they would have planned to empty the safe altogether."

His deceit mixed with the truth in such an intricate fashion that she had difficulty pulling the two apart. But from the accusing looks on the jury's faces, they accepted them all as fact. Why wouldn't they? He was a respected community member. Celeste and Noelle were not.

"Moreover, they have cast a pall of trepidation over the bank, irreparably damaging our reputation. Naturally, we'd like to assure all our investors that—"

"No further questions." The prosecutor cut him off before he could launch into a speech.

Mr. Forbes left the stand, passing Mrs. Pierce as she moved to take it. They traded looks. What seemed like a warning from him and agreement from her. Celeste had no doubt that Mrs. Pierce would support his testimony. She needed to protect her own job. Celeste supposed she could hardly blame the woman.

"Yes," Mrs. Pierce said, when asked, "I concur with Mr. Forbes's testimony in relation to the procedures with the notes. I never saw evidence that any other process was followed." Her first lie. What others would follow?

"What about the defendants?"

Mrs. Pierce looked at Mr. Forbes, who sat in the front row behind the prosecutor. She raised her fingers to her mouth as if to bite her nails, then lowered her hands. Clutched them together, then glanced at the jury. Celeste followed her gaze. Something seemed not quite right with a few jurors, but she couldn't figure it out.

"Miss Celeste Haché was, I believe, the only one involved."

Celeste yanked her eyes back to Mrs. Pierce. Was she helping them?

"Based on my careful supervision of the two, Miss Noelle Haché is innocent."

A male spectator behind Celeste muttered, "Not likely. One Acadian is the same as another. Good for nothings."

"Shhh," whispered a woman beside him. "I want to hear this."

"I respect Mr. Forbes's opinion, of course," Mrs. Pierce continued, "but I was in more frequent contact with the sisters. I grew to know them well."

Mrs. Pierce was a woman, so her testimony didn't have the same legal weight as a man's, but the justice seemed to consider her words. The cleanliness of the bank and supervision of the cleaners was, after all, her responsibility. A few members of the jury nodded as Mrs. Pierce explained the differences between Celeste and Noelle: one untrustworthy and impertinent, the other honest and reliable. Mrs. Pierce was helping Noelle, risking the wrath of Mr. Forbes for going against him. Celeste silently pleaded with her to continue, for Mrs. Pierce had given Celeste the chance she needed. If she changed her plea to guilty, the justice and jury might believe Noelle had nothing to do with the theft, especially if Celeste agreed to committing the crime in the manner Mr. Forbes mentioned, by breaking into the safe. Much worse than simply snatching up loose notes. The judge might not sentence her to execution if she pled guilty. But even if he did, at least Noelle would be freed. Her safety was worth the risk. Celeste would finally choose the right thing willingly. Thanks to her vision. And Mrs. Pierce.

The justice declared a short recess. The courtroom erupted in chatter as the prosecutor shuffled papers and the doors were opened to allow the air to circulate.

Celeste ignored it all. She turned to Noelle, hooked their pinky fingers together, and leaned close. "Little goose, it's going to be all right."

"What do you mean?" Noelle's eyes were wide.

Celeste was unsure if she'd been listening to the testimony, if she understood what was going on. "I'm going to plead guilty."

"You can't," Noelle said. "You heard the penalty ..." Her voice faded as if she couldn't say the words.

"It's the only way. Mrs. Pierce, she's given us a chance. Now I can be assured they'll believe me when I say only I was involved."

"I'm sorry," Noelle whispered, her voice barely audible. "For calling you twisted. For threatening to betray you."

"It is I who should apologize. You were right. About everything." Celeste stood and turned away so she couldn't see her sister's tears. She stepped towards the prosecutor, who was surrounded by a crowd of well-wishers. The bailiff motioned her back but the prosecutor, noticing her attempt, waved her forward, a delighted grin on his face. No doubt he guessed at her intention and was already calculating how he'd benefit from winning the case.

As she approached, heart in throat, shaking, forming the words in her mind so she would be able to speak them, Mr. Campbell rushed in. Sweat dripped from his forehead and he wheezed, trying to catch his breath. He searched the crowd, found Celeste, and elbowed his way to her. The prosecutor pushed towards them.

"Were you afraid you'd miss the moment they found me guilty?" Celeste asked.

"It would make a good photograph," he said, "but not as great as the one I have planned." He winked and a smidgeon of hope hummed through her.

"Miss Haché," the prosecutor interrupted. "Did you have something you wanted to say to me?"

"I have some information for you," Mr. Campbell said to him. "Though I don't think you'll like it much."

"Later," the prosecutor said. "Now, Miss Haché—"

"I could tell it straight to the justice," Mr. Campbell said. "But, as we've helped each other in the past, wouldn'tcha rather hear it from me?"

"Is it relevant to this case?" the prosecutor asked.

"It is."

"Fine." The prosecutor tilted his head towards an unoccupied corner on the left side of the judge's bench. "Let's talk."

Mr. Campbell winked at Celeste again. "Found out a few things even you didn't know." He followed the prosecutor. She tried to join them, but the bailiff stopped her and led her back to her seat.

"What's going on?" Noelle asked.

"I don't know." Celeste tamped down the hope now roaring through her, knowing to feel it and then have it dashed would be worse than having none at all.

She watched as the prosecutor and the reporter spoke. The prosecutor glared at the jury, shaking his head. Mr. Campbell handed him three photographs, then pointed out three jurors. Celeste strained forward and could just catch Mr. Campbell's words, as if she were meant to hear them.

"You can refuse to do anything, of course, but this'll be on the front page of the newspaper. It's going to come out, and if you don't act now, the judge'll be none too pleased with you."

The prosecutor grumbled and swore. Celeste examined the three jurors, finally remembering why they seemed familiar. They were three of the bank's ex-officio directors. It wouldn't be common knowledge that they worked for the bank, but their service as jurors was a clear conflict of interest. The trial might be stayed. When she and Noelle were re-arraigned, she might get a chance to do it properly from the first. Plead guilty, send her sister home. Redeem herself. She smiled at Noelle, embraced her. Memorized holding her close, for this might be the last time they ever touched.

When the justice returned, the sisters disentangled themselves. Mr. Campbell was now at the back of the courtroom, on the side closest to the jury.

The prosecutor stood. "Your honour, if it please the court, may I approach the bench?"

The judge nodded and beckoned him forward. As the prosecutor spoke, the justice frowned. "Is this true?" he asked in a raised voice that echoed through the courtroom. The prosecutor's reply was too quiet to hear. The judge scrutinized the jury. Celeste followed his gaze and watched with satisfaction as a few jurors began to squirm.

The prosecutor handed over the photographs and associated documents. The justice examined them. "Step back," he said.

"Your honour," said the prosecutor, "please be aware that I had no knowledge ..."

"Step back," the judge repeated, his voice rough. He fixed his stare on the jury box. "It has come to my attention that there are those on the jury with an undisclosed conflict of interest. I'm going to give you the benefit of the doubt and assume you weren't trying to intentionally influence the verdict in an inappropriate manner when you put yourselves forward for jury duty. But let me be clear." He raised his index finger and pointed at three of them in turn. "You might have political and economic influence out there"—he gestured beyond the courtroom doors—"but, in here"—he thumped his finger on his dais—"I reign supreme. I will not have my authority in question. Case dismissed."

Celeste sat, frozen. It appeared he wasn't so much freeing them as punishing the bank. But it was a more than welcome outcome.

Mr. Forbes jumped to his feet and protested the decision. The three jurors appeared stunned. Mr. Forbes approached them and they jabbed fingers at each other, spittle flying from their mouths. Mr. Campbell raised his camera, taking what was sure to be a front-page photograph.

"What now?" Noelle asked. "Are they just going to start again? Are they going to continue with your other trial?"

No one was paying them any attention in the ruckus. The justice had left the bench, the bailiff was trying to separate Mr. Forbes from the jurors, and Mr. Campbell continued framing photographs.

Mr. Murphy tilted his head towards the now open courtroom doors.

"We're going to walk right out of here, little goose," Celeste said. She'd found her peace with who she was. Her abilities. Now it was time to go home.

To Rustico.

CHAPTER 19

Madeleine

As the moon slipped behind a cloud, Madeleine and Elinor, with the three children and Marie-Blanche's feux follet in tow, approached *La Terreur*, ready for the journey home. The shadowy docks were otherwise deserted, with little sound except for the scurrying of rats and lapping of waves. A lantern hung by the ship's gangplank, its flames casting flickering lights against the night sky that reminded Madeleine too much of the phantom ship. But it wasn't accompanied by a warning vision, so she ignored the comparison.

Charlotte clomped down the gangplank. "About damned time. I bet my handsome husband you'd show, but he was about to collect my wager." She tugged on her purple skullcap as if it were the source of her frustration. "Though I'd give it to him anyway," she said with a leer, "I don't much like being wrong."

"When I make a decision, I follow through," Madeleine said.

"Good thing for it," Charlotte said. "I'd be in a mighty poor mood if I lost my soothsayer."

Sébastienne stepped forward. "Are you the woman pirate?"

Madeleine shushed her and pulled her back, while Charles hid his face in Madeleine's skirts and Rose peered at the stars.

"I am indeed." Charlotte crouched in front of Sébastienne. "You're an interesting one, aren't ya?"

Sébastienne pointed at the woman's neck. "That's Maman's necklace."

"It's mine," Charlotte said.

Sébastienne leaned forward, not in the least concerned with facing Charlotte down. "Why do you have it?"

"Enough, Sébastienne," Madeleine said.

"Ah, she's fine. I like curiosity in a woman." Charlotte patted Sébastienne on the head like she'd never touched a child before. "Or a girl."

"Pleased to meet you," Elinor said, successfully diverting Charlotte's attention towards herself.

"Argh. Forgot you were British," Charlotte said. "Guess I can't much hold it against ya, though. Madeleine's told me your story."

"I assure you I hold no allegiance to them," Elinor said. "I'm Welsh."

"Whatever you are," Charlotte said, "just obey our rules and everyone gets to keep all their body parts."

"We have every intention of doing so," Madeleine said, having learned this was the key to dealing with Charlotte. Honesty and transparency. "We'll abide by our agreement if you will."

"You're questioning my honour?"

"Simply confirming our bargain."

"You've a persuasive tongue." Charlotte said. "But I see you're telling the truth, so you'll be safe enough with my crew. Can't guarantee the same if we're attacked, but ain't nothing guaranteed in life, is there?" Her eyes grazed over the area where the feux follet flashed, but couldn't seem to focus on it. Charlotte returned her attention to Madeleine and Elinor. "Besides, you two are going to be my good luck charms. Maybe three, if the girl turns out to be as remarkable as I think."

Madeleine exchanged a look with Elinor.

"I see you eyeballing each other. No need to worry about me. Funny how like finds like, ain't it? How you two found each other. Added little Sébastienne to the mix. And now you've found me." Charlotte rubbed her hands together. "This journey is going to be more promising than most, I can feel it."

Rose struggled in Madeleine's arms, her hands grabbing for Charlotte's hair.

"Keep that one away from me, though. Babies are more trouble than they're worth. Too bad it takes them so long to grow up."

"Have you any children?" Elinor asked.

Charlotte guffawed. "You have quite the sense of humour." A slight wind blew the clouds away from the moon and the docks brightened. "Mother moon is giving us our cue. Time to get aboard. The crew is confined to their bunks—can't have anyone shirking their service agreement the night before we sail—so no concerns about selling news of your presence." She turned to the sailor beside her. "Not a word to anyone until we're out at sea, or it'll be twenty lashes for ya."

"Yes, Madame," he said.

They stepped onto the gangplank and boarded the ship, right foot first. Madeleine scrutinized the pier for signs of pursuit, but the shadows were quiet.

Grégoire walked past the mainmast towards them.

"Take them below," Charlotte said. "Quarters are cramped, but no need to spend much time in them once we're out of sight of land, long as the weather's fair."

Their quarters turned out to be a storage hold in the bow. Two mattresses stuffed with hay lay on the floor beside the trunk Elinor had sent ahead earlier that day, packed with blankets, a few sets of warm clothes each, herbs, jerky, preserved fruits, and dried vegetables. Madeleine paused outside the hold, fighting off a fear of confinement, though Charlotte had permitted them to leave the hatch secured open. She reminded herself that this journey across the Atlantic would be nothing like their first one. This time, they had more resources and privacy, and would travel in the summer instead of the winter. More importantly, they were not prisoners, although they had to tread carefully, to stay on Charlotte's good side.

Elinor squeezed Madeleine's hand. "Between the two of us, we'll keep everyone healthy and free from harm."

Madeleine nodded. The sun had set in a red sky that evening, a sign of clear skies and good weather. Paired with the blackbird that flew past when she first met Charlotte and the positive tea leaves that had nestled at the bottom of both their cups, she was fairly certain she had made the right choice. But she was wise enough to realize that a better choice did not mean a lack of risk. "Let's get the children settled."

Charles flopped on one mattress and was asleep in seconds. Sébastienne sat beside him. "I'm staying awake. I don't want to miss anything," she said.

"There's nothing to see," Madeleine said. "Close your eyes and it'll soon be morning. Then we can enjoy the day."

Sébastienne crossed her arms, shook her head, and leaned against the bulkhead, just as Rose let out a wail.

"Shh, little one." Madeleine sat beside Sébastienne and brought her baby to her breast. She drank hungrily. Sébastienne put her head on Madeleine's shoulder. Soon, all the children were snoring softly.

"You didn't tell me you gave her your necklace," Elinor said.

"It was part of her price."

"You parted yourself from a tie to your ancestors—and your descendants."

"It had to be done."

They sat in silence as the ship rose and fell with the waves in the harbour. Madeleine must have fallen asleep, for the next she noticed, the familiar sway of the ocean held them in its treacherous embrace, the wooden beams of the ship creaking. At a knock on the hull, Madeleine flinched, thinking of the woman in white. But it was only Grégoire, notifying them that they were far enough away from shore to go above deck.

Charles groaned that he wanted to sleep, while Sébastienne jumped up, ready to explore. Elinor agreed to stay with Rose and Charles. She looked a bit pale. "I'll bring hot water for ginger tea," Madeleine said. "Then we can all get some air. It'll make you feel better."

Elinor groaned and waved her away. "I'll get used to it," she said.

Madeleine kissed her forehead, allowing the fib. Elinor had once let slip she was sick the entire voyage from Wales to Belle-Île-en-Mer. This voyage would not be an easy one for either of them, not simply due to seasickness, but also to haunting memories.

When Madeleine and Sébastienne left the cabin, each crew member they passed stared as if they were mysterious sea beasts caught in their fishing nets. Grégoire paid the crew no mind, so Madeleine tried to do the same as they climbed two sets of ladders and emerged into the growing sunlight.

Sébastienne ran to the rail, drinking in the sun and the sea. Some of Madeleine's tension released. Now there was no chance of Alexis following them. She had not truly thought he would leave their farm to search for her; indeed, even if he had wanted to, he had no way of knowing where she had gone, not for sure, although he could have discerned their destination of Saint-Malo. Part of her had kept watch for him, just in case. Now, that part of her switched focus, her whole being centred on keeping the woman in white away from her family, and her family travelling safely home.

She wondered if she would have to prepare Charles against any comments Grégoire might make about their father's supposed illness, but she need not have worried. They barely saw her stepson after that first morning. He kept close with his pirate kin, and she with her own.

They soon settled into a rhythm on the ship, much less grim than their last. Each morning, they ate their meals in the galley after the crew had finished, chasing away any vermin brazen enough to swoop in during the switch. If the weather was fine, they climbed above decks. Charlotte had dictated they stay between the mainmast and foremast. When any change of sail was required, they were to stay clear of the workings. Charles soon bored of watching the crew and turned to pacing the siderails, eyes on the water in search of sea life. Sébastienne followed Charlotte and the captain as they worked together to command the crew, fascinated with *La Terreur*. Madeleine and Elinor were worn ragged trying to keep the children within arm's reach at all times. Still, their relative freedom aboard was a blessing, so different from being a prisoner crammed into a hold.

Charlotte called for Madeleine every late afternoon, wanting her to read tea leaves, cure boils, converse with her, or give her something to help her sleep. Sometimes the feux follet trailed Madeleine, sometimes not. Marie-Blanche's presence waxed and waned like the moon. So far, the wind had been in their favour and they had thankfully seen no other ship since the day after leaving France. The possibility that *Le Terreur* would attack or be attacked occupied Madeleine's thoughts. She prayed constantly against it, searched for omens that might give her warning, laid a broomstick at the entrance to their quarters as protection against evil.

At first, Madeleine prohibited Sébastienne from accompanying her to Charlotte's cabin, but the girl snuck away from Elinor and poked her nose in the door, asking for permission to enter. Charlotte always granted it, and Madeleine had no desire for Sébastienne to roam the ship alone, so she now brought Sébastienne with her. Her daughter curled up with a large pillow and listened to their every word. Once they returned to their own quarters, Madeleine told Sébastienne stories of her own life, and of their family's.

"Is it true you can tell when someone is lying?" Sébastienne asked Charlotte one day, two weeks into their journey.

"Let's test it, why don't we? You tell me something and I'll tell you if it's a lie." Charlotte scrunched down so she could look Sébastienne directly in her eyes.

Sébastienne grinned. "I am one hundred years old."

"That's impossible. Try something that might be true, if I didn't know better," Charlotte said.

"Let me think." Sébastienne tapped her fingers on her lips. "I know. You will return that necklace to my family."

Madeleine gasped at the impertinence, while she yearned for the remembered warmth of the necklace on her now empty neck.

"That's a foretelling, wrong that it is," Charlotte said. "Try again." She crossed her legs in what she called her yoga pose, something she had said she learned in a place called India.

Madeleine shook her head at their interaction. A pirate's wife and an Acadian girl, the best of friends. No one would have predicted that. At least it further guaranteed their protection. She settled herself further into her own cushions and closed her eyes.

"My mother is a witch," Sébastienne blurted.

Madeleine jolted up. "Where did you hear that word?"

"From Papa. When you were sick over the winter." She looked down at her hands. "He said I had better watch out, or I'd become one too. He said it was bad. That I was bad."

"Accused of being a witch?" Charlotte asked. "Nasty business. Saw one burned at the stake. I'd rather drown, myself." She gestured towards the portholes that held a view of nothing but fog settling on the ocean.

Sébastienne grimaced and Madeleine shot Charlotte a dark look.

"Sheltering the girl serves no one." Charlotte shrugged. "And I deal in the truth. Though I'm careful to sometimes appear to make mistakes about what's true and what ain't in front of the crew. Who stole a tot of rum, who lied about his share of the spoils, who voted against us in a bid for captainship. They need to be scared of me, just enough so they follow my orders, but not so terrified they think mutiny's a better option." She slid her cutlass out of its scabbard and sharpened the blade. "The thieves, liars, and traitors get their due eventually, even if they don't understand why."

Madeleine pulled Sébastienne onto her lap. "Why didn't you tell me about Papa before this?" she asked.

"I was going to. Once you were back to yourself, after I took you to Elinor's. But then you decided we should leave, and I didn't want to make you sad."

"Oh, darling. Yes, it's sad, but you must share everything with me." This news allowed Madeleine to shed her last tether to Alexis, her guilt. Leaving him had been the correct—the only—choice.

"So, I'm to answer if your statement about your mother is truth or lie," Charlotte said.

Sébastienne made a small nod, chin tucked into her chest.

A flickering out one of the portholes caught Madeleine's attention. *La Terreur* was headed west, but the light was too low to be the setting sun. "No," Madeleine whispered.

"You don't want me to answer?" Charlotte asked.

Madeleine lurched to the front porthole. There, on the horizon, growing brighter with every moment, as the sky darkened, was the phantom ship. Why was it here, now, after so long, so far from Île Saint-Jean?

Sébastienne pushed between her mother and the porthole to peer outside.

"Do you see it?" Madeleine asked.

"The phantom ship," Sébastienne breathed.

An image of a cat's cradle flashed in front of Madeleine. "Marie-Blanche," she whispered. The feux follet appeared and flew over Madeleine's hands, seeming to land on her palm, the first time she'd done anything more than flicker.

"Is she communicating with us?" Sébastienne asked, tilting her head at the feux follet.

"I think so." Madeleine's hands tingled. "We must be near the waters where we laid Marie-Blanche to rest." Though the girl had never found peace.

The phantom ship blurred, then reformed. Two ships, firing ghostly cannonballs at each other. Spectres flitted and dashed from ship to ship, in a battle between the dead.

Madeleine gasped.

"What is it?" Charlotte shoved past them. "What do you see?" She looked one way and the other. "There's nothing there."

"It's a warning," Madeleine said. "We're going to be attacked."

Charlotte's eyes lit. "Truth," she said. "Get below." She brandished her cutlass and roared out of the cabin, her feet thumping up the stairs. "Action stations," she yelled. "Prepare to be attacked."

Madeleine grabbed Sébastienne and pulled her away from the porthole. They dashed up the stairs, as the only way to access their quarters was from a hatch on the deck. When they emerged topside, sailors rushed past them, loading muskets, readying cannonballs, drawing water, and climbing the rigging in a kind of organized chaos. The fog closed in around them such that water droplets skimmed Madeleine's skin. She strode towards the hatch that would take her to Rose, Charles, and Elinor.

"Charlotte, my dear," the captain said. "Is this a drill? Ya know I hate those things."

"Not a drill." Charlotte lowered her voice to a whisper. "Listen."

The ocean slapped at their hull and the sails flapped. The sound echoed. As if there were two ships, not one.

"Enemy, ho," yelled the boy in the crow's nest just as a six-masted schooner emerged from the fog.

"Attack," called the captain. "Fire at will!"

Gunshots reverberated from one ship to the other. *La Terreur* rocked sideways as a cannonball splintered the hull just above the waterline near the bow. Madeleine's pulse raced. A musket shell dropped on Sébastienne's arm and she screeched as it scorched her skin. The hatch they had been aiming for popped open. Elinor emerged with Rose and Charles.

"Our quarters are taking on water," Elinor shouted in the din.

"Don't let them broadside us," yelled the captain. "Turn about."

The ship listed in a spray of water. Tears streamed down Charles's face and Rose howled.

"The galley," yelled Madeleine. "It's midship. We'll be safest there. Hold onto whatever you can as you go."

Cannons boomed in quick succession. The deck tilted, sending Madeleine careening away. She let go of Sébastienne just in time to avoid pulling her daughter with her. Madeleine slammed against the gunwale, holding fast so she wasn't swept overboard. "Go!" she yelled, motioning desperately for Elinor and the children to get below. One of the sails was sent ablaze, casting smoke and soot into the fog so it was impossible to see anything other than flames and musket fire.

More cannons fired. A triumphant cry went up from *La Terreur*. She sensed rather than saw the other ship begin to pull away. Had they done it? Had her warning saved them? She leaned onto her elbow, tried to push herself up.

The air cleared just enough for her to watch an enemy sailor leap from his ship's rigging onto *La Terreur's* deck. He held a pistol in one hand and a knife in the other. His eyes flashed. He looked back at his own retreating ship in surprise. He was trapped. He turned in a circle. *La Terreur's* sailors were occupied fighting fires and shoring up holes in the hull. No one else had noticed him. The enemy sailor's head tilted and he grinned, stuck out his bleeding tongue. Walked towards Sébastienne, who was all alone near the starboard rail, which had been damaged in the attack. Sébastienne held up shaking hands and backed away until she was far too close to the edge of the ship. The woman in white appeared, hovering behind her.

Madeleine shrieked. Jerked to her feet. Ran at the sailor at full tilt. Hurled herself at the side of his body, her momentum carrying so they both flew towards the siderail, past Sébastienne and through the woman in white. The siderail smashed apart, sending the sailor and Madeleine over the side. As she fell towards the ocean, she twisted around, ensuring Sébastienne was safe. The woman in white had disappeared. Sébastienne stood on the deck, screaming, reaching for Madeleine, who was beyond her grasp. The feux follet appeared in Madeleine's hand, flashing in time to the rhythm.

Tap-tap-tappity tap.

The seas closed over Madeleine's head.

CHAPTER 20

Raina

The ambulance turned towards its dedicated emergency entrance as Raina steered her Jeep into the visitor parking lot of the Queen Elizabeth Hospital. She averted her eyes from the harbour and the ocean beyond, jolting to a stop in the first empty space she found. "Any update from my dad?" she asked Simone. Her father had jumped into the ambulance with her mom while Raina and Simone followed in the Jeep. It had been a harrowing thirty-minute drive from Rustico to Charlottetown.

"Nothing since the last one," Simone said.

The paramedics suspected her mom had had a stroke, so administered treatment through an IV and hooked her up to oxygen. Her mom's vitals were stable. Usually when Raina heard that assessment, her next thought was how to go about getting whatever information she needed, depending on whatever incident or crime a victim had experienced. It was an entirely different feeling when it was her mother.

"The woman in white only knocked twice," Simone said. "Before you and the spectres fought her off."

"As far as we saw. If Mom heard her knock three times..." Raina didn't finish the sentence. Instead, she placed her hands on Madeleine's book, stacked on top of Celeste's journal on the centre console, taking comfort from the strength of her ancestors. "Thanks for grabbing these." For the first time since she'd met Simone, Raina's thoughts when leaving the house hadn't included the journal or book at all, chased away by concern about her mother.

"Anything to help," Simone said.

The phantom ship had been quiet during the drive, due to the book and the journal, perhaps. Or maybe the spectres had their own problems, struggling with the woman in white. The phantom ship was friend *and* foe to Raina. Feeding her nightmares, increasing her abilities. Luring her, protecting her. Tormenting her, helping her. Madeleine's necklace might make the ship a constant ally. If she could find it.

A dark grey minivan pulled up beside them and Brian hopped out. He'd raced over to their parents' house when the ambulance arrived, then bundled the kids into the minivan to follow when it left. He hadn't wanted to waste any time looking for someone to watch the girls.

Raina grabbed Madeleine's book and Celeste's journal. She and Simone exited the Jeep, and they both hugged Brian. "Dad texted they think it's a stroke," Raina said. "She's stable."

"I know, Maeve read out his texts while I was driving."

Maeve opened the back door, unbuckled herself, and climbed down. "I did good. Only had to spell out one word. O, x, y, something something. I don't remember now."

"You did a great job," Brian said, ruffling Maeve's long red hair.

Simone walked to the other side of the minivan and helped Nora out. "Where's Gramma?" Nora asked, turning her freckled face up to Raina.

"Inside," Raina said.

"Stay close." Brian took one of each girl's hands. "Mommy will be here in a few hours. Granddad and Grandma will arrive soon." Claire's parents had been in Summerside, visiting Claire's sister. "They'll take you back home."

"Want to see Gramma," Nora said.

"You can't right now," Simone said. "The doctor is taking care of her. But I can take you to the cafeteria. How about some hot chocolate? We can colour for a while." Simone pointed at Maeve's clear carrying case, with a labyrinth colouring book and pack of crayons at its front. "I'm the best at picking colours. Green for the sky, blue for the grass."

"That's not right." Nora laughed as they all walked across the parking lot, stopping for every car that came anywhere near them. Raina shoved down the urge to run ahead.

When they arrived at the sliding doors of the emergency room, Brian pointed to a sign for the Crema Coffee Shop. "Thanks, Simone." He turned to the girls. "You two go with her. You can even have doughnuts if you want." He dug into his wallet but Simone waved him off.

"My treat," she said.

Nora bounced up and down. "Lemon glazed?"

"Yes, if they have it," Simone said. "What do you think, Maeve?"

Maeve considered. "Okay. I'll go with cousin Simone." She turned to Brian. "Tell Gramma I love her." She leaned into Raina to give her a hug and her eyes grew wide. "Tell Gramma she'll be okay," Maeve whispered.

"That's a nice hopeful outlook." Brian said. He kissed each of his girls and they left with Simone, Nora skipping and Maeve with careful steps.

"Don't give them false hope," Raina said.

"I'm not taking parenting advice from you," Brian said, striding into the waiting area and away from her. "Or any family advice. Mom was working too hard, and you know it."

Raina tapped her fingers on her thigh, willing herself not to respond. It'd only escalate into a fight. She'd watched it happen too many times. Some families pulled together during a crisis. Others tore into each other. She and Brian, they weren't the pulling-together type. Silence was the better option. Besides, he wasn't angry at her. Not really. He was worried.

Raina had cause to be angry, though not at Brian. At herself. She and her mom had spent the day before together, openly discussing Raina's abilities—and her mom's lack thereof—after so many years of animosity about them. But despite every opportunity, when her mom reached out, tried to repair the misunderstandings and hurt, Raina had ignored the effort, too focused on all the ways she thought her mother had failed her, too obsessed with the call of the phantom ship. Fuck that ship. It had ruled her life long enough.

She checked in with reception, even flashed her badge for good measure, but all they could tell her was that her mom was being seen by a doctor. She found an empty seat in an adjacent row to Brian, between a young woman pushing a stroller back and forth and an elderly man who sat with his head in his hands. The waiting room was calm at the moment, people talking quietly, a few with their eyes closed, working through whatever physical or emotional pain they were in. They looked up every time the swinging doors opened to the treatment rooms in anticipation of their name being called, having kept track of who arrived before them and who after, disappointed when someone with a more serious issue bumped them down the priority list. It wasn't reassuring that her mother's condition had the paramedics whisking her directly to a doctor. She'd rather be sitting with her mother beside her for some innocuous problem, complaining about how long they'd been waiting.

Raina resisted texting her dad for an update. When he had one, he'd give it. No need to add her worries to his. She texted the chief instead, telling him about her mom. He replied that his thoughts were with her and her family during this difficult time. Textbook response. No offer to delay her tasking with the Coast Guard. Not that she'd expected one.

She texted Liam and Hattie, who both sent their love. Then, she opened Madeleine's book, needing to learn anything she could about the phantom ship while equally wanting to lose herself in the story. She shut out the squeaking of shoes on the hospital floor and the constant paging of codes over the public address system. She travelled with Madeleine across the Atlantic, around France, and back again. Cheered Madeleine when she attacked the pirate to save her daughter, then mourned her death. She'd been dead for centuries, but that didn't make it any less of a loss.

The book related how Sébastienne had been inconsolable after her mother died, so Charlotte had tried to distract her by teaching her to read and write, skills Sébastienne later used to write out her mother's story. Charlotte had given the necklace to Sébastienne, who'd correctly predicted its return to the family, as a thank you for Madeleine's warning. Without it, *La Terreur* would've sunk, with everyone aboard either taken prisoner, drowned, or killed. When they arrived at Île Saint-Jean, Sébastienne begged to stay on board, but Charlotte forbade it, though it sounded as if she wished she could keep her. Elinor settled with the children in Rustico. It was here that Sébastienne ended the story, but Celeste's journal had picked it up. Sébastienne eventually married, and had a daughter, Lottie, who must've been named after Charlotte. Lottie had a daughter without special abilities, who then gave birth to Celeste, who did. Through their line, Raina and Simone gained their own abilities, the generations in-between lost to history.

Both Madeleine and Celeste had wished the necklace back into the family. It belonged in the hands of a Doiron woman. Raina wanted it. Needed it. To carry echoes of her ancestors with her. They were a part of her—her abilities and her family—that Raina wanted to embrace once again. But more than that, the necklace was tied to the phantom ship. Somehow. Finding the necklace meant controlling the lure. And if she could control the lure, she could work to discover the mysteries of the ship without joining the crew in death. Learn about its origins, its secrets, its possibilities.

Raina's phone pinged and she jumped. It wasn't her dad, though. Just Rustico's constable, checking in on her mom's condition. Brian had texted him. It'd be constant now, neighbours and friends sending their support and love. A stack of coolers with casseroles was sure to be already piling up on her parents' front stoop. She gave the constable an update. He said to tell her mom he'd stop by when he could. He was busy with work and looking for a house in Summerside. He wanted a transfer there, where his fiancé lived. She told him not to tell her mom that. She'd chide him for being another one to abandon his hometown.

She checked her email and reviewed the joining instructions: CCGS *Earl Grey*, docked at Coast Guard Base Charlottetown, report to captain upon boarding, bring required police kit including wet-weather gear, read attached Standard Operating Procedures. Much less interesting than Madeleine's story. She skimmed the SOPs, though there would be nothing in them on dealing with the phantom ship. That she still needed to figure out on her own.

The swinging doors swooshed open. She glanced up. It was her father, face pale but smiling. Raina's body flushed with relief. He strode over to her and Brian. "It was a mini-stroke," he said. "She's fine now. She'd love to see both of you."

For the first time in a long while, Raina was eager to see her mother as well.

RAINA AND SIMONE STOOD ON THE STREET OUTSIDE THE ARCHIVES, WHICH WAS situated in a large four-storey brick building with a peaked roof, a few miles from the hospital. Raina had left Madeleine's book and Celeste's journal in the Jeep, not wanting to bring either into the archives, as that seemed like tempting fate.

As soon as she'd stepped out of her vehicle, the call had started up.

Raina, Raina … It's time, Raina.

She glanced towards the harbour, where both the phantom ship and the Coast Guard vessel waited for her. She tapped her fingers on her thigh. Tap-tap-tappity-tap. The call dimmed enough for her to ignore it. But it promised to come back with a roar.

"Aunt Kate is going to be fine," Simone said.

"I know. It just feels wrong, leaving her." So odd to think, when she'd spent her entire adult life avoiding her.

"Well, she basically kicked you out to go find the necklace already, so no guilt needed."

"Easy to say. Tough to do," Raina said. But it wasn't as if there was anything she could do to help her mom's health, just let her talk to the doctor about aftercare, follow-up tests, and being discharged. Her father would take her home, make her tea, and ensure she rested.

Raina checked the time on her phone. The archives had just opened. No time to waste. By that evening, she'd either have reported to the CCGS *Earl Grey* or not, the latter meaning she'd be officially disobeying an order. That'd be the end of her promotion chances for sure. And maybe her career.

"Are you really going to go in there and lie?" Simone said. "What would your cop friends think?"

"I'm not going to lie," Raina said. "Just leave a few things out." She'd decided, since they were in town, going in person was better than phoning. It was always easier to get information face-to-face.

"If the archivist doesn't have long blond hair in a ponytail, then text me that it's safe to come in. She's the only one who might recognize me. I'm not even totally sure if she saw me take anything, but still …"

"Sure," Raina said, with no intention of doing so.

"Want me pull the Jeep up? Keep the engine running?" Simone asked. "In case you need a quick getaway."

"Not funny," Raina said, though she grinned.

"Do you think Celeste walked by here in her search for photographs? Maybe even sat in this park?" Simone snapped a photo of two women in hoop-skirted dresses playing croquet with two men in coattails and top hats. "Does someone pay them to dress like that or are they just serious history geeks? I bet they're sweating like anything under all those clothes. Maybe the women will let me team up with them. I'm queen of striking my opponent's balls clear off the field. You ever play?"

"Sure, as a kid." Her mom had gotten them an indoor set one year for Christmas. Raina and Brian set up a course in the basement, around pillows and boxes. It kept them busy for hours. It must've been the quietest morning her mom ever had. Probably just as much a present for her parents as for her and Brian.

Now, Raina could give her mom a gift in return. Time with her daughter. If Raina could find the necklace, then she could handle visiting Rustico. Get her promotion, board a Coast Guard ship, and get her family back. All in one fell swoop. She said goodbye to Simone and walked up the concrete steps into the archives.

A grey-haired security guard signed her in and directed her to the fourth floor. "Elevator or stairs. Your choice." Raina picked the switchback stairwell to stretch her legs.

At the top, she walked into the reading room and addressed the archivist on duty, a man with short curly hair standing behind a long wooden counter. Good. Though she wasn't telling Simone to come up, she was glad the archivist wasn't the same one who might have seen Simone acting like she was up to no good after requesting Celeste's journal. "Good morning," Raina said, introducing herself and flashing her badge. "I'm here for background info for something I'm working on."

"A case? What about?"

"I'm not at liberty to discuss. Just a simple question. What's the name of the person who donated ..." She pulled her notebook out of her back pocket and flipped through the pages, as if refreshing her memory. "A journal written by a Celeste Haché." She read out the reference code she'd copied from the journal's retrieval request.

"It should be listed in the finding aid," he said.

"That field is blank," Raina said. Simone had told her she'd looked herself, when she'd first visited. She'd asked about it but was refused the information. Some donors wanted their names kept confidential, for one reason or another.

"How can it help a case?" the archivist asked.

"I'm afraid that's privileged."

"Not even a hint?"

"I really wish I could. Sorry."

"Okay, let me check." He turned to an old library index card filing cabinet that was set against the back wall, off-limits to anyone but the archivists. He trailed his finger over the small white labels, tugged on a metal hooked knob, and pulled out a long drawer. "One of these days we'll have these digitized." He selected a card and handed it to her.

"Mr. James and Mrs. Erica Murphy," Raina read out the familiar names. She stared at them a moment longer. Hands shaking, she gave it back.

"Are you all right?"

"Absolutely. Thanks for your help." She restrained herself from racing down the stairs. Once outside, she motioned for Simone to join her, dashed to the Jeep, and jumped into the driver's seat.

"Why are you hurrying? Did you steal something?" Simone asked as she settled into the passenger seat. "I knew I should've kept the engine running."

"I know the family who owns the journal."

"Really? Who?"

"They must be related to Celeste's guard. The name is so common, I never even thought …" She turned the key in the ignition.

"Who, who, who?" Simone leaned over the gear shift, her nose practically touching Raina's.

Raina pushed her back. "My sister-in-law, Claire. Her parents. James and Erica Murphy."

"What, it was in the family all along? I didn't need to steal it?"

"It's not just our history," Raina said. "It's theirs as well."

CHAPTER 21

Raina

Although the Murphys' sedan was parked in Brian's driveway, the whole family was sure to be at Raina's parents' place. To her mother, company fit the doctor's definition of "rest."

"Just follow my lead, Simone," Raina said as they walked up the front steps. Behind the house, in the distance, she glimpsed the ocean. The phantom ship sailed past, its sails afire and crackling, the spectres cavorting over the rigging, soaring through the flames.

Raina, Raina.

Raina had once again tucked Celeste's journal into her waistband, but the call had increased with their return to Rustico. Luring, taunting. Simone carried Madeleine's book, having skimmed through it during the drive. If the call kept up with its strength, Raina might have to ask for the book back.

"Don't you want a specific plan?" Simone asked.

"No, I'll assess their reactions, adjust as needed."

They entered the house and followed the sound of quiet conversation to the kitchen. Raina's mother sat at the table with Erica and Claire, a mug in front of each of them, with plates of squares and cookies between them. Clacking and laughing drifted up from the basement. Her father, brother, and nieces must be playing mini-sticks with James, whose booming voice called out, "Score."

"My goodness, Raina," her mom said, her voice softer than usual, her skin pallid. "You're back. I expected you to drop off Simone and leave." She picked up a pill bottle and shook it. "I must be seeing things. Have I taken too many pills?"

Erica leaned forward, slipping the glasses that hung from a chain around her neck onto her nose. "I hope not," she said. "Let me check the dosage."

"She's kidding, Mom." Claire fiddled with the button of her cardigan. She always seemed nervous when the Murphys and the Cormiers were together, as if her role was to play translator and referee.

"I have a few hours before I have to report to the CCGS *Earl Grey*," Raina said. Though she didn't dare board it with only the journal and the book. She bent down and hugged her mom, who clasped her back. What if she never felt her mom's hug again? Never heard her voice, or looked in her eyes, shared a cup of tea with her? "I'm so glad you're okay," Raina said. "I'm sorry about everything. It was all too … complicated, and weird, and unsettling." She looked her mom in the eyes. "I love you."

"Oh my," her mom said. "I'm not dying, remember?" But she smiled, not bothering to hide how pleased she was by Raina's words. "I'm the one who's sorry," her mom said. "But there's not exactly a rulebook for all this, is there? We're fine, you and I. You're my daughter." She slapped her hands on the table, as if that was the last word on the subject.

Raina placed her hands on her mothers', not able to resist a tap-tap-tappity-tap with her fingers. Then she stood and glanced at Simone, who grinned.

"How are you feeling, Aunt Kate?" Simone asked.

"I'm right as rain, now that I'm home. Though the dream I had just before the mini-stroke was unsettling. It's never good to be visited by the woman in white, even if she only knocks twice."

Erica smushed her lips together.

"More tea, anyone?" Claire asked.

"My goodness, any more and I'll float away," Raina's mom said.

"I'll take some," Raina said. Only two knocks was good news, but she still didn't trust her hands to stay steady if she poured a cup herself. The phantom ship was now clearly visible through the patio doors. At least it was a fair way offshore.

Simone peered in the ship's direction and tilted her head at it. She raised her eyebrows at Raina. So Simone could see it, now. She walked closer to the patio doors. Raina readied herself to grab at Simone, if she tried to join the ship, but Simone looked only curious, not compelled. Simone turned back to Raina and mouthed, *Wow*.

"Simone, come back over here," her mom said. "Meet Claire and Erica."

"Nice to see you, dear," Erica said. "Your aunt has been telling us all about your trip. You've seen a lot of the Island, have you? What's your favourite part?"

"Actually, the view from here is kinda wild," Simone said.

Erica glanced out the patio doors. "It's beautiful, isn't it? Have a seat. Eat something. You too, Raina."

"I actually wanted to talk to you and James," Raina said as she sat.

"Nothing criminal, I hope? Did we witness something?"

"No, you didn't witness anything," Raina said, in answer to the second question.

"That's good, dear. Don't know how you deal with all that." Erica turned as Raina's mom pushed up from the table. "Kate, are you sure you should be—" Erica said.

"I'm completely fine," Raina's mom said. "I'm going to heat up one of those casseroles." She opened the fridge, reading off the masking-tape labels. "We have ham and rice, tuna noodle." She shuffled a few containers. "Which one is Hattie's? She makes a mean enchilada casserole."

Erica motioned at Raina, gesturing to Raina's mother and to the chair she'd been sitting on. Raina raised her hands, palms up. As if her mother would listen to her.

"Wait a minute," her mom said. "Here's one with eggplant. Who in their right mind puts eggplant in a casserole?"

"I'll take care of that." Simone placed Madeleine's book on the table and stood. "You rest, Aunt Kate." Simone selected a long rectangular dish, closed the fridge door, and steered Raina's mom back to her chair. "Didn't you say you were starting to get tired this summer, wanted a break from managing the business and the house?"

"It's one thing to want that on your own terms, quite another to be told to do it," her mom said, but she sat. "Mini-strokes only slow down the women in our family for a quick bit. When your great-aunt," she pointed at Raina, "had a mini-stroke while playing cards, she just zoned out for a few seconds, same as I did out there." She fluttered her hand at the back deck. Raina kept her focus on her mother, away from the ocean. "When she came back to herself," her mom continued, "she didn't want medical help. Someone called 911 anyway, and when the paramedics arrived, she offered to feed them. Only agreed to go to the hospital because her friends refused to finish the card game."

"That sounds like something my mother would do," Simone said as she put the casserole into the oven and turned it on.

"You have to preheat that," Erica said, starting to stand.

Simone waved her back down. "It'll be fine."

"Did you find any information at the archives?" Raina's mom asked.

"We did," Raina said.

"The archives?" Erica squinted towards Raina, but she didn't make eye contact. "Why were you at the archives? Seems an odd place for a police officer to go on the day her mother's released from the hospital." Erica reached for a chocolate macaroon but withdrew her hand and settled it in her lap.

"Go ahead," Raina's mom said to her. "There's more in the pantry."

"Mom, you seem jittery," Claire said. "Kate is okay, you don't need to worry. Is something else wrong?"

"No, nothing, nothing at all," Erica said.

"Maybe you tell them, Simone," Raina said. That way she could keep all her attention on Erica. Claire's mom had more tells than a juvenile facing a first charge.

"Tell us what?" James said, as he walked into the kitchen. "Those kids plum tuckered me out." He plopped down in a chair. "Any tea left?"

Claire poured him a cup. He took a long sip. "That's better," he said.

Claire looked at Erica, Erica looked at her nails. James looked around the room. "No one's talking," he said. "Why isn't anyone talking? You lot are always talking."

"It's about Celeste's journal," Simone said.

James froze, cup halfway to his mouth. He placed it carefully back down on the table.

"Who's Celeste?" Claire asked.

"Someone you should thank for your existence," Simone said.

"Wait," Raina's mom said. "Mr. Murphy is one of *their* Murphys? The necklace worked for him?"

"James's great-great-grandfather, maybe a 'great' more or less," Raina said.

"James," Erica said. "Handle this, will you?"

James grabbed a Nanaimo square and shoved it in his mouth, glancing around at each of them as he chewed. "Cat's out of the bag, isn't it?"

"What is going on?" Claire asked.

James wiped his hands on a paper napkin. "We've a bit of, um, interesting family history. Something rather mystical."

"Conjecture," Erica said. "It's all conjecture."

"Why are you interested in Celeste?" James asked.

"She's our great-great-great-grandmother," Raina said.

Erica's mouth dropped open. James laughed. "You're related to the Doirons, Kate? To Madeleine Doiron, the one in the Miscouche exhibit?"

"From way down the line, yes."

"Well, I'll be," James said. "Claire and Brian must've been destined to fall in love. Bringing the Murphys and Doirons back together."

Brian and Claire had unknowingly played a part in all of this, the couple connected through the generations just as much as Raina, Celeste, and Madeleine.

Brian and their father tromped up the basement stairs, faces sweaty.

"Are you taking care of your hip?" her mom asked.

"I was goalie." Her father opened the oven and looked in. "What's cooking?"

"A choose-your-own-casserole," Simone said.

"The girls are watching TV," Brian said.

"What is going on?" Claire asked.

"I gave them an extra hour, what with all the excitement today."

"Not you," Claire said. "Them." She pointed around the table.

Raina explained the relationship between their two families, that they'd read Celeste's journal and Madeleine's book. Brian listened with growing discomfort. Claire asked question after question, wanting more detail, more information about the woman in white and the phantom ship. "That is the most amazing story I've ever heard," Claire said.

"Is this connected to what happened to you that last summer in high school?" Raina's dad asked.

"It is," Raina said. "It wasn't your fault. I think it was fated."

Her dad leaned back in his chair.

"Where did you find Madeleine's story?" James asked. "I'd always thought it was sad that Celeste lost it, and that necklace."

"The book was in the wall at the Union Bank. We didn't find the necklace, though," Raina said, trying not to let hope fill her voice.

"That's too bad," James said. "I always hoped it had managed to find its way back into the hands of a Doiron woman, somehow."

"You don't have it?" Raina asked. "You're sure you don't know anything about it? Maybe a family member said something about it? Even in passing?"

"Sorry, no."

The phantom ship roared in victory, its sea of spectres seeming closer to shore. The captain separated himself from the others and held out his hand to her. *Raina, it's time.* Raina clenched her fists, dug her nails into her palms, and focused on the feel of Celeste's journal against her skin. When the captain's voice faded, she opened her hands and tapped her fingertips on the table top. Tap-tap-tappity-tap. Simone reached over and squeezed her shoulder, tapping her own fingers lightly on her arm.

Simone turned to James. "Why did you put the journal in the archives?"

"Erica wanted to burn it," James said. "The archives were a compromise."

"That's a dangerous book," Erica said.

"It's just family lore," James said.

"Did you plan on keeping it there?" Raina asked. If they said no, that they wanted it, then it would officially stay lost, maybe assumed misfiled in the archives, in any of hundreds of boxes. She couldn't give it back.

"Now that I know Celeste is your ancestor," James said, "I'd prefer you had it. We can get it out of the archives next time we're in Charlottetown."

Simone looked at Raina, who nodded.

"We've saved you a trip," Simone said.

Raina removed the journal from behind her back and set it on the table, her hands still touching it.

"How did you get that?" Erica asked.

"In my defence, I didn't know it was yours when I, um, took it," Simone said.

"You stole that from the archives?" Brian asked.

"It was more like, reappropriating," Simone said. "Bringing it back into the family."

"It's part of the Murphy family as well." Claire reached for it. "May I see?"

"Claire, don't," Erica said.

"It's fine, Mom." Claire slid the journal out of Raina's grasp, towards herself.

The phantom ship roared. Raina jerked.

"Here." Simone handed Madeleine's book to Raina. "This'll help."

But it didn't. There was no tingling, no sizzling, no change to the call. Raina turned it over in her hands, eyes wide. "Nothing," she said.

"That doesn't make any sense," Simone said.

Raina held out her hand to Claire. "I need the journal," she said in a trembling voice. "Please."

Claire pushed it back to her as the girls ran in. Raina's hands closed around the spine and the call dimmed. She let out her breath. Before this, whenever she'd held Madeleine's book, she'd also held Celeste's journal. So, was it only ever the journal that had power? Why? Madeleine was the stronger one. Wasn't she?

Nora tugged at the fridge door. "Orange juice, please. I said please. Juice."

"Just a moment," Claire said. "I'll get it. Maeve, do you want some?'

Maeve shook her head and approached Raina. She reached up and touched the journal. "I love this necklace," she said.

Erica's face paled.

Raina's hands tightened on the journal. "What necklace?" She scanned everyone's jewellery. Rings, earrings, bracelets. No one wore a necklace.

"The one with a plus sign and a capital C," Maeve said.

Raina pushed off her chair and crouched in front of Maeve. "Did you hear us talking about a necklace?"

Maeve shook her head.

"Did you have a vision?" Raina asked.

"Why would you ask my daughter a question like that?" Brian said.

Maeve ignored her father and shrugged. "I dunno, Aunt Raina. But you should take the necklace out." She pointed at the spine. "It's in there." She tapped the journal. Tap-tap-tappity-tap.

Raina stared at her niece, then tore her gaze away to examine the twine stitched on the journal in the shape of flowers. She'd assumed it was only decoration, but now saw that it also secured the journal's spine, which was bulky, just like Celeste had written when she'd found a fountain pen tucked into it. But it hadn't been sealed then.

"It wants to be around your neck," Maeve said. "It'll make you feel better."

Erica pushed herself up from the table. "That's why I wanted that journal out of the house," she said. "Maeve pulled it off the shelf one day and started … saying weird things about ghosts and ships and premonitions."

"Damnit, Raina," Brian said. "You started all this."

"Blame Madeleine, not me," Raina said. Though she was wondering if she should *thank* her ancestor, instead.

"Why didn't you tell me?" Claire asked her mother.

"I thought it better to just ignore the whole thing, dear," Erica said. "Which is what I think we should do now."

"Not a chance," Raina's mom said. She reached out, pulled a drawer open, and handed Raina a pair of scissors.

Raina, the phantom ship called. *Raina, Raina …*

Raina took the scissors and clipped at the twine, slitting a knot in two. She pulled at the twine and cloth until she had a hole in the bottom of the spine. She tipped the journal up and a necklace fell into her open palm. Wooden cross and crescent moon.

The phantom ship's call disappeared. She scanned the ocean and found it in the distance, still there but amorphous, like a faraway mirage.

Maeve whispered in Raina's ear. "It worked, didn't it? Made them go away."

Had Maeve seen the ship, or just intuited that Raina felt better? "Maeve…" she said. "Did you feel it…anything, calling to you?"

"No. Just the necklace, when I touch the book. It's pretty."

"I bet Mr. Murphy hid the necklace there," Simone said. "Or his wife. To keep it safe."

"Put it on," Maeve said.

Raina placed it around her neck and let it settle against her skin. The necklace's warmth tap-tap-tappity-tapped against her skin. A sense of comfort overtook her.

It had been the necklace all along—not the journal—that had given her the ability to fight off the phantom ship. Not the stories of her ancestors, though they had a power of their own: understanding and connection.

Combined, the necklace and the stories provided something even stronger.

Hope. For her future, and that of Simone, and Maeve, and beyond.

CHAPTER 22

Raina

Raina picked up the takeout bag from the passenger seat of her Jeep. She walked towards Your Morning Sludge as Hattie turned the sign in the café's window from *Open* to *Closed—Please come back soon*. The sunset was obscured by clouds, thick with the coming rain. Madeleine's necklace thrummed against Raina's skin, staving off the phantom ship, which was nowhere to be seen. But it'd be back.

The phantom ship with its cursed crew had shadowed the CCGS *Earl Grey* the entire time Raina sailed on the patrol vessel. But it soon learned that she had strengthened her resistance to it. Only once, in the middle of the night, had she found herself with her hand on the lever that opened her cabin door. That'd been the only time she needed the handcuffs. A drastic improvement. And a sweet relief to be living, working, and sleeping on the water, waves crashing against the vessel, the ocean's briny scent filling her lungs with life, rendering her whole again.

Still, she kept her guard up. She'd never be free of the phantom ship. It was part of her, just like her abilities. Like her family.

She glanced at the harbour one more time before entering the café. Several fishing boats bobbed at the docks. No phantoms.

Hattie held the door open. Raina stepped over the broom handle in the bottom sill, with a somewhat new appreciation for it. Brian was already sitting on the back bench seat at their old corner table. He looked up, then back at his phone. Undoubtedly readying himself to text a play-by-play to Claire.

"Are you prepared for this?" Hattie asked.

"Do you have the whisky poured?"

"I'm not licensed, remember? This is a coffee shop."

"Yeah, yeah," Raina said as she strode across the café and sat down. Hattie grabbed three soda waters from the counter and took the chair beside her.

Raina pulled three boxes out of the bag. "I sprung for a seafood platter each." She dropped a pile of condiments in the centre of the table.

"Thanks." Brian doused his fries with malt vinegar and dug in, focusing on his meal, not Raina.

"Look at that," Hattie said. "This peace deal is already going swimmingly. What more do we need?"

"An apology?" Raina said. "Now that Maeve ..." She trailed off, not sure how to finish the sentence without sending Brian into fits of discomfort.

"It was never just about your ..." He waved his hands around. "Abilities, whatever. You know that. It's about how you abandoned your family."

"I didn't abandon anyone. Besides, now that you know about Maeve, can't you understand me? My choices?"

"How is Maeve?" Hattie asked, picking at her fried clams and sending a warning glance at Raina.

"Seems fine, for now." Brian said. "Claire and I? Not so much." He glanced at his phone, then turned it facedown with a sigh. "This is uncharted territory for us."

Maeve had explained that when she sensed the necklace—when she picked up the journal at her grandparents, leaned on Raina at the hospital, and touched the journal in the kitchen—she saw things. The phantom ship. Her grandmother healthy. The necklace around Raina's neck. So she'd inherited the Doiron women's abilities, through Brian, and maybe through the Murphys, if something had passed through the necklace to the guard's child. It seemed that, somehow, the abilities could affect men who were close to the Doiron women, the way Celeste's twin Yvon could sense the phantom ship, even when it hadn't intended to appear to him. It remained to be seen what unique form Maeve's abilities took. Raina's focus on finding lost people, animals, or mysterious objects? Simone's on predicting babies? Or, something else entirely? If Raina had to guess, she figured Maeve's had something to do with well-being.

"You can understand how Brian feels, right?" Hattie said to Raina. "You've been used to this your whole life. It's new to him."

"I understand it can be overwhelming." Raina scanned the ocean through the café's large windows. Fog settled in.

"And, Brian, if you're scared of this, you can see how Raina felt too. Why she had to leave."

"That's what I'm worried about," Brian said, leaning towards Raina. "That something will go wrong with Maeve. That the phantom ship will take her."

Raina's voice softened. "She won't have to go through what I did. All alone. She'll have me to teach her. Maybe Simone." Her cousin had flown back to Montréal, with promises to return when she could. "And I don't think the phantom ship will try to lure Maeve to it." Near as Raina could tell, dangerous as it was, the lure had emerged as Madeleine's way to connect Raina to her ancestors, to find the necklace, and return it to the Doirons. In a way similar to how Marie-Blanche's feux follet had convinced Madeleine to travel back to L'Acadie, for the good of their family.

"'Think' isn't good enough. I don't want you to teach her." Brian dropped his fork on the table. "I want you to tell her how to stop it. How to avoid everything about it. That's what you did for years. Show her."

"You can't mean that," Hattie said. "Her abilities are part of who she is."

"No, they're not," Brian said. "She's a little girl who should be playing with dolls, and Lego, and toy cars. Not having visions of who knows what."

"Ignoring her abilities is not a solution," Raina said.

"What if we move away?" Brian asked. "Would that work? Inland, far from the ocean and any lakes. No water, no phantom ship, no abilities."

"Rustico is where our abilities are strongest, because it's our hometown, where Celeste and Madeleine lived most of their lives, but the abilities will stay with Maeve wherever she goes," Raina said. "Better she learns how to use them."

"Shit," Brian said.

"Maeve's younger than I was when my visions first started. Closer to the age Sébastienne was. Likely because she has a guide nearby. In me. Even if we didn't know it. But without assistance …" She trailed off, let Brian come to his own conclusions. He'd read the book and the journal. So had Claire. They knew everything Raina did.

"Just because you want it to be different, doesn't make it so," Hattie said, her hand on Brian's arm. "Claire's okay with this, isn't she?"

"She's worried, but she wants to know more. I seem to be the holdout," Brian said. "What the hell is the phantom ship, anyway? Where did it come from? Why's it so interested in our family?"

Raina shrugged. "I wish I knew." She'd keep searching for an answer. It was important to their family, their abilities, their history. Maybe, one day, she could ask the crew herself. She shuddered at the thought.

"I propose a trade," she said. A bargain. "You let me help Maeve, and I'll help with the family business."

"I'm not trading anything that affects Maeve," Brian said.

"And Raina, do you really want to give up your promotion? Your career?" Hattie asked. "After you worked so hard for it, for so many years?"

"I have it all figured out," Raina said, not wanting to say any more until Brian asked for details. That way, Brian would feel as if he had control of the situation, like when a suspect thought he had the upper hand and made a concession he might not have previously considered. She'd never hurt or mislead Brian. But she needed to do whatever she could to advocate for Maeve. Defend her future.

As Brian poked at his fish, she gazed just over his head into the fog. A car drove through the parking lot, cutting towards a side street, its headlights briefly illuminating the water that lapped at the docks. The waves advanced and receded, as the phantom ship would, for the rest of Raina's life.

She resisted reaching up to touch the necklace, instead contenting herself with its warmth on her neck. She'd had the rope that threaded through the cross and moon replaced with a thin chain. The rope was now in a fireproof lockbox, with Celeste's journal and Madeleine's book. They wouldn't be lost again. She'd seen a vision of the box passed down, from generation to generation. To Maeve's own daughters. And their daughters after that.

"Tell me more," Brian eventually said.

Raina forced herself not to smile. She didn't want Brian to think she was gloating. Rebuilding trust between them would take time. "A constable position in Rustico just opened up. I'm putting my name in for it."

"Isn't small-town constable work a demotion?" Hattie asked.

"Not this time," Raina said. "I've managed to create a bit of a new role." One that would help her connect with family. With Maeve. Maybe Nora. Help with the family business. Safeguard the Island, by working in her hometown.

If she'd learned anything from Celeste and Madeleine, it was that Doiron women were meant to protect and care for each other. Ancestors and descendants alike.

EPILOGUE

Raina

Early the next summer, Raina rolled up her jeans, slipped off her sandals, and sat on the dock beside the *Spirit of Rustico* tour boat. She'd finished her official police shift by helping a woman file a report after an out-of-towner tried to mug her. With the help of two passing locals, the woman had fought him off and he was in custody. Now he knew this town protected their own. Raina's unofficial shift, the one she'd created with the help of her chief that resulted in a promotion and a pay raise, started now. It hadn't taken too long to convince the chief of the advantages of a plainclothes officer on the water, without having the department buy and maintain a boat and a crew, or engage in long-term collaboration with the Coast Guard.

With only a slight hesitation, she stuck her feet in the cold water. It lapped at her legs, sending chills through her body. She focused on her breathing, looked out over the ocean's calm surface with the sun glinting off it, and tapped her fingers on Madeleine's necklace, secure around her neck. It hummed against her skin. She closed her eyes, pictured Madeleine, Sébastienne, and Celeste. Repeated their names. Breathed in the sweet briny air. The ritual kept her balanced on the precipice of past and future, mystical and rational. A threat still lingered under the surface, but it was dim and subdued.

Her ears and eyes were attuned to the fishers and tour operators around her. She wasn't undercover, but when she was on the docks or on the water, people seemed to forget who she was, giving her a window into their thoughts and actions. She never arrested anyone in her off hours, just passed on the info to whoever was on duty. Their detachment's success rate was the highest on the Island. She got to her feet and boarded the boat to prep for the evening's tour.

A few hours later, after loading the tourists and setting out to sea, Raina and her crew waited for dusk. She peered into the distance as the sun set over the glimmering water. "There it is," she pointed. The phantom ship, sails afire, flickered in the distance. Burning bigger and brighter, showing itself to far more people than in the past. But it still only called to Raina.

The tourists rushed to her side of the boat. "I see it," one said. "Me too," said another. "Creepy," said a teenager, drawing out the vowels until the word fairly drifted in the air.

"Isn't it awesome?" Simone said from the wheelhouse. She throttled the engine down until the boat came to a stop, the only sound that of waves lapping at the hull. She'd transferred to UPEI and changed her major to folklore, and was helping with the tours during the summer.

One of the other teenagers reached into the cooler and sneaked out a beer. Hattie smacked his arm, made him put it back, and handed him a container of homemade lemonade. Hattie had become their caterer and spotter. Raina swore people signed up for the tour just for the food, which was fine with her. Hattie was also a whiz with the life preserver. Never missed whenever they practiced person-overboard drills.

Her mom and dad had their feet up at home, playing Scrabble and watching movies. Brian was scurrying around the Island, buying and selling houses. Raina chased criminals during the day and the phantom ship at night, both jobs made easier now that the necklace allowed her to cautiously tap into her premonition abilities. On weekends, she helped Maeve practice with her own abilities, though soon enough, it was likely that Maeve would be teaching Raina. The girl was strong. Nora liked to watch. She was learning as well. The future held awesome possibilities for both of them.

A spectre from the phantom ship broke her reverie, with a smaller one by her side. They raised their hands and waved, their flames flashing in time to a tap-tap-tappity-tap. Madeleine and Marie-Blanche. Madeleine's bargain with the phantom ship—that she'd join their crew when she died, if it ensured her familial line survived—was a capricious one. It hadn't quite played out as she'd expected, but such was the way with the supernatural. As a crew member herself, Madeleine's power only grew, fuelled as it was by the eternal presence of her long-lost daughter. They'd both found a certain peace, together.

Tap-tap-tappity-tap.

Raina copied the rhythm. Forced down the urge to join the sea of spectres. Every tour was a victory. Approaching the phantom ship and then leaving it behind. Maybe one day she'd succumb to its call, but not today.

Author's Note

This is a work of historical fiction based on actual events and Prince Edward Island legends. Though the character of Madeleine is loosely based on my several times great-grandmother (eleven generations back) from the Doiron line, her story, and that of the other characters, is entirely fictionalized (and indeed diverges from the real Madeleine's life partway through the novel). I was inspired to write her story when my mother sent me an article, "The Saga of Alexis Doiron," by Georges Arsenault. The focus of the article was on Madeleine's husband, Alexis, and how his family was deported to France in 1758 as part of the Acadian Expulsion. There is brief mention of Madeleine, with the statement that "Alexis Doiron soon found a new wife to help him raise his three children and take care of the household....in the course of the next 25 years, she would give birth to at least 15 children" (p. 14). Madeleine's life, and the way it was largely absent in the article, fascinated me. It was her story that I wanted to tell. The exhibit about her at the Acadian Museum of Prince Edward Island is real, as is the step-dancing exhibit (be sure to try it if you visit).

In the telling, much had to be changed. In addition to decreasing the number of children Madeleine had, I also separated her from Alexis. Her abilities are invented, based on Acadian folklore. In real life, she and Alexis, with several of their children, returned to Rustico, PEI, years after their deportation, though it is unknown how they secured passage home. I stayed mostly true to what is known of their time on *Patience* (which was one of the five ships they could have possibly been transported on). Three of their children did die on board and Madeleine gave birth to another, who died soon after they reached France. After landing in Saint-Malo, the real Doirons lived in St. Servan and St. Enogat before leaving for Belle-Île-en-Mer. For narrative reasons, I eliminated their time in

St. Servan and St. Enogat, moving them straight to Belle-Île-en-Mer, with the result that they landed there, in 1759, before the British did (occupied between 1761–1763). I therefore had to move the dates of the occupation backwards. As far as I know, the real Alexis was a perfectly nice man, although he would've been just as likely to be wary of any preternatural abilities as the Alexis in this novel.

The woman in white, phantom ship, and feux follets are PEI legends. Thanks to Georges Arsenault for his excellent source books, including *Acadian Legends, Folktales, and Songs from Prince Edward Island* and *The Island Acadians 1720–1980*, and the co-written (with Jacinthe Laforest as lead author) *Les Acadiennes de l'Île-du-Prince-Édouard: Trois Siècles d'Action.* Although I changed some of the facts of Madeleine's life as outlined here, the general context of her life is historically accurate. As Islanders will know, I increased the reach of the phantom ship (it is sighted only in the Northumberland Strait) to suit my narrative. Please forgive me. I also had to be a bit creative with the location and staffing of Island police stations.

Celeste and Noelle were inspired by two women who stood trial for counterfeiting bank notes in 1864, as mentioned in *The Public Archives 2014 Almanac and Miscellany Celebrating 1864: A Look at Prince Edward Island in the Year of the Charlottetown Conference.* My father asked everyone in the family to enter a contest so he could get one for my mother. Turns out, most of us won copies, and I ended up with two, wondering what I would ever do with them. One day, I flipped through it, found information about the case of Joanna Connors and Ellen Jane Coombs, and they ended up as a focus in my novel. Records indicate they worked as cleaners at the bank and had access to the notes. The almanac states, "the case against the suspects fell apart, however, when it was discovered that some of the jurors were in fact directors of the Union Bank" (p. 84). Although the Union Bank existed in 1864, the actual building I've set the story in wasn't built until 1872. At the time of writing, the building wasn't being turned into condos but still held government offices.

Raina is entirely fictionalized, although situated within the Island context. She initially gave me the most difficulty as a character but I ended up having the most fun with her, her mother, and Simone.

Charlotte Dieu-le-veut is the fictional granddaughter of Anne (Marianne) Dieu-le-veut, a seventeenth-century Frenchwoman who spent much of her life as a pirate.

A note on last names: I would have loved to have all my characters have the last name Doiron, but, alas, as surnames are typically patrilineal, I had to restrict it to Madeleine. As I'm related to much of PEI, I decided to stay away from maiden names of family members, which left out Gaudet and Gallant for main character names, as I didn't want anyone thinking the character was modelled after a real contemporary person. So, I chose Haché for Celeste and Cormier for Raina, in a nod to Michel Haché-Gallant and Anne Cormier, who are considered to be the founding parents of the PEI Acadian community.

In this novel, I focused on three questions: How would an eighteenth-century young mother (Madeleine) help her family survive during the Acadian Expulsion? Why would a nineteenth-century bank cleaner (Celeste) consider stealing bank notes? How would a twenty-first-century police detective (Raina) navigate the rational and the fantastical in her work and her family life?

Huge thanks to my agent, Alice Speilburg, for seeing the potential of this novel and my career as a fiction author, helping me develop the story through multiple revisions, and suggesting its final title. My family and friends know her better as "Amazing Alice," as that's how I preface every mention of her, for her knowledge, support, editorial comments, and assistance. Thanks to P2P and Kathy Ver Eecke for helping me find her.

Special thanks to Else Khoury, my steadfast friend and critique partner, for reading and commenting on my ever-again almost final version, for our lunches and our walks, and for helping me figure out what the heck was going on with the necklace.

Thanks to Acorn Press, especially Tracy Belsher for all things publishing, as well as the beautifully haunting cover, and my editor, Penelope Jackson, for loving this novel as much as I do. Penelope's insightful edits, comments, and questions helped me improve the novel, particularly with respect to fixing pesky gaps in character and plot. Thanks to my copy editor, Danielle Metcalfe-Chenail, for catching and fixing so much more than grammar.

Thanks to Donna Morrissey, my mentor for Humber College's Graduate Certificate in Creative Writing, as I was working on an early draft of this novel. I always remember her guiding question for any character's actions, feelings, or thoughts: "What's the psychology of it?"

Thanks to my beta readers who gave me feedback on separate chapters in the Fiction Critique Group of the Niagara Branch of the Canadian Authors Association as well as in Brian Henry's writing courses (thanks to Brian for helping me ramp up the tension with Raina's teenage encounter with the phantom ship), and to beta readers who read a much earlier version of the novel, Dale Rutherford and Maryann Breukelman.

More thanks to my parents, Linda and Allan Callard, for their support as well as their comments on PEI geography, culture, and nautical details. And my PEI mug.

Love to Mike, for pulling me back into the twenty-first century when my brain was immersed in the nineteenth and eighteenth; to Nick, for always asking about my fiction; and, to Dylan, for his ability to lose himself in the world of a book. Hugs and thanks to Jenny for solving my rental car problem.

Mom, Paula, Marsha, Donnie, George, and Glenn, I hope you discovered my nods to each of you. I think Anna, Edmond, and Reit would've enjoyed theirs.

For anyone looking to be entranced by Island music, I highly recommend Lennie Gallant's *Searching for Abegweit* album, particularly the song "Tales of the Phantom Ship." I was lucky enough to see the live show, which incorporated beautiful artwork by his sister, Karen Gallant. I listened to the album often when writing, while drinking coffee out of the Island mug my mother sent me.

A previous version of Chapter 6 was published as "Flickering Hope" in *Fifteen Stories High* (2019), for which I retain copyright.